HUGH FINCH

Arctic Revelation

A Thousand Lifetimes in the Blink of An Eye

NEW LONDON PUBLISHING

First edition

Cover art by Daniela Bertua
Editing by Shannon Roberts
Editing by April Kelly
Proofreading by Melanie Scott

This book was professionally typeset on Reedsy.
Find out more at reedsy.com

Dedication

To my mother Sharon.

If you look up 'unconditional love' in the dictionary, you'll see her picture, beaming with love for her children.

Had it not been for her, this book would still be on a thumb drive,

somewhere in an unpacked moving box,

somewhere in the depths of my basement.

Chapter 1

Allen trudged through the unfamiliar lumber yard, his footsteps softened by a thick blanket of sawdust. Something was off—he couldn't scream and wasn't sure why he wanted to. How did he get there? A feeling of unease took root.

In the distance, a rusted orange machine shredded scrap wood into small chips, its clanging loud enough to penetrate the silence that surrounded him. The piercing call of a majestic eagle lured his gaze across the clear blue sky and straight into the blinding sun.

As his vision slowly recovered from the trauma, the eagle's song began transforming into the rhythmic pinging of a heart monitor. The sun turned into a bright surgical light.

And to Allen's shock and confusion, the clanging wood chipper had morphed into the low metallic whir of a medical saw.

Shadowy figures toiled in the periphery of the overhead surgical light. Every sound echoed, bouncing off the chamber walls as if they were in a large cave or tunnel.

Despite the unsettling circumstances, Allen felt relaxed and weightless, much like the feeling one has after a deep, renewing sleep… or after being drugged and kidnapped.

As his head began to clear, so did his memories from earlier that evening. One at a time, then all at once, they came flooding back. He remembered meeting a strange, masculine woman at the bar. The rum and coke she gave him tasted bitter. Moments later, the music and surroundings began to distort as he watched the glass fall to the floor, shattering in slow-motion. The patrons feigned concern, but no one intervened as Allen tried to scream with paralyzed vocal cords.

Helpless and trapped in his own body, all he could do was watch as this same woman awkwardly walked him out of the bar, apologizing to onlookers along the way.

Becoming more alert with each passing second, Allen tried to sit up, only to find his entire body rigidly locked in place by a series of inflexible leather straps.

His screams for help reverberated through the cold, sterile air, mingling with his pleas for answers. "Where am I?" he cried out, his voice tinged with fear and confusion. "What are you doing to me? Please, let me go!"

Adrenaline coursed through his veins, consuming any remnants of the sedatives from the tainted rum and coke. A rush of panic and terror engulfed him, fueling his fight for freedom as his desperate cries evaporated into the abyss of darkness surrounding him.

Finally, one of the shadowy figures leaned into the dome of light. Allen rolled his eyes up to see the person looking down upon him. In a mixed state of confusion and relief, Allen exclaimed, "Hey, I know you, you're..."

Cutting him off mid-sentence, the man announced, as if addressing an audience, "I am The Surgeon."

The momentary relief faded faster than the lumber yard. The truth of the situation was an exploding volcano that bathed him in molten reality. Accompanying the painful acceptance were tears of horror that welled in his trembling eyes. The circumstances left little doubt that this man was, in fact, The Surgeon.

Everyone in Europe, including Allen, knew of The Surgeon. He also knew he would never see his friends or family again. All he could do was stare, without hope, into the psychotic eyes of the most notorious serial killer since Jack the Ripper.

Chapter 2

On the other side of the Atlantic, Christian Yates raced to present his first lecture as a newly graduated psychologist.

"What was I thinking?" Christian cursed the day he had purchased the hard-soled Italian shoes, as they announced his tardiness long before his arrival. He imagined the four hundred Psych 101 undergrads sitting quietly and listening as the ridiculous click-clack of his shoes drew closer and closer. One peek through the tiny window in the door reinforced his fears.

The silence amplified his already pounding heartbeat as he watched the carnivores, drenched in the early morning sun, anticipating their prey. The nervous tic in his right eye was an inescapable reminder of how much he needed this Assistant Professorship.

This tic had cursed Christian since his father's brutal death when he was just nine years old. Years of childhood therapy had taught him how to suppress it in all but the most stressful situations. Those same years of therapy were the sparks that ignited Christian's passion for psychology. He desperately wanted to help others the way he had been helped, but, deep inside, he also prayed it might finally liberate him from a lifetime of suffering and shame.

Longing to be just another student, Christian rallied his courage as he slowly turned the squeaky brass doorknob. The unfortunate, high-pitched squeal echoed throughout the acoustically enhanced lecture hall, drawing everyone's attention to Christian's late arrival.

The ensuing barrage of penetrating stares and indistinguishable whispers carried him down the crowded stairs to the lonely podium. The short decent felt like an eternity as he finally reached the stage like an avalanche settling at the base of a mountain.

Christian knew all too well what some of the whispers were about.

Light tapping on the unresponsive microphone only drew more attention to the late start. This was a painfully poor prologue to what could be the most important lecture of his life.

Dr. Jamison, the department chair, stormed up to the podium and grabbed the microphone, hissing, "This isn't rocket science."

The dandruff on Dr. Jamison's shoulders accentuated his over-rehearsed Freudian expression, which fooled nobody. While making several crude adjustments, he further contaminated Christian's personal space, whispering, "Half the psychology department is watching. You'd better stick to the preapproved talking points, or else..." Christian couldn't tell which was more offensive, Dr. Jamison's breath or his threats. "You're only here because you bring out the 'savior complex' in Dean Edwards."

He wasn't wrong. Dean Edwards was the reason Christian was at the university in the first place. Very few people knew Christian was from the South, and even fewer knew that Dean Edwards was once his pediatric psychiatrist down in North Carolina. Edwards had run the county mental health facility where Christian received years of therapy after his father's death.

Christian's case led to a series of groundbreaking publications on dissociative amnesia and repressed memories that elevated Dr. Edwards to the top of his field, eventually landing him the deanship of the university.

Dr. Jamison couldn't resist adding just a little more insult to the injury. "If it were up to me, you'd never step foot in this university again. And for God's sake, stand up straight!"

Christian was a textbook product of childhood trauma. Nervous tics aside, he was constantly trying to shrink his six-foot-four frame in the hopes of avoiding a repeat of whatever horrific thing it was that he locked away as a child, much like a beaten dog cowering and tucking its tail when threatened. It was so ingrained that he only noticed when reminded by people like Dr. Jamison.

Amazing how times they change, Christian thought to himself. Just two years ago, Dr. Jamison couldn't stop singing his praises. "Everyone, come meet Christian, the psychology department's Golden Boy! His case study on Collin Trevor has given our program unprecedented exposure in the most prestigious journals and media around the world!" A wave of nausea washed over Christian as he chanced a brief memory of Collin.

Chapter 3

~*~ Two Years Earlier ~*~

How could he not cringe when reflecting on his time with Collin Trevor? The passing of two years had done little to heal those wounds.

He remembered being lost, half-running, half-walking through the never-ending corridors of the university hospital. It was an ecosystem of constant sights and sounds—between the pinging of medical devices, he heard nurses calling over the PA system as white-coated doctors reviewed charts—everything seemed so random and chaotic, yet there was an underlying harmony to it all.

Upon reaching the psych unit on the fifteenth floor and stepping off the elevator, one of the strangest-looking people he'd ever seen greeted him.

His late father's words crept in, as they often did— "Son, always remember, beauty is only skin deep, but ugly goes all the way to the bone!" That pretty much summed up his dad's sense of humor.

The strange man extended his hand as Christian wrestled his gaze away from the gargantuan beard that engulfed his cheekbones right up to the rims of his round, blacked-out sunglasses. "Greetings, my name is Dr. Nilsson," he said with a thick, singsongy Swedish accent. Christian fought to maintain focus, but all he could see was the Swedish Chef from *Sesame Street*.

"Hi, I'm Christian, the psychology graduate student here for my month-long hospital rotation," Christian said nervously, fighting to suppress a tic.

Dr. Nilsson raised the massive, bushy eyebrows that framed the top portion of his inappropriate sunglasses. "I'm so glad to meet you, and it glads me even more for you to meet Collin!" he exclaimed in broken English.

Christian tried to keep up as Dr. Nilsson, like a mole in a tunnel, scurried through the dark corridor into an even darker observation room, never removing his sunglasses. Christian stumbled along behind, pupils dilated, straining to capture what little light was to be found. A large observation window at the far end of the room was their saving grace as it emitted just enough glow to guide them safely to their destination.

Several towers of audiovisual equipment roared in the corner, masking the sound of their arrival. The scene playing out in a bright room on the other side of the one-way mirror was mesmerizing to the point that Christian barely noticed the two attending psychiatrists huddled to the left of the window.

Unable to blink, Christian just stood frozen as the images and sounds washed over him through the observation glass and AV system. A young man sat motionless in a chair, normal but for the small gray cable running from the side of his head to a box on the table.

Consumed by the experience, Christian didn't initially see the bolts anchoring the chair to the floor, or the straps anchoring Collin to the chair. When he finally noticed them, it just deepened the intrigue.

They could have been watching a dramatic Broadway monologue as Collin looked across the table to an empty chair while holding a perfectly timed conversation with a phantom of his imagination. Christian had to keep reminding himself there was nobody in the other chair as he watched this one-way dialogue play out for ten minutes straight.

Everyone suddenly leapt back as Collin, without warning, began violently thrashing and contorting. His head twisting and craning in such unnatural positions that Christian feared his neck would break.

This continued for about ten seconds as the limits of the bolts and straps were tested, then ending as abruptly as it began. The seizure was replaced with a completely new and beautifully composed personality, holding another perfectly paced conversation.

One of the attending psychiatrists began turning away from the window towards Christian and Dr. Nilsson. As she swiped through Collin's chart, the glow of her tablet revealed an ID badge that read 'Isabella Scola MD, Attending Psychiatrist.' There was a yelp, and the tablet went flying when she finally looked up and noticed them for the first time in the darkness.

"I'm so sorry, I didn't see you there," Dr. Scola exclaimed as she tried to gather her tablet and composure.

Christian could only imagine what it must have looked like to Dr. Scola, turning to see the giant and the Swedish Chef just lurking there in the darkness, "We're so sorry for startling you like that." Christian replied apologetically.

"It's not your fault," she confided, fear and defeat evident in her voice. "You just missed Archbishop O'Dwyer. He was here with the Governor and an entourage of Vatican experts."

"Vatican?" Christian asked, puzzled.

"They don't think this is a mental illness," she said, taking a trembling deep breath. "They believe Collin may be possessed by a *non-human entity*, whatever that means."

Christian tried to draw perspective from his Southern Baptist upbringing, but all he could summon were sun washed memories of late arrivals to the back pews with his dad, potluck dinners, baptisms, and a desperately missed sense of belonging.

"Holy shit!" were the first words that came out.

Before Christian could apologize again, Dr. Scola's colleague, Dr. Smith, interrupted. "I believe those were my exact words to the exalted Archbishop and Governor!"

Their nervous laughter was followed by Christian's pathological inability to withhold his inner feelings-another byproduct from years of childhood therapy cautioning the danger of suppressing emotions, "That must be the scariest thing I've ever heard. Shouldn't we have some bibles and holy water, or maybe a few ordained guards?"

Dr. Scola agreed. "We felt the same way, but they assured us that we should be OK since the *occupied* has shown no signs of aggression."

An involuntary shiver coursed through Christian's body. He could have just as well been in a horror movie standing there in the dark psych ward with only a thin pane of glass separating him and the would-be Antichrist, were it up to the Archbishop.

Dr. Scola snapped him back to reality as she vented, "We think they belong in the psych unit more than most of our patients, but the Governor and Archbishop go way back. He's insisted the hospital take this seriously." With a shrug of frustration, she continued, "Hell, maybe they're right. We've tried every medication and therapy possible, with absolutely no perceptible changes."

Suddenly, an all-consuming mixture of bliss and revelation washed over Dr. Scola's face as she beamed at Christian, the way an unprepared student beams at a blizzard forecast the night before a final exam, "You must be Christian, the psychology grad student here for your rotation?"

Christian just nodded, unable to speak or swallow, as all the saliva in his mouth had been consumed by his sympathetic nervous system in preparation for a possible fight or flight.

All he could do was recall his father's three Ds of avoidance: Defer, Deny, and Delegate. He suspected *delegation* was in his not-to-distant future.

"Dr. Smith and I need to do our rounds and manage about thirty other patients on the floor. We don't have the time to babysit Collin and everyone else."

Dr. Scola's gaze panned to the strange person next to Christian as her plan came into focus. "Dr. Nilsson is visiting from Stockholm University in Sweden. He seems to know his stuff, but his background check will probably take a few weeks or longer. Since you are technically credentialed here, we'd like to leave Dr. Nilsson in your charge for a little while. Here's my cell number, call if anything strange..." she glanced at Collin, "stranger... happens."

"Wait!" Christian blocked their exit as he rapid-fired a series of panicked questions, "What's his medical background? How did this happen? What do we do if his condition worsens? Why me?"

Dr. Scola passed the baton to Dr. Smith, who, based on his posturing and speech, had clearly served his country in exchange for medical training, student debt relief, and hopefully a sense of national pride at having helped defend his country and its citizens.

Christian had applied to the Air Force Health Professions Scholarship Program (HPSP) but was rejected, ironically, due to his history of psychiatric trauma.

Dr. Smith calmly but firmly repositioned Christian away from their exit trajectory, "At ease soldier. Consider this a baptism by fire! We just need you and Dr. Nilsson to observe and report any changes. Collin's medical records are on a locked-down, need-to-know basis, and you do not, I repeat, DO NOT need-to-know! The nursing staff will take care of any medical issues… Oorah!"

With that, Dr. Scola and Dr. Smith resisted the urge to run as they rushed out the door "like a couple of long-tailed cats in a room full of rockin' chairs." *Nice, Dad!*

Chapter 4

~*~ Present Day ~*~

C hristian tried to suppress the memories of Collin as he surveyed the room of students and professors. Only now did he realize how limited his career options had become. The Collin Trevor incident from two years ago was an insidious cancer that had since consumed everything good in its path. His licensure application to practice in Rhode Island had been denied due to the circumstances of that debacle.

There was nothing more Dean Edwards could do for Christian. Conflict of interest was in his rear view mirror, getting smaller and smaller by the moment. Any further interference on his part would put his career at risk, if it hadn't already. Christian would never forgive himself if the man who had worked so hard to help him was also consumed by this terrible thing.

Christian knew this lecture would play a significant role in the committee's decision, or perhaps it wouldn't.

The sudden screech of the microphone echoed throughout the lecture hall, jolting everyone's attention to the podium. Dr. Jamison shriveled back into his seat.

The lecture began.

Christian stuck to the boilerplate speaking points on schizophrenia and dissociative identity disorder (formerly known as multiple personality disorder.) He tried his best to make the material interesting.

Alas, the students could have learned more from watching a 1980s psychological thriller, and had more fun doing it.

Chapter 5

The Surgeon reveled with mercurial excitement as Allen thrashed and fought his restraints. He had performed this procedure enough times to know that there was no escaping the workbench. Even if he did, where would he go? They were five stories underground.

Exhausted, Allen finally gave up struggling and pleaded, "Please, let me go. I swear, I won't tell anyone about this. I'm only nineteen years old; there's so much of the world I haven't seen, and so many things I haven't done."

To Allen's surprise, the buzzing stopped. In the silence, he wondered if his pleas had triggered a moment of clarity in this psychopath's rampage. Maybe he had a son of Allen's age and realized the madness of what he was doing.

"You're right," The Surgeon replied in a nurturing, almost apologetic tone. "There is so much left for you to see and experience. I'm glad you shared your feelings with me..."

Allen let out a sigh of relief.

The Surgeon continued, fighting to suppress a chuckle, "It makes what I am about to do much easier."

14

The familiar buzzing resumed as Allen's heart sank. *What have I done?*

The Surgeon bellowed with enthusiasm over the saw, "You see, Allen, if this procedure is a success, you'll have access to more experiences and memories than you could have accumulated in a thousand lifetimes... You're welcome."

Allen felt a surprisingly painless pressure on the top of his head. The buzzing sound became bogged down and muffled. Allen smelled something but was unable to identify it.

Although, it would have been strange if he recognized the smell of a saw cutting through his skull.

Chapter 6

~*~ Two Years Earlier ~*~

D r. Nilsson turned to Christian as the attendings fled. "Finally, they go!"

"What the hell!" Christian exclaimed as Dr. Nilsson lunged for his neck with both hands. His attempt to duck and weave was unsuccessful as Nilsson quickly snatched the lanyard from around his neck. Nilsson then pulled out the ID badge that read "Christian Yates MS, Graduate Student, Department of Psychology" and held it to the sensor on Collin's door. There was a click, followed by Christian's objections as they entered Collin's room. Both fell silent as Collin went into a seizure, followed by a new personality.

Christian strained to understand Collin's words, but they made no sense. Dr. Nilsson quickly explained, "Collin is speaking German, a very old dialect of German that I can barely understand."

Of course, Dr. Nilsson could understand German, Christian thought to himself. Dr. Nilsson continued, "He is arguing with his wife. He is saying Martin Luther has liberated them." A pause occurred as if Collin were listening to an invisible person. "Now he's denying that they are blasphemers, and they have a right to speak directly to God."

16

Christian waved his hand in front of Collin's eyes, but there was no reaction. He was perfectly still. They spent the next hour observing Collin cycle through at least five different personalities. They witnessed him speaking flawless Greek, British English, and what appeared to be some form of Arabic. Neither Christian nor Dr. Nilsson understood Greek or Arabic, but it sounded amazing. Collin was speaking with an English cockney accent in one of the episodes. He seemed to be warning his daughter to come home straight after school. There had been a series of murders, and they were all women.

Dr. Nilsson finally broke Christian's trance. "Collin was admitted to the Psych ward three days ago. I arrived from Sweden twenty-four hours ago. I've been observing for eight hours now. He revealed at least thirty different personalities and ten different languages that we recognized. There were another twenty that either made no sense or sounded like caveman grunting. Not that we would know what caveman grunting would sound like! This has to be the most extensive case of dissociative identity disorder ever discovered."

Christian thought about this for a moment. "I don't have a license yet, but this seems to be more of a hybrid between schizophrenia and dissociative identity disorder. If Collin was assuming these personalities and interacting with us, then it would be more clean-cut, but what he is experiencing is more of a hallucination with one-way communication. It's almost like he's a recorder playing back scenes from the past. That's just ridiculous to think he's possessed!"

Nilsson commented with melodramatic enthusiasm and praise, "It's clear they chose the right guy for the job when they assigned you. Amazing deductions!"

The praise rubbed Christian the wrong way, but he wasn't sure why. As such, he resisted the urge to ask Dr. Nilsson to stop pissing on his back and telling him it's raining. His father would have approved, or he may have just asked him to stop blowing sunshine up his ass.

Chapter 7

~*~ Present Day ~*~

T he first half of the lecture ended like *Old Yeller*. Christian feared the students would leave less enlightened than when they arrived. This didn't seem right. Be that as it may, he couldn't postpone the inevitable. "Any questions?"

Christian surveyed the auditorium. The only people paying any attention and not sleeping or fidgeting with smartphones were the professors. And why not? It was their mundane subject matter Christian was being forced to regurgitate. He was doing his best, but the specter of Collin Trevor's tragedy continued to pervert everything in its path.

What nobody in the department realized was that Christian had spent much of his time over the past two years researching Collin's unique past life memories and only the bare minimum on his dissertation topic of dissociative identity disorders.

It was a surprise to everyone, including Christian, when the university granted him his PhD after defending his dissertation. He suspected Dean Edwards had a hand in that one also. Once again, his father's words haunted him, "Son, don't ever look a gift horse in the mouth."

Christian wasn't kidding himself. He desperately needed a good job. And in six months, when his three hundred thousand dollars of student loan deferment ended, he was also going to need a good bankruptcy attorney.

One after another, Christian's efforts were falling short. Everything kept circling back to one simple truth.

Despite being cleared of any wrongdoing, Christian would always be remembered as a person of interest in the murder of Collin Trevor.

Chapter 8

~*~ Two Years Earlier ~*~

T he weeks that followed proved to be a fantastic journey of scientific
exploration and enlightenment.

Christian and Dr. Nilsson spent their days taking full advantage
of the hospital's robust translation services. One by one, they translated
and deciphered each of Collin's conversations, at least the ones that were
recognizable. The fact that he was speaking numerous languages that
could not be identified by expert linguists posed an entirely different set of
questions.

At night, Christian would secretly log into the AncestryDNA account that
he had illegally created with an unauthorized saliva sample from Collin. He
had tried to get permission from the hospital's administrative powers, but
just like Collin's medical records, it was a no-go.

After the third denied request to create the account, he finally deferred to
his late father's wisdom: "Buddy, as unfortunate as it is, sometimes all you
can do is ask for forgiveness when permission isn't in the cards."

At first, he struggled to match Collin's personalities with his ancestors,
but the deeper he dug and the more he developed the family tree, the more

matches began to emerge.

Christian couldn't help but appreciate the dichotomy between his past and Collin's present. He would have given anything for just a fleeting memory of the day his father died. Collin, on the other hand, would surely give anything to forget the unbridled flow of memories, even if just for one fleeting moment.

The fruits of Christian's and Nilsson's endeavors yielded a small case study that quickly found its way into scholarly journals around the world. This greatly elevated Christian's status in the psychology department and garnered a lot of outside attention.

None of it seemed real, but Christian had an instinct to make the most of every moment and do everything in his power to understand Collin's condition. He was really paying it forward. On the rare occasions his resolve would waver, Christian simply recalled his father's words: "Don't forget, the sun doesn't shine on the same dog's ass every day."

Meanwhile, like a broken record, Dr. Nilsson relentlessly hounded Christian to sneak a peek at Collin's medical background. "My dear Christian, we are making tremendous progress, but we really need to dig into Collin's medical history and go over the details of how he came to be here. I know you can access his records."

After a particularly aggressive barrage of begging, Christian reached his limit. "Trust me, Dr. Nilsson, I want to know those details just as much as you, if not more. The thing is, HIPAA laws are serious business. You mess with that bull, and you'll surely get the horns. This, I promise you."

Nilsson tilted his head and gave Christian a strange look. Embarrassed, Christian realized he had inadvertently slipped into his old southern accent. He had spent many years trying to erase this southern drawl, just as he had done with his southern roots. Little did he know this would do nothing to erase the pain he carried with him wherever he went.

Christian regrouped and continued the explanation with his New England accent, "The hospital and Collin's treating doctor still refuse to give us access to his medical records. Just between you and me, I can't help but wonder if someone messed up, and that's why they've refused us permission to Collin's history. Sometimes I think there are more attorneys walking these halls than doctors."

A rare grin emerged from Nilsson's giant beard as he jested with his Swedish Chef accent. "How does your American joke go... 'Are you injured? I don't know, I haven't spoken with my attorney yet!'"

Trying to suppress his own smile, Christian continued, "What I do know is that, just last year, a very prominent physician lost his job here. All he did was take a quick peek at a high-profile celebrity's electronic health record after an ER visit from an injury sustained while filming in the area. Unless you have permission, you cannot access a patient's medical records. Of course, the database is designed so that anyone with a login can see anyone's records. It's the forbidden fruit of the hospital ecosystem."

After that interaction, Dr. Nilsson never again asked for Collin's medical records. Things went back to business as usual, or so Christian thought.

One morning, towards the end of his rotation, Christian was the first to arrive at the observation suite. The nursing staff was out in the hall finishing their handoff to the next shift. While in the room with Collin, he noticed the wire running out of Collin's head was unplugged from the machine on the table. He had no idea what it did but had never seen it unplugged before. No nurses were in sight, so he reached for the cable to plug it back in. "There's no reason to be afraid," he told himself as he slowly took the cable and plugged it in.

See, no demons or zombies. Turning away from Collin with a sigh of relief, Christian was about to log into the computer for the day when a weak trembling voice emerged behind him, "How many billions of years have I been gone?"

Terrified, Christian slowly turned back to Collin. The vacant stare was gone. In its place was the ghost of a human, writhing with tears of horror flowing down his face.

"Billions of years? You've only been here for three weeks. They won't let me see your medical records, so that's all I know."

Collin began to slip into one of his seizures, "Kill me, kill me, please. The world ends if anyone sees what I've seen!"

"What do you mean?" Christian asked, but knew it was too late. Whatever he had plugged back in was working. Collin had already begun reciting another memory. The AV equipment had not been turned on for the day, and no nurses witnessed what happened.

Christian resisted the urge to confess to the nurse who came strolling into the room just as Collin's seizure ended and a new personality emerged—she should have been the one to reconnect the cable. For all he knew, maybe they purposely disconnected it, and he screwed things up by reconnecting it. Whatever the reason, he decided to play this one close to his chest for now.

Chapter 9

~*~ Present Day ~*~

Musing the question of whether the students had absorbed everything so far, Christian prepared to start the second half of the lecture.

Just as he began, high above in the back row, he saw a timid hand emerge from the masses, but the young girl spoke with strength and clarity, "Earlier, you said there was a statistically significant higher prevalence of schizophrenia and dissociative identity disorders in Native American, Inuit, and Aboriginal peoples. Do you have any idea why they may be more susceptible to these disorders?"

He was hesitant to answer the girl in light of Dr. Jamison's forbidding look. His words were a flashing neon sign in Christian's head, "If you can't prove it, don't say it."

Christian had spent years on a dissertation that his heart wasn't in. He knew deep down that Collin's death was not his fault, yet he couldn't let it go. He knew better than anyone how to navigate the landscape of grief and tragedy, but knowing and doing were two very different things.

Had he courted Dr. Jamison's abuse these past two years? Did he believe it might absolve his guilt and ease the suffering? It didn't.

Suddenly, as if the answer had always been there hiding behind a thin veil, Christian knew what he had to do to honor Collin and free himself from the necrotic grip of self-loathing and guilt. It was suddenly so clear and so easy.

With a simple nod toward Dr. Jamison, Christian began to answer the question in a way that would surely end this job prospect, but possibly liberate his embattled soul.

"As some of you may know, many scientists believe the minds of pre-historic peoples possessed memories that had been passed down through genetics. These memories, or instincts, as some call them, were necessary for prehistoric peoples. With limited communication abilities, they needed an alternative method of avoiding dangers such as poisoned berries or lethal predators.

"It's like the way certain butterflies can emerge from their cocoons and, having never met their parents or made the journey, migrate thousands of kilometers to the same tree to meet them for the first time, with no instructions.

Another example is the earthworm and the light study. Shining a light on a worm normally causes no reaction."

One student quickly raised his hand.

Anticipating his objection, Christian expounded, "Earthworms don't have eyes, but they do have light receptors to help them differentiate between light and dark. Was that your question?"

The student slowly lowered his hand while giving an affirming nod.

Christian continued, "But in this study, scientists introduced an electric shock each time they shined the light, which caused the worm to recoil. Eventually, the worms were conditioned to recoil every time a light was shined on them, even without the electric shock. This was not overly impressive..."

Out of the blue, A student leapt to her feet, revealing a tie-dyed shirt with a peace sign. "That's animal cruelty. Free the worms, free the worms, free the..." She paused, scanning the audience as her face turned red, clearly disappointed and a little embarrassed that the rest of the class didn't join in.

The timing of the interruption couldn't have been better as Christian quickly took a much-needed drink of water; his mouth parched from the decision to finally take a stand against the department's oppression.

The class settled and he continued, "What was astounding was the fact that all the offspring of these worms and all their offspring, who were all separated immediately at birth, from then on would automatically recoil in the presence of a bright light despite never having experienced the shock. The worms' reaction to the light was somehow coded into their DNA and passed to all future generations. This is just one of many examples of learned behaviors being encoded into DNA and passed to future generations. But what is learned behavior if not a memory?"

Several of the professors observing the lecture stood up and stormed out. Unfazed, Christian continued. "Modern science will tell you we know everything about genetics, the mind, and the body. It's all been mapped out, dissected, and documented. This simply isn't true.

"On one hand, I believe that, over the years, modern advances such as reading, writing, computers, robotics, the internet, and artificial intelligence, among others, have reduced the need for humans to access memories that have been genetically encoded and passed from parent to child, but I believe the actual recording process is still happening.

"On the other hand, to answer your question," he said, addressing the girl, "I believe ancient peoples who have not so readily and easily given up their ancient ways may still possess more direct links to their inherited memories. These ancient people all have a common thread of communing with their deceased ancestors in some form or fashion. Most of the time, achieving this with the aid of natural psychedelics, such as peyote, mushrooms or other mind-freeing mediums."

Numerous hands simultaneously shot into the air as Christian finished his sentence. "You, third row back wearing the Coachella T-shirt."

With great enthusiasm, the student stood up and brushed his dreadlocks to the side. "Hi, my name is Clay, and I know exactly what you're talking about. We were road-tripping through the Arizona desert on our way back from Coachella just last week and got lost."

A few impressed oohs and ahhs rose from the crowd.

"Anyway, we ran out of gas way deep inside a Navajo reservation in the middle of the night."

More oohs and ahhs.

"We got out of the car, and it was darkness as far as the eye could see in all directions. Luckily, it was a full moon, and there were more stars out than I had ever seen in my life. After our eyes adjusted to the darkness, we saw a fire way off in the distance and started hiking towards it."

Everyone in the class was hanging on his every word, including Christian.

"The fire light was coming from inside this giant mound of dirt with a doorway. Then, from out of nowhere, this Native American appeared with a tomahawk…"

A few students jumped with surprise, clearly enjoying his story.

"We were scared out of our minds. Thank God, he could tell right away that we meant no harm or disrespect. He ended up inviting us into their sweat lodge. We spent the whole night there. It was hot as hell, but after smoking some of their peyote, I didn't even notice. That stuff was way stronger than any weed I've ever smoked. It was a total trip, and I'm pretty sure I saw my gramps, which was crazy because he's been dead for almost ten years."

The student looked around and took a bow. The class roared with applause as he sat down.

Christian continued having enjoyed the story as much as the students, "Thank you for sharing, Clay. Clay had the extremely rare opportunity to experience a very sacred and enlightening Navajo tradition that dates back many thousands of years. As I said before, almost all ancient people who have retained their traditional ways have rituals like the one Clay experienced. Most of these ancient indigenous peoples also live in balance with nature and their past.

"Modern-day mental-health providers have only recently begun to utilize these various techniques and psychotropics to help patients. Had we spent more time appreciating and protecting the indigenous peoples around us, we could have long since learned what they've known for countless generations.

We are just scratching the surface of a vast reserve of untapped access to the mind, memories, and subconsciousness via psychedelics. As scientists, we need to take a step back and make sure we've explored all avenues before labeling ancient people such as the Inuits, Native Americans, and Aboriginals, as mentally ill.

"We have to remain open to the possibility that some of these mental illnesses could instead be their DNA expressing an ancient ability; an ability they never lost because they never traded their traditional ways for modern conveniences."

Another roar of agreement rose from the crowd.

Christian took a deep breath and looked around the classroom. As a well-educated academician, he knew that much of what he was saying sounded like the rantings of a thirsty conspiracy theorist. However, the difference was that his beliefs were a result of seeing irrefutable proof.

He witnessed in Collin an unending flow of ancestral memories and languages that no human could have learned or faked. Christian had witnessed truth in its purest form—his problem was one of trying to reverse-engineer the route to that truth.

With unwavering faith in what he knew to be true, Christian continued the lecture. "I believe our DNA is far more dynamic, responsive, and interactive than we could have ever imagined. Let's take a straightforward process that happens every day with human teeth. Humans, for the most part, no longer need their third molars, a.k.a wisdom teeth. So, in many people, their genetic code has stopped expressing wisdom teeth. As a result, some or all four wisdom teeth never grow in these individuals. Can I see a show of hands for those who never got one or more wisdom teeth?"

Close to a quarter of the class raised their hands.

"What if it didn't take a thousand millennia of random mutations and natural selection of the strongest for you to stop getting your third molars?

"What if, instead, it just took a few generations of your ancestors eating a softer diet or simply lacking the space in their jaw?

"What if this was enough for your DNA to detect the changing environment and stop growing wisdom teeth?

"We are trained from day one to believe without a doubt that our DNA is a 100% static, rigid code that can only change through totally random chance mutations or scientific intervention. We see mutations in DNA every day, but what if they are not all random? What if there is a yet-to-be-discovered feedback loop between our DNA and the environment?"

Christian's thoughts drifted to Collin as he took a much needed sip of water.

Chapter 10

~*~ Two Years Earlier ~*~

R eporters, onlookers, and paparazzi zigged and zagged, trying to gain access to Christian as he entered the hospital. Everyone wanted to know about this mystery patient with a thousand personalities. Trying to remain polite and courteous proved a challenge with all the cameras and microphones being jammed into his face.

"Be good to the people you meet on the way up, because you'll be seeing them again on your way back down." Christian grinned at how easily his father's proverbs surfaced in these situations.

It had been almost four weeks, and there was no improvement in Collin's condition. Christian had developed a routine each morning that included coffee, wading through the mob, and then spending the day with Dr. Nilsson and Collin.

This day was different. After breaking through the crowd and entering the elevator, two campus security guards stepped in and stopped anyone else from joining them.

Christian thought to himself, *I could get used to this kind of VIP treatment.*

The elevator pinged its way to the fifteenth floor.

No sooner had the door begun opening than four police officers grabbed him from out of nowhere.

Christian struggled as they forced him to the ground, cuffing his wrists behind his back. "You have the right to remain silent. Anything you say can be held against you in a court of law…"

Ignoring the pain of being lifted back to his feet by his almost dislocated arms, Christian wrenched his head around with great effort. He stole a brief glance down the corridor and into the observation room.

An eerie red glow was filling the room. He was confused until a sudden burst of camera flashes revealed a blood-soaked observation window.

Behind the window was an image that would forever be burned into Christian's memory—an image of Collin's headless body, tied to his chair.

Chapter 11

~*~ Present Day ~*~

Christian looked at the class with renewed hope coursing through his veins. The memory of Collin was foremost in his thoughts.

"I know, without a doubt, that somewhere in our body lies an undiscovered interface with our DNA. This interface allows for dynamic changes to our genetic code based on environmental feedback, not just random mutations. I also believe this same interface allows us to record and store everything we see, hear, smell, touch, taste, and feel from the moment we're conscious until we die."

Christian paused, realizing that this was the true hypothesis that would set him free. This hidden interface between our fragile mortal bodies and our immortal DNA is the key to solving Collin's puzzle.

Christian wasn't distracted by the rude departures of more faculty as he continued, "Back to our original topic. I believe the ability to store and transfer memories to our offspring is still alive and well in the human race. The only difference is that we aren't as aware of these memories in our conscious mind the way our ancestors might have been. Maybe we don't need them anymore, the same way we don't need wisdom teeth. Apologies if I sound like a broken record."

A quickly raised hand from the crowd gave him pause as the student asked, "What's a record?" Before Christian could answer, the student had asked their AI ChatGPT app, nodding with comprehension. "Never mind, I see. The record player uses a sensitive needle to translate music from a crudely coded vinyl disc, known as a record, that slowly spins in a circular motion. If that record becomes scratched or damaged, each revolution will cause the needle to skip back and play the same line repeatedly. Hence the 'broken record' comment. Sorry for the interruption—please continue what you were saying, I was really into it!"

Christian just smiled and continued with a deeper appreciation for this next generation of learners. "If you think about it, it makes sense. Prehistoric humans didn't have the luxury or time to learn how to stay warm, avoid dangerous predators, or figure out which berries were lethal. They relied on these memories to keep them alive. As humans developed more complex communication skills, learned to read, write, and make records, no pun intended, they no longer needed these memories to stay alive, and, like we've seen in previous examples, maybe our genetic code removed our access to these memories. Science has explained away the existence of these memories by calling them instincts, but again, what is an instinct if it's not a memory passed down from our ancestors?"

The remaining professors, except for Dr. Jamison, fled the lecture hall. Christian didn't fault them; they were more afraid of Jamison than he was. Dr. Jamison gave an approving nod to his fleeing colleagues, then turned to Christian with renewed vengeance.

Christian paid little attention. He thought about Collin and looked at the students, who were clearly interested in the discussion, daring to abandon their note-taking requiem for a brief stint of critical thinking.

A student across the room interjected with a question. "Are you saying I have my parents' and grandparents' memories stored somewhere in my DNA?"

Christian replied, his voice full of emotion, "That's exactly what I'm trying to say. In fact, I believe you have every one of your ancestors' memories, from the beginning of time, stored in the DNA of every cell of your body. I also believe they're only accessible with external intervention."

"External intervention?" The student asked, raising an eyebrow.

Christian recalled his father's story of the pessimistic kid versus the optimistic kid. Both were presented with a six-foot-high pile of horse manure. The pessimistic kid ran away, looking for hand sanitizer and someone to clean up the mess. The optimistic kid dove into the giant pile and thrashed around like a college freshman on spring break. When asked what he was doing, the kid simply responded, "With all this horse shit, there must be a pony somewhere!"

Christian knew exactly where that pony was. "I believe we can only access our genetic ancestral memories through select psychedelics and possibly unique forms of head trauma."

Four hundred Psych 101 students sat paralyzed, waiting and anticipating the next words.

"There's little to no empirical data proving these memories exist, thus I'm not supposed to discuss them with impressionable students. However, fate doesn't always adhere to departmental policy. Two years ago, I had the honor of working with a young man named Collin. He had clearly and unequivocally gained access to countless memories from countless generations past..."

An unexpected and unidentifiable sensation paused Christian mid-sentence as he fought for the words. "Collin was..." An invisible pair of hands began crushing his throat, preventing the words from escaping. "Collin..." A wave of nausea and disorientation almost buckled Christian's knees as memories of Collin's blood-soaked, headless body flashed like a strobe light in his mind. The antique walnut podium groaned under his full weight as his equilibrium was challenged by the sights and sounds of concerned students blending with the ringing in his ears and the blurring in his eyes. Christian steadied himself, wondering if this was what his father experienced daily with his PTSD flashbacks.

As the episode began to pass, Christian remembered the parable of the shoemaker's family and their neglected shoes. It was only now that Christian realized he had not once sought therapy for himself in the two years since Collin's murder. He glanced over to Dr. Jamison, who was fighting to conceal a smug grin as he gathered his papers.

"In light of Dr. Yates's condition," Dr. Jamison said while standing and addressing the concerned students, "I feel it's only appropriate to adjourn class for the day and resume next time."

"A rustling of backpacks and closing laptops slowly filled the auditorium as students reluctantly prepared to leave. Then, like a phoenix rising from the ashes, Christian's voice boomed over the microphone, halting everyone in their tracks. "As I was saying," the words resonated with hope and reverence, "Collin was brutally murdered before we could conduct the proper research to fully understand his condition. I have, and will continue, to dedicate my life to uncovering the mystery of these genetic memories and finding Collin's killer."

Dr. Jamison quickly sat back down as the captivated students leaned into Christian's every word, some dangerously close to cascading off their seats onto the students below.

"Wow, I remember you from the news," the same student said with revelation. "They tried to pin that murder on you, but it didn't stick," a low murmur spread through the audience as the students who hadn't already made the connection did so. The student continued with another question, "So, if I'm understanding you correctly, you're saying everything that I'm seeing, hearing, tasting, smelling, and feeling is being recorded, in real time, and stored somewhere in my DNA?"

Christian pounded the podium with unexpected excitement, startling himself and the students. "Yes, yes, yes! This is EXACTLY what I'm telling you. Not in a million years would I have believed a word of it, had I not seen it with my own eyes. I spent a month with Collin, and, during that time, I was humbled by the limitless abilities of the human mind and body. Collin cycled through roughly two thousand distinct personalities. He spoke, with fluency, over eighty different languages and dialects that we could identify and confirm with translators. We were also able to identify who, when, and where many of those personalities came from. They stretched all the way back to the beginning of recorded history. I ran an AncestryDNA test on Collin and was able to accurately match over thirty ancestors in his family tree dating back almost seven hundred years."

The boy who had asked the question stared at Christian with a look of awe as he continued to speak. "I've taken an intro to biology and learned a little about DNA. I know it's made up of four different nucleotides arranged in different combinations to store all of our genetic information. I'm a computer science major and couldn't help but think how similar it was to computer data, which is made up entirely of various arrangements of ones and zeros. My first question is how it's possible to store a lifetime of sensory data in the DNA, and second, they've mapped out most of our DNA, so why haven't they found anything like what you're talking about?"

Christian had numerous theories on these exact questions. Countless sleepless nights and long days at the library had been spent researching the possibilities. These theories were even more outlandish than the existence of genetic memories. But once again, having seen it firsthand in Collin was enough to overcome any doubt or obstacle in his way.

"What's your name?" Christian asked the young man.

"It's Chad."

"Well, Chad, now you're asking the million-dollar question, and I've literally spent hundreds of hours contemplating this."

"Wow," Chad said, nodding in anticipation.

With a calm but excited tone, Christian continued, "The topics we are now discussing would have gotten us labeled heretics and blasphemers not that long ago. The good news is they no longer burn you at the stake, at least not literally, for free thinking and brainstorming." There was a low murmur of laughter as Dr. Jamison squirmed in his seat. "The only thing I ask is that you keep an open mind and take everything I say with a grain of salt. Your guess is just as good as mine, if not better!"

Christian could tell the students appreciated his honesty and transparency. "First, I may have a slight advantage as I've taken advanced courses in psychology, anatomy, biology, chemistry, biochemistry, genetics, physics, physiology, and neurology. Please forgive the humblebrag!"

Another rumble of laughter.

"With that said, most of what I'm about to discuss is more like science fiction than science, so you may have the upper hand. The bottom line...your imagination is the limit!"

Chad, along with everyone else, nodded their heads in agreement.

"Fasten your seatbelts and let's take a little ride down the rabbit hole and see where it leads."

Chapter 12

~*~ Two Years Earlier ~*~

T he flashing cameras and police lights were a muted blur as they escorted Christian, cuffs and all, out of the hospital. He wasn't worried about the reporters' questions or the rapid-fire camera flashes. There were just two simple thoughts dominating his mind as the detective pushed his head down into the police cruiser: Why Collin, and where was Dr. Nilsson?

Christian couldn't help but take in the scene at the police station as they made their way down the dimly lit hallway. The windowless walls were constructed of gray cinder blocks. The dismal, flickering fluorescent lighting cast a hopeless hue that made the already depressing environment feel even more morgue-like.

Every noise became a hollow echo in this environment devoid of any soft, sound-dampening materials. The ambiance was not helped by the intermittent sounds of metal cell doors closing and rusted chair legs dragging across hard institutional floors. This was all accented with the smell of body odor and fear that is to be expected in a place that routinely manages the people we try so hard to avoid in our daily lives.

Christian slowly gained his bearings as the officers awkwardly led him through the police station, weaving between random desks and bustling personnel. As he attempted to block out the judgmental stares from all sides, his attention was piqued by a spirited argument taking place behind a closed glass door with the name Chief Williams stenciled across it.

A man in a disheveled suit, who Christian assumed to be Chief Williams, was having a heated conversation with another man and a woman, both wearing dark navy FBI wind breakers. Standing above them all was a remarkably handsome, rugged-looking gentleman. This mysterious man's shoulder-length, dirty-blond hair flowed over the back of his black military vest, emblazoned with large white lettering that simply read INTERPOL. Christian estimated him to be in his early fifties, and the natural authority he exuded was apparent without so much as a word.

Christian's observation was cut short as one of the escorting officers gave him a harsh shove, refocusing his attention towards the interrogation room ahead. As he was forcibly seated in an uncomfortable gray metal chair and handcuffed to an equally drab table, his eyes were drawn to a camera with a blinking red light strategically placed high up in the corner to his left.

Despite the rush of adrenaline and the initial shock of the situation, the hour he was forced to spend there felt like mere minutes. His numb legs and back disagreed. Nonetheless, he understood the interrogation room and long wait were most certainly standard operating procedures aimed at frightening and intimidating suspects like himself. Rather than dwelling on the possible consequences of a crime he did not commit, Christian focused his thoughts on Collin—the only thought that mattered to him in that moment.

Without warning, a detective stormed into the interrogation room, slamming the door and snapping the blinds shut before turning towards Christian. With no introduction or eye contact, he flung a thick manila folder alongside an evidence bag containing Christian's bloody ID badge onto the table.

Christian wondered if this man even knew he was in the room. The detective opened the manila folder and began to speak in a calm, collected voice as he leaned over, rifling through the paperwork, still making no eye contact.

"Here are the facts. At 10:45 PM last night, this university ID badge with your fingerprints on it was used to enter Collin's observation suite. At 10:58, your login and password were used to access the computer in the observation room, where you downloaded Collin's complete medical history, including all CT scans, MRIs, and other related reports. We don't know how yet, but you managed to erase all of Collin's records, not only on the hospital database but also all the remote backups located at the Iron Mountain facility in Pennsylvania. If that wasn't enough, you then released over three thousand confidential patient medical records onto the internet. The HIPAA violations alone could land you a decade in jail, but then you had to go and cut poor Collin's head off."

As the detective spoke, a sick, visceral feeling consumed Christian. Despite this, he refused to show his discomfort to the interrogator.

"But wait, there's more," the detective exclaimed. "You used your badge to leave the observation suite at precisely 11:14, dropping it on the elevator floor as you fled the building, which means you did all of this in less than thirty minutes. As of a few minutes ago, we have not discovered a single eyewitness or camera catching you in the act. However, we did find your fingerprints all over the computer and the room in which Collin was decapitated. Unless you have a bulletproof alibi for last night, I believe we have more than enough evidence to bring formal charges against you."

The detective slowly closed the folder, stood up straight and crossed his arms. Seething with condemnation, his gaze met Christian's for the first time, "So… what say you?"

Chapter 13

~*~ Present Day ~*~

To both his, and their surprise, Christian abandoned the safety of the podium and moved closer to the students, "Everything Chad said is correct! Scientists have mapped most of our DNA, and there are no indications of some vast repository of 'memories.' Even if such a place existed, the DNA strand would have to circle the planet a million times to store that much information."

Christian continued, "Sometimes, the most important step in answering a question is figuring out what the answer is not. In this case, I believe we should eliminate the possibility of memories being stored in DNA through the traditional nucleotide bases—adenine, guanine, cytosine, and thymine.

"Have you ever heard the phrase, 'I saw *my entire life flash before my eyes*'?"

A low roar of positive affirmations reverberated through the room.

"We've all heard it at one point or another in our lives, but probably never really gave it much thought."

Another wave of agreement.

"As it turns out, this phenomenon has been observed more frequently than any other throughout all religions, cultures, and societies since the beginning of recorded history. It occurs most often when someone has a near-death experience. But we can assume it also occurs when someone has an actual-death experience." More agreement and some laughter rose and fell.

Christian queried, "My question is as follows: how can a person see their entire life in just a split second? For a seventy-year-old individual, that constitutes over half a million hours. Is it possible to see over half a million hours of your life in less than a second?"

More expressions of wonder suffused the room.

"If that example wasn't effective, think of one of your favorite movies. Does everyone have a movie in mind?"

Another murmur of agreement rose from the audience. "Most films run for an hour and a half to two hours, but in your mind, you can speed through the entire movie in just a few seconds. I challenge each of you to give it a try."

Slowly, more waves of oohs and ahhs emanated from the students.

"Space-time is not as simple and linear as we assume it to be. Can anyone explain how you just watched a feature-length film in your mind in just a few seconds?"

Initially, there were no responses, but a hand gradually rose in the back of the class. "Hi, I'm not actually in this class. I'm here for Professor Fielding's graduate class in quantum physics. I was going to take a quick nap, but this is too intriguing."

Christian grinned and said, "Please feel free to share your thoughts. We value everyone's opinions."

It was apparent that the quantum physics student appreciated the invitation and spoke confidently. "To experience an entire lifetime in a moment, the normal laws of physics would need to be suspended. This can theoretically happen when approaching the speed of light or nearing the event horizon of a black hole. Therefore, I speculate that these hypothetical memories could only be stored and manipulated at a deep subatomic quantum level."

The graduate student continued, "I agree with your assessment of the space-time assumptions we all make. We live in a constant state of false security when it comes to time. I believe we choose to live that way as the concept can be overwhelming. Another example of us accepting time anomalies is the Time Perception phenomenon that every creature on the planet experiences throughout their life."

"Could you elaborate on that for me and the class?" Christian asked with genuine interest.

"Absolutely!" The physics student accepted the request with enthusiasm. "When we recollect childhood memories, each minute, hour, month, and year seems to last much longer than they do now. Accompanying this is the impression that every subsequent year passes faster than the previous one. Have you all experienced this?"

The entire class agreed in unison.

"This is not a trivial mind trick," the student stated. "Time is indeed accelerating, and we are all conscious of it in our daily lives. Rather than trying to comprehend it, we choose to use it as a casual conversation topic when we run out of things to say!"

The students were clearly taken by this idea, and silence ensued as they pondered what the physics student had just introduced.

Christian thanked the graduate student for her contribution. "I think she's exactly right! For those of you who haven't studied chemistry or physics, most visible matter in the universe consists of atoms. For our discussion, DNA is composed of the four peptides mentioned before, arranged in millions of various combinations to store our genetic code. One strand of DNA has millions of each of those four peptides. Let's take adenine as an example. One of those millions of adenine molecules contains carbon, nitrogen, and hydrogen atoms. Its chemical formula is $C_5H_5N_5$. One hydrogen atom from one adenine molecule theoretically has enough subatomic space to store a million lifetimes of memories a million times over."

More waves of awe filled the lecture hall. Christian completed his example. "To summarize, I believe there exists a dynamic mechanism within the body that interacts with our DNA, and is yet to be discovered. Among its many functions, it uploads and downloads all of our sensory data—a.k.a memories—into a subatomic space located somewhere in our DNA. The same space where all the memories from countless previous generations are also stored."

Dr. Jamison abruptly interrupted the explanation, lunging out of his seat and violently throwing his notepad aside. "You're finished here!" he exclaimed before storming towards the exit.

Christian lifted his arm towards Dr. Jamison's disgruntled exit. "There's a pillar of individual expression and free thought, give him a hand!" A mocking ovation, boos, and a few paper balls were hurled at Dr. Jamison as he fled the lecture hall.

A student protested, "They can't do that to you."

Christian responded in a calm and reassuring tone, "Unfortunately, they can, and frankly, I wouldn't have it any other way!"

Chapter 14

~*~ Two Years Earlier ~*~

"What say you?" Of all the things Christian could have said at that moment, questioning the detective's English syntax should have been the last on the list. "Is that even proper grammar?" Christian replied.

As the detective violently dove across the table at Christian, he regretted not asking a more benign question like, "Don't I need a lawyer?" or, "Don't I get a phone call?"

The one thing Christian didn't want to tell the detective was that he was alone in his loft all night with absolutely no witnesses or alibis.

Christian gritted his teeth and prepared for the blow, but it never happened. Instead, the detective froze in midair and was flung backward towards the wall. As Christian opened his eyes, he saw the imposing Interpol agent pinning the detective against the wall. A quick pan downward revealed the detective to be suspended half a foot above the floor.

The two FBI agents and Chief Williams rushed in to intervene, but it was like a toddler trying to move a parked car from its space.

The Interpol agent finally released his steel grip as he turned to face the group. The detective flaccidly slid to the floor gasping for breath.

Christian noticed the name 'Soren Müller' Stitched on the front breast pocket of the agent's body armor as he addressed everyone with a neutral German accent, "I don't know how you cowboys do things around here, but where I'm from, we don't assault our handcuffed detainees who haven't even been offered a lawyer or a phone call."

The detective hoarsely proclaimed, "Time was of the essence; we needed to get vital information."

Soren addressed the group as he approached Christian's table, turning his back to everyone else, including the camera, "If you had just listened to me, you would have saved yourself a lot of excitement and pain."

Christian watched in amazement as Soren winked at him with a "follow my lead" gesture, before turning back to the others and continuing his explanation.

"I arrived from Switzerland late yesterday evening after receiving an alert about a doctor in Rhode Island whose death matched the MO of a serial killer we've been tracking for the past five years in Europe. Her name was Dr. Emma Goldstein. We were able to link her to Collin, who matched the type of victim this serial killer has been stalking."

"And you didn't think it prudent to notify us?" Chief Williams demanded, making no effort to mask his contempt. "This kids death may be on your hands as well."

Soren continued with a look of regret, knowing there was probably some truth to Chief Williams accusations, "I went straight from Logan International to Christian's place."

The female FBI agent quickly chimed in, "How did you know Christian was involved?"

"Fair question," Soren admitted, "during our investigation, we came across the case study Christian and Dr. Nilsson wrote. I had strong reason to believe Christian's life was in imminent danger, and I needed his help."

"We also found their little scientific article," The chief boasted waving the manila folder, "but what does that have to do with the price of rice in China, and what do you mean you needed Christian's help?"

"Because," Soren revealed with a calm and declarative tone, "Dr. Nilsson does not exist."

The chief was reaching a fever pitch as he bellowed, "The hell you say! He's more legitimate than you! We have his hospital background check from Stockholm University right here." Once again waving the manila folder as his patience wore even thinner if that was possible.

"I can see how it would seem that way," Soren cautioned as he began pacing away from the chief, "but, on a hunch, I had one of our Swedish Interpol agents visit Stockholm University and ask a few questions."

"And?" both FBI agents asked in unison with bated breath.

"They never received a background check, and have never employed a Dr. Nilsson. This person we're calling Dr. Nilsson intercepted the university hospital's background check before it reached Stockholm University. He then responded with a completely false identity, including a twenty page CV and a perfectly forged signature from the rector of the university."

Christian was speechless at this point as Soren continued, "The serial killer we've been investigating for the past five years is so elusive that we've never even found an eye witness to describe him. I think your Dr. Nilsson is our serial killer."

The male FBI agent asked rhetorically, "Does your serial killer normally cut the victim's heads off?"

"That's a first." Soren said, acknowledging the agent's point.

"You still haven't answered my question," Chief Williams snarled through clenched teeth, "why did you need Christian's help?"

Christian was impressed with the convincing guilt Soren expressed as he delivered the closer that would sell everyone on his lie, "I needed Christian to lure Dr. Nilsson into the open this morning where I was going to detain him for questioning." Chief Williams face was turning bright red as Soren continued, "Christian and I stayed up all night planning the operation. I was with him right up to the moment he entered the hospital this morning, so there's no way he could have murdered Collin."

Chief Williams exploded with rage as he drew his pistol on Soren, "You're under arrest you arrogant bastard. Who the fuck are you to come sneaking into my jurisdiction playing God like you own the place?"

A ping from the female FBI agent's phone broke the tension as she read the message and simultaneously addressed Williams, "Stand down Chief Williams. The Department of State just sent a verified communication regarding Agent Müller. According to them, he is some kind of Interpol special forces agent with security clearance far above any of our pay grades. Effective immediately, all local, state and federal authorities are to aid and assist Agent Müller in any way possible."

Chief Williams reluctantly lowered his weapon from Soren, knowing this was checkmate, "No hard feelings, right friend?", he then turned to Christian, "Looks like you're off the hook. No harm, no foul…"

Christian paid little attention to Chief Williams. His focus was directed towards a wall mounted TV just outside the door as a special report interrupted the regularly scheduled programming, "We're reporting from the university hospital where Christian Yates, the person of interest in the decapitation of a helpless psychiatric patient, has been apprehended."

Everyone in the police station watched in silence as a video of a handcuffed Christian being pushed into the police cruiser played over and over.

"Sure, no harm, no foul…" Christian vacantly mumbled, more to himself than anyone else.

Chapter 15

~*~ Present Day ~*~

Another student raised his hand. His T-shirt read 'The Truth is Out There.' Christian knew he would have something interesting to say.

"Hi, my name is Eric, and I know it may sound strange, but what if humans are just high-tech recorders placed on earth by higher intelligence to gather information? If your genetic memory theory is true, then we could have memories stored in our DNA from the beginning of time. That would explain why aliens abduct people. I bet they take us to the mothership and upload our memories into their database for research!"

Eric's expression then faded, and it was apparent he had drifted into deep concentration as he continued, speaking more to himself than the class, "But that still doesn't explain the anal probing..."

As the laughter subsided, Christian looked at Eric and then at the rest of the class. "I know some of you may think Eric's idea is a little far-fetched, or maybe not, but he's done something that I want all of you to see. He's expressed an idea without fear of repercussion. This action represents a core principle of a free society: freedom of speech and thought. This kind of thinking is vital for the progression of humankind, and I applaud your courage, Eric.

"In response to your theory, I think we must first question whether or not extraterrestrials have ever visited our planet." A tidal wave of disagreements and gasps flooded the room.

Christian had clearly trodden on sacred ground and had to act fast. "I understand your concern, but please hear me out! If any of you decide to study Philosophy, you may come across a school of thought that has pondered the probability of extraterrestrial visits. In fact, the US government conducted some studies on this topic back in the day. Instead of looking into space or sending random radio signals into the cosmos, the government hired an elite group of philosophers and influential thinkers to ponder this probability. Their conclusions were both enlightening and sobering."

Christian walked over to one of the giant blackboards and started writing down numbers. "The first part is a simple matter of statistics. In our galaxy alone, there are literally hundreds of millions of stars just like our Sun. Of those hundreds of millions of stars, there are millions of them with planets in that sweet spot 'Goldilocks' zone where the elements of life, including liquid water, can exist freely. If you believe in evolution, as many people do, then you will quickly see from those numbers that it would almost be impossible for life not to evolve on some of these water-supporting planets. This group concluded there is an almost certainty of life on other planets."

A gasp of renewed interest filled the room. It was a close call. He'd almost lost them, but he could tell by the refreshed postures that they were back. "This leads to the second part of their conclusion. Do any of you know what powers our Sun and all the stars in the known universe?"

The quantum physics student happily chimed in, "Stars are basically great big balls of subatomic fusion."

"Thank you...?"

"Amanda," the quantum physics student quickly answered.

"Thank you, Amanda! The gravity and heat of a star are so intense that it ends up fusing hydrogen atoms together and creating helium. This reaction releases enormous amounts of energy that we receive as heat and light radiation here on Earth. These philosophers concluded that nuclear fusion and fission are the most obvious forces in the visible universe.

"I say visible universe, because all the stars, planets and everything else we can see and measure in the known universe only makes up about five percent of the total matter. The other ninety-five percent or so of the universe is made up of dark matter and dark energy. These are the things we can't see or measure, but we know they are present and account for many of the mysteries we cannot see or explain... Yet.

"Back to the point. These philosophers and great thinkers inferred that any species that developed intelligence in this universe would eventually discover the secrets of fusion and fission, just as we have done here on Earth. They also deduced that once a civilization had discovered the secret to nuclear manipulation, they would destroy themselves long before discovering a method of traversing the vast distances of space, which would be necessary for discovering life on other planets.

"Their conclusion, due to this reasoning, was simple. Despite the almost certain probability of life on other planets, these civilizations would inevitably destroy themselves long before making first contact with other beings."

Eric was clearly unsatisfied with this conclusion. "What about all the crashed flying saucers and alien autopsies in the late forties and early fifties? The government has evidence and has been hiding it for the last seventy years!"

"Okay, let's think about this," Christian said, clearly enjoying the discussion. "Firstly, let's think about these flying saucers that crashed. How could a craft designed to cross countless light-years of brutal and unforgiving space simply crash upon reaching Earth? Secondly, you mentioned that most of these crashes occurred back in the late forties and early fifties," Christian said, asking Eric, "Why haven't there been any crashes in recent history?"

Eric thought for a moment. "You know, that makes sense. How can all these advanced spaceships just crash? And why haven't there been any crashes in recent history?"

Christian had an idea but wanted Eric to figure it out. "Can you think of anything we humans were doing for the first time in the forties and fifties that could have caused such an advanced craft to simply crash?"

Eric never had the chance to answer. Amanda stood up and exclaimed, "EMP! Holy shit. That makes perfect sense!"

Eric turned to the quantum physics student and asked, "What the heck is an EMP?"

Amanda enthusiastically explained, "An EMP is an invisible electromagnetic pulse that is released in all directions every time a nuclear device is detonated. It totally disrupts anything with electrical or magnetic components. Aliens would probably utilize dark energy and gravity drives to travel vast distances. Back in the forties and fifties, we were testing and detonating nuclear devices all over the place. We probably caught the aliens off guard. Since then, we haven't seen any crashes because either they adapted, or we stopped detonating nukes so openly; maybe a combination of both."

Christian had lost track of the time, and so had the class. They sat in silence and considered what had just been discussed. The aisles were filled with the remaining quantum physics students and their professor, who gave an approving nod and a smile to Christian.

Christian relished one last survey of the class, knowing it might be his last. "I wish you all the best. Remember, never compromise your beliefs. In the end, they're all we have." He gathered his books and left the classroom to a standing ovation and cheers.

Chapter 16

Christian demanded answers as he and Soren left the police station. "This is crazy, you weren't..."

"Shhhhh," Soren quickly interrupted, "there are cameras all around the police station. Is there a place where we can talk?"

Christian only had to think for a few seconds before replying, "OK, let's go back to the pub below my loft. It's just a few blocks north of here."

As they entered Ian's pub, Christian ducked and turned his head to avoid being noticed by the reporters camped out by the entrance to his loft. Soren had removed his Interpol body armor a block earlier, having already anticipated the reporters.

Ian, the pub owner, rushed them past a heavily lacquered bar and a number of weathered, dark wooden booths to a private table near the back of the room, "My God Christian," Ian whispered with his thick Irish accent, "You've sure gone and stepped in it this time. Is it true what they're saying?"

"No, of course not," Christian whispered, trying not to draw any attention their way. "Would I be out and about walking the streets if I had done that?"

"Fair enough," Ian exclaimed as he juggled three remotes for the three bar

TV's; searching for a channel that wasn't broadcasting Christian's face. He then walked away nervously as Soren slide the Interpol body armor under the table.

"OK, talk!" Christian demanded.

"I'm so sorry you've been pulled into this," Soren said apologetically.

Christian appreciated Soren's apology, but had so many questions, "What else do you know about this serial killer?"

"All the victims in Europe had severe cases of dissociative identity disorder and sometimes schizophrenia. They were all kidnapped, experimented on extensively, and murdered by way of a lethal injection of fentanyl. All the bodies were found with fifty to sixty times the tolerable amount of LSD and various other psychedelics, some we could not even identify."

"I'm still a little unclear how you tracked the killer here?" Christian asked, struggling to understand.

"To elaborate on what I said at the police station, Interpol is set up to get alerts anytime someone dies in a manner that matches an active investigation. We received an alert about Dr. Goldstein because she died of an extremely high level of fentanyl under suspicious circumstances. I was able to get an immediate warrant through the International Court at The Hague and cross-referenced all her patients. Collin jumped out because he matched the MO of all the serial killers' victims. Severe dissociative identity disorder and/or schizophrenia."

Soren continued, "Collin initially had run-of-the-mill schizophrenia, but was receiving treatment and leading a normal life. Then one day, he was found unconscious, having suffered severe head trauma. He was in a vegetative state, and his family was about to take him off life support. That's when a young neurosurgeon, Dr. Emma Goldstein, proposed a radical surgery that included placing an experimental electrical amplifier of her design between the two lobes of Collin's brain."

So entranced was he by the story, Christian barely noticed the two massive Guinness beers being placed in front of him and Soren. Soren protested to the server, "I think there's a mistake, we didn't order this."

The server said nothing and turned to Christian. Christian grinned, "I'm kind of a regular… is Guinness OK?"

"That'll be just fine after the day we've had!" Soren said as he gulped down half the glass and continued his explanation. "Last week, Dr. Goldstein went missing, along with all her research notes and data. Her body was found on the beach two days ago with high doses of fentanyl. This couldn't be a coincidence. I commandeered a seat on the first flight over the moment I made the connection. I clearly arrived too late but have no doubt that your Dr. Nilsson is the serial killer we've been following."

"Everything you're saying makes sense," Christian said, "but why on Earth would you stick your neck out for me?"

Without hesitation, Soren replied, "This person you call Dr. Nilsson is a master manipulator and destroyer of lives. His resources and skills are like nothing we've ever seen before. He clearly wanted you to take the fall for this. I wish I could say I did it out of some greater good or cunning checkmate move, but that's just not the truth. I did it because I'm sick of this asshole always being one step ahead and always getting what he wants. I wanted to send him a message. This was a no-brainer. I was able to foil a small part of his plan and save an innocent person from a terrible fate." With an extended hand, Soren finished, "Nice to officially meet you, I'm Soren."

Christian's physical appearance was not that of a stereotypical doctoral graduate student. At six foot four, when he wasn't slouching, and with a muscular build, Christian's classmates would routinely tease him, saying things like, "OK, Jack Reacher, how do you think this neuroscience final will play out?" Christian would laugh it off, because for every Jack Reacher comment there were two gentle giant references, which summed him up much better.

Christian was used to cutting his handshake strength by roughly two-thirds so as not to visibly injure the person whose hand he was shaking. As he grasped Soren's hand, this clearly wouldn't be the case. It took all his strength to match Soren's apparently effortless grip.

"What I said about this murderer back at the station is true," Soren exclaimed, trying to contain his excitement out of respect for Christian's suffering. "Nobody has ever seen this serial killer and lived long enough to identify him. You are the first. Please tell me everything you can about him."

"I wouldn't get my hopes up too much," Christian said, trying to temper the mood.

"How so?" Soren asked with apprehension.

"I never actually saw his face, nobody did. He had this unnatural beard that pretty much covered his entire face up to the bottom of his eyes. Then, he would wear these blacked out sun glasses night and day. About the only part of him I could describe would be his forehead."

Soren was clearly disappointed, "You spent four weeks with him. Was there anything else that stood out?"

Christian thought about it for a while, "Now that I think about it, there were two incidents during our time together that stood out, and I haven't told a soul."

"I'm all ears!" Soren said putting his drink down.

"First, I arrived early one morning at the hospital. When I entered the observation room, Dr. Nilsson was in the room shaking Collin." Soren raised an eyebrow as Christian continued, "He was shaking him and saying over and over, 'The golden cube, the golden cube, the golden cube!'"

"Interesting," Soren said, deep in thought, "what do you think he meant?"

"I called out to Dr. Nilsson over the intercom from the observation room, 'What are you doing?' He immediately stopped and looked at the window."

"Without breaking stride, Dr. Nilsson responded, 'I think Collin is going hypoglycemic and needs a sugar cube. I was hoping a nurse would hear me. He seems OK now though.' I just added it to my list of peculiar Swedish behavior and didn't really give it much more thought."

Soren thought this over for a few minutes. "I have many Swedish friends and colleagues. I wouldn't form an impression of all Swedes based on Dr. Nilsson's behavior. As for the golden cubes, I can't think of any way that relates to Collin or Dr. Nilsson. That said, I'll run it through the database to see if anything turns up."

"The next thing that stood out was a whole other kind of strange." Christian told him about Collin waking up and begging to be killed. He also mentioned the billions of years comment and the end of the world warning.

Soren took his time contemplating what had been told to him. "You did the right thing by not mentioning those little tidbits. I'd continue to keep them to yourself. I've worked on a lot of cases, and this one is different. I keep getting the feeling this is part of something bigger than anyone suspects. Is there anything else you can think of that stood out as particular?"

There was a long silence and suddenly Christian exclaimed, "Duh!", startling Soren and several other patrons. "I totally forgot the weirdest thing of all about Dr. Nilsson..."

"And?" Soren said, clearly desperate for any information.

"Well, he spoke with this really strange accent." Christian finally admitted.

Soren seemed a little let down, "Listen, I know the Swedish accent can be a little melodic and I'm sure he was faking it, so that probably made it even worse."

"I could have handled that," Christian said, "but this was different. His accent was off the charts silly, he sounded just like the Swedish Chef from Sesame Street. It was like he was purposely trying to sound ridiculous. Nobody could believe it."

With that last sentence, Christian watched as all the blood drained from Soren's face. Something about what Christian said had triggered the reaction, "Are you OK?" Christian asked, genuinely concerned.

Soren just sat there staring at his Guinness-white as a ghost, repeating over and over in between rapid shallow breaths, "No, it can't be..."

Christian was preparing to call 911, worried Soren was having a stroke or some kind of mental break. Then, as quickly as it set in, Soren snapped out of it.

"I have to go," Soren apologetically informed Christian while taking a card out of his pocket and writing a number on the back. "This is a very private and secret number. You must protect it with your life and only text or call if it's a life-or-death situation."

Clearly confused, Christian pleaded for more information. "What just happened? Did I say something to upset you?"

Soren looked at Christian with pain and compassion in his eyes. "The smartest thing you can do is forget we ever met. Death follows me like a biblical plague, and I can't have your blood on my hands."

"Wait," Christian pleaded, but it was too late. As quickly as Soren had flown into his life, so did he leave as he snatched up his Interpol vest and dashed out the door.

Late that night, Christian turned on the news halfway through a report, only to be shocked once more. "We believe this German male to be the eighth victim of a serial killer people are now calling 'The Surgeon.' He last struck in a small college town in the United States just one day ago. This is the second in a row of his eight victims who has been found with their head decapitated and missing."

...

Christian spent the next two weeks enduring a grueling university disciplinary hearing.

The university powers-that-be were prepared to expel Christian, even though the district attorney had never actually charged him with anything.

They concluded that Christian was at least partially responsible for the patient's medical records leak, as he had not properly safeguarded his ID badge and login credentials. They had also discovered his unauthorized saliva sample and AncestryDNA activities.

In the end, it was once again Dean Edwards who persuaded the council to settle for probation and a notation of the incident on Christian's permanent record. Christian wouldn't fully understand for another two years that this was still tantamount to a death sentence, and would not have cared if he did. The only things that mattered to him were understanding Collin and finding his killer.

Christian tried to change his doctoral thesis to focus on uncovering the existence of genetically inherited memories. Unfortunately, the psychology department refused to have anything to do with it, despite the clear evidence collected from Collin before his death.

Undeterred, Christian spent the next two years putting the bare minimum effort into finishing his dissertation on dissociative identity disorders while secretly devoting much of his time to researching genetic memories.

Chapter 17

~*~ Present Day ~*~

The faint echoes of seagulls reflected off the ivy-covered walls as Christian emerged into the early spring Rhode Island day, just in time to see the last of the morning fog lift.

As he stepped away from the shadowed archway, sunlight glistened on the dewdrops. Christian experienced the unveiling of a new world for the first time in the two years since Collin's murder. Despite his most promising career option being obliterated by the lecture he had just concluded, Christian was surprised that he didn't feel more remorse.

Instead, a nervous undercurrent of excitement coursed through his body. It was the feeling of being on the brink of a great adventure that had yet to be written but was undoubtedly his adventure to do with as he pleased.

Reluctantly, Christian moved away from the confining yet comforting university walls that had surrounded him for so long. A bit dazed, he struggled to grasp this new reality and shook off the heaviness of the past. Living with the specter of Collin and the guilt it generated for the past two years had crushed his spirit more than he had realized.

In a way, he felt like thanking Dr. Jamison for pushing him to and beyond his breaking point, inadvertently allowing him to shed this burden. The world was slowly coming into focus.

As he surveyed his surroundings for one last time, the attempt to gain a final moment of closure was interrupted by the extended hand of a former classmate and now colleague, Todd Brody. "Congratulations on your PhD, Dr. Yates!"

"Same to you, Dr. Brody." The words sounded strange and uncomfortable, but Christian knew he would have to get used to the title. He hoped, at least.

With a condescending tone, Todd asked, "So, what are your plans now?" The question was clearly rhetorical as he immediately shared his own good news. "Dr. Jamison just offered me the Assistant Professorship in the psychology department. Tough break for you, buddy, but I'm sure you'll land on your feet just like you did with the whole Collin thing."

Christian wanted to warn Todd but was torn between two of his dad's favorite cautions, "If you lie down with dogs, be ready to wake up with fleas!" and, "The higher up the ladder you climb, the more of your ass you show!"

In the end, as he watched Todd gloat with his smug, shit-eating grin, Christian decided to let him figure these things out on his own. *Who am I to be giving advice, anyway?*

"Congratulations! You're the perfect man for the job," he finally said. And he meant it. He knew that Todd would have no problem making the compromises the department would surely demand of him. In fact, he probably wouldn't even notice.

Todd had always planned on teaching at the university. He had everything plotted and scheduled, down to his third child. Christian envied that ability as he couldn't see his own future at a glance. Lately, his long-term goals seemed to have the foresight of a grocery list, and after the Collin tragedy, that list got a lot shorter.

An uncomfortable silence reminded them both of just how little they had in common. Todd left with a nod and a half-hearted "Best of luck," leaving Christian to his spoiled moment.

After the sudden jerk back to reality, Christian took one last look at the university and its Gothic spirals before heading across the grass-blanketed quad towards his loft.

His modest loft atop Ian's Pub had magnificent views of the cobblestone street below and the university beyond. During the day, this street was a bustling hub of commerce and New England college town charm. It was renowned for its commercial and recreational value, attracting a mix of tourists, students, and locals.

But with the setting sun came a transformation that could rival that of a werewolf under a full moon.

Without fail, each dusk, the gas lamps that adorned the storefronts would ignite, revealing the hidden world of discarded inhibition and libation that is to be expected in any good college town.

Around ten o'clock, oceans of students would begin to emerge from their respective days of note-taking and exam-cramming. Most of them were happy to drown their worries, if only for an evening of inebriated flirtation and a morning of shameful regret. Christian had observed but seldom participated in this world from his residence above Ian's since his sophomore year.

Fumbling for the right key as he faced the weathered door, Christian heard the distinctive Irish accent of his landlord, Ian Callahan. "Top of the day to you, lad."

Instinctively, Christian turned and began to ask Ian how much he owed for the bar tab plus rent, realizing the end of the month was upon them. But before the words were out of his mouth, Ian interrupted, "So, how did your first lecture go as a full-fledged PhD?"

Christian tried to be positive. "I enjoyed it, but I won't be holding my breath for a job offer."

Ian was a successful self-made businessman who took great measures to conceal his disdain for the world of academia, which was ironic, as it was his bread and butter.

With some hesitation, he asked how Christian's job search was going. "Did the licensing board process your appeal yet?"

Christian replied, "Not yet, but hope springs eternal!"

Sensing an unusual strength and defiance in Christian's response, Ian backed off and gave him a puzzled look. "Something's different about you, but I can't quite place my finger on it... yet!"

Before Ian could prod any deeper, a Guinness truck pulled up to the curb. With inventory and profit on his mind, Ian quickly lost interest in their conversation, which was odd, as he hadn't collected the rent yet. He excused himself to supervise the truck's unloading.

Finally uncovering the correct key, Christian finagled the old door open with a turn of the lock and a kick of the foot. He collected the strewn mail from the floor and creaked up the narrow staircase.

Chapter 18

The loft had become Christian's stronghold. Over the years, he had transformed a drafty and neglected space into a cozy, well-appointed home.

His gaze drifted to the street below as he procrastinated in front of the panoramic bay window. The miniature dramas that unfolded below were always a welcome distraction.

While scanning the street, a family of three caught his eye. The mother, in a confrontational stance, was speaking to the agitated father in her most controlled angry voice. The father began to tap his watch with growing impatience. The daughter, most certainly a prospective student touring the campus with her family, had her face buried in her hands, concealing her embarrassment from passing onlookers.

Christian knew exactly how he would help that family if they were his patients. Suddenly, he almost doubled over in physical pain, his guts churning at the thought of his denied license and assistant professorship. Hopelessness loomed at every turn.

I can't practice, and I can't teach.

So, where does that leave me?

Christian felt himself drifting further up the metaphorical creek without a paddle.

With the drama below dissipating, Christian sought a new source of distraction. He spotted the TV remote and pressed the power button. Before the picture fully brightened, the news anchor was giving an update on three mass shootings that had occurred over the weekend.

The reporter interviewed an expert on mass shootings and gun violence who explained, "This isn't an issue of violence. It's a mental health crisis. We have a nationwide shortage of mental health providers to combat the ever-growing surplus of angry, disgruntled individuals who desperately need help."

This wasn't helping.

The news anchor suddenly paused and brought his hand to his ear as his regular programming was interrupted. "This just in—we're receiving reports of a violent confrontation between a terrorist cell and a group of Interpol agents in the Czech Republic."

The screen flickered to live footage of a historic building in the heart of Prague, surrounded by wailing and flashing police cars, ambulances, and fire trucks. The camera panned to a third-story window with smoke pouring out, then back to the entrance as three bodies were rolled out on gurneys covered in bloody white sheets. The paramedics were in no rush.

A procession of Interpol agents and local authorities followed the gurneys, leading several individuals in handcuffs with cloaks over their heads. One Interpol agent towered above the others, and Christian immediately recognized him despite the helmet and goggles covering most of his head and face.

The anchor continued narrating the scene. "We've just received reports of several casualties and a stash of bombs and other illegal stockpiles. We've also received reports of something unusual hidden inside one of the walls—a duffle bag filled with tiny golden cubes, each measuring about one inch on each side. We are unsure what, if any, relevance this has to the terrorist activities, but will keep you posted."

Christian's breathing quickened as he fumbled through a desk drawer, praying he still had the card with the emergency number Soren had given him.

Just as he found the card, his phone pinged with a message from Soren on the emergency number, "Hi Christian, I hope all is well."

Christian responded, hands trembling, "I'm OK over here. Was just about to text you."

"I take it you saw the news," Soren texted back.

"Yes, I can't believe it. Are those golden cubes related to The Surgeon?"

There was a pause, then Soren responded, "Yes, but please don't share with anyone."

"Mum's the word, just happy there's progress."

"I have to go," Soren texted. "But please take care and be careful. He's still out there somewhere. I'll keep you posted with any news."

"Will do. Thank you."

Christian's heart raced as he paced the room. The interview with the mass shooting expert resumed. Christian quickly switched to a history channel, reminded of his inability to help due to his lack of a license.

The host of the show walked by a World War II memorial in Nagasaki, Japan. In the background, half-crumbling walls with dark, ghostly images on them caught Christian's attention. The host explained, "Behind me are the actual shapes of people. The light and heat from the nuclear detonation were so intense, they bleached all the surfaces except when blocked by people or objects. Thus, these eerie reminders of the unimaginable atrocities of war."

This wasn't helping.

He needed something more uplifting, and fast. With a remote in one hand and his iPhone in the other, he ended the TV show and started a playlist.

The familiar voice of Johnny Cash filled the room. The songs reminded him of his father and a time when life was simpler, before everything went to hell.

Without hesitation, Christian impatiently tore open a very old and expensive bottle of Johnnie Walker Blue Label that he'd been saving. He prayed it could now return the favor.

As he felt the burn of the first gulp going down, Christian tried with all his might to remember his father's face. It was useless, and to make matters worse, he couldn't remember when he forgot.

There were pictures, but they just weren't the same. His father had been shot and killed in a violent confrontation with four other men, who all died in the incident. Christian was only nine years old and the sole witness to the murders.

He had no memory of the event. Even after years of therapy, there was nothing. His saintlike grandmother had raised him after his father's death, but Christian always felt the void of losing his best buddy, as his dad would frequently call him.

Earlier that day, he had sacrificed his strongest and, quite frankly, only career option.

As he paced in front of the large bay window overlooking the street, a cold draft from the poorly insulated single panes reminded him of winter's resilience.

Anticipating a chilly evening, Christian threw some wadded-up newspaper, kindling, and a few small pieces of timber into the disproportionately large fireplace, then searched his coat pocket for his trusted lighter to start the fire. After some groping, he found the lighter, along with his mail. The fireplace was in the far wall, close to the front window. A worn brown leather chair from his childhood sat patiently by the hearth, beckoning Christian to sit.

By the time Christian finished his second drink, the fire was blazing, and the drafty room was soothingly warm. The bottle of Johnnie Walker Blue Label clinked against his rocks glass as a third round rushed out.

Christian vaguely remembered a time when opening the mail was a joy as he now begrudgingly scanned each piece. The first, a donation request from the alumni board, met a fiery demise with prejudice. The second was a statement for Christian's deferred student loans. He had six months left on his deferment of three hundred thousand dollars with an interest rate of forty-five dollars a day accruing. The third round of Johnnie Walker was empty before the statement hit the flames.

The final letter was from the Center for Advanced Human Studies in San Diego, California. Though he knew with certainty the contents of the letter, his twitching right eye refused to let him incinerate it.

Dear Dr. Yates,

Thank you for your recent inquiry and application. After reviewing your credentials and application, it is clear you have much to offer the field of mental health. Your experience and expertise are commendable. However, we regret to inform you that we do not have a current need for someone with your particular skill set and notoriety.

We wish you the best in your future endeavors.

Thank you,

Dr. Craig Hartman, M.D., Ph.D.

Director of Clinical Studies

Christian stood up, walked over to his desk under the window, and casually tossed the letter into a side drawer. This rejection was not alone; there were at least ten others in what he fondly referred to as the drawer of shame.

As courteous and professional as the rejections were, they all circled back, in one way or another, to his connection with Collin Trevor.

A manic storm thundered and roared, with black clouds of despair closing in. Christian poured a fourth drink and paced the floor. The Johnnie Walker only added to the waves of hopelessness drowning him, one after the other.

Christian thought, *It wasn't supposed to be this way. I faced my demons today and did the right thing. I should be on top of the world right now. So why does it feel the other way around?*

Christian felt the soft, worn leather of his favorite chair embrace his body as he reclined with his drink. The flickering flames lulled him into a buzzed slumber as he recalled the countless bedtime stories his dad had read to him in that very chair.

Chapter 19

The crashing embers of a burning log jolted Christian from his slumber. He had been in the middle of an epic dream and was sure he'd been asleep for days, but the clock indicated he'd only been napping for five minutes.

He struggled to hold onto the traumatic dream but wasn't sure why. He was ten years old and had been lost in his elementary school for days, trying to escape. Suddenly he was surrounded by a group of kids running around him, chanting repeatedly, "Son of a crackhead drug dealer, son of a crackhead drug dealer!"

Christian had spent every waking moment with his father before his death. His memories were of a wise, kind, and loving father with the patience and understanding of a saint. He remembered helping his dad feed the horses and muck the stalls; every second had been priceless.

Christian knew his father, like many who faithfully served their country, suffered from post-traumatic stress disorder (PTSD). His father had seen things no human should ever see, having served as a Navy SEAL for almost two decades.

Nevertheless, his dad regularly attended therapy and support group sessions and always took his medication. Christian never once felt unsafe, nor did he ever see his dad acting high or using drugs.

Tears streamed from Christian's clenched eyes as he smashed his fist into the arm of the chair, screaming, "Why did you have to leave me?" Then, with trembling rage, he continued, "And why the hell can't I remember a single second from the day you died?"

The exhaustion and trauma from the rebellious lecture and his nightmare had taken a toll on Christian. He spread the glowing embers in the fireplace and corked the remaining three quarters of his Johnnie Walker. Shutting down the last lamp, he fell onto his low Ikea bed with a thud, pulled up the down duvet, and drifted into deep, now dreamless sleep.

The next morning, the soothing sound of light classical music from his iPhone gradually roused Christian from his alcohol-induced slumber.

Mentally ready to resume his previous day's work, Christian turned the corner to face the first obstacle of the day: at least a foot of thick snow had replaced the early spring grass, rendering his sun-drenched world a gray, wintry wonderland.

Christian showered quickly and rummaged through his wardrobe, emerging with waterproof boots, a thick wool overcoat, leather gloves, and an old scarf. He was ready to face the elements.

Christian's first order of business for the day was settling up with Ian. As he cautiously stepped onto the sidewalk, he noticed the short, stout, red-headed man whistling an Irish tune while shoveling snow. Ian greeted Christian without missing a beat, "Top of the morning to you, lad!" Waving his checkbook in the air, Christian hoped to avoid any small talk and said, "Just wanted to settle up with my rent and bar tab."

Ian halted mid-scoop, with a look of sympathetic concern that troubled Christian. "Come on in, son. Let me make you a nice Irish coffee to knock the chill off." Christian had never refused a free drink, and this day would be no different.

As they walked in, Christian admired the festive decor that could easily have been in the heart of Dublin. The grand wooden bar with shiny brass accents dominated the center of the room. Dark, glossy wood paneling and leather booths reflected the light from the scattered flickering candles and sconces. A few tables and armchairs sat near the back of the room, in front of the large fireplace, while everything else was either tinted green or featured some form of a cloverleaf. To complete the ambiance, an endless mix of U2, Sinead O'Connor, and random Irish jigs played continually in the background.

Leaning back in a comfortable bar chair, Christian admired Ian's artful crafting of the Irish coffee as steam billowed and hissed from the shiny stainless-steel machine with unending levers and buttons.

But more than anything, he admired Ian's ability to embrace his heritage. Christian missed the Southern past and accent that he had worked so hard to abandon. The child inside of him had truly believed the distance would ease the pain. Of course, this wasn't the case. By the time he realized it, he was too far along in his New England academic journey to change course.

The more Christian tried to focus on Ian and his Irish Coffee, the more he was pulled into the past. Christian had always called his past trauma quicksand of the mind. You never know when you're going to step in it, and once you're in, resisting only pulls you deeper.

Since he couldn't remember the day his father died, he couldn't confirm or deny any of the headlines that read things like, "Disgraced Navy SEAL war hero turned addict dies in a drug deal gone bad," or, "Suspected cartel hit deep in the mountains of North Carolina. The only survivor, a nine-year-old boy, remembers nothing."

He didn't want to believe that his father was a drug dealer and addict, but he was only nine. Perhaps he had blocked out other bad memories and chosen only to remember the good ones about his dad. He knew all about trauma-induced amnesia and was well aware of its ability to alter one's recollection.

Christian was still lost in his thoughts when Ian placed the steaming Irish coffee in front of him. "What's on your mind, lad?" Ian asked, noticing Christian's distant gaze. Christian calmly returned to the present, took a sip, and responded with a smile, "Just thinking about the past, great drink by the way."

After another sip, Christian decided to broach the topic that had been eluding them both, "So, how should we work out the lease renewal?"

Christian's lease would be running out in a few months, and he assumed that Ian had some kind of insane rent increase in mind. He was also sure that there would be some very reasonable reason behind the increase, which would have explained the interrogation yesterday.

Ian fumbled around a bit before replying, "Actually, I wanted to talk to you about that."

Mentally preparing to argue against the increase, Christian was caught off guard as Ian pulled a picture of a beautiful, fiery, redheaded girl off the wall. "You remember my daughter Maureen, don't you?"

Christian's heart raced as he tried to maintain composure. "I've seen her around. You must be very proud."

Ian continued, "Well, we just found out that she's been accepted here, and we want to give her the loft."

Christian had feared this might happen, but he hadn't lost much sleep over it. Based on the wild stories Ian had told him over the years, he assumed that Maureen would either not get accepted here or go to one of the more social Southern schools. Seeing that was not going to be the case, Christian clung to the fact that he would have at least four months to prepare for the move before the fall semester started in August.

Ian continued, "I know the timing is terrible, but we actually want to renovate the loft and need to start at the end of this month."

And just like that, Christian's last security tether had been severed, triggering a free fall. The warm feeling inside from the Irish coffee quickly turned into heartburn as Christian resisted the rising sense of impending doom.

Ian could see the unrest in Christian's eyes and tried to ease the blow. "I know this is of little consolation, but you don't have to worry about this month's rent, the security deposit, or the bar tab." Neither of them was sure which was larger.

"I know this is short notice, and by law, you could challenge it, but we just didn't think she would get accepted here. Until a few days ago, we were pretty sure she would find her way to a school down South. They all rejected her.

"Hell, the only reason she got in here was that I caught some bigwig arsehole professor from the psychology department in the bathroom fooling around with an undergraduate. When I finally got him to stop begging and squealing like a trapped piglet, he asked if there was anything he could do to keep me quiet. Maureen got her acceptance letter the next week!"

Christian could only guess who the bigwig from the psychology department could be and thought about how useful that information could have been twenty-four hours ago. He quickly shook that thought from his head. That path leads nowhere.

Christian knew he had to pick his battles at this critical juncture in his life. "You've been a friend and pretty fair with me over the years, Ian. I'll take your offer, and please send my congratulations to Maureen."

Christian gulped the last mouthful of his Irish coffee as Ian sang his praises for being a stand-up guy. "I'll start getting my things in order and find a new place by the end of the month."

As Christian stood up to exit, Ian followed, "If there is anything I can do to help, just let me know."

The sidewalk appeared perfectly dry as Christian left Ian's pub. As his feet flew out from under him, Christian thought, Of course, this is happening, as he braced for the body-wrenching impact. He landed with a thud on his side. Without a word, he stood up and tried to ignore the radiating pain from his hip as Ian rushed out, fearful of a lawsuit.

"I'm alright," Christian mumbled while staggering to his feet. Ian apologized profusely as he dumped a full bag of rock salt to cover the icy scene of the accident. Christian tried his best to walk off the injury as he made his way down the street to Ed's newsstand.

Ed the news guy gave a hearty greeting that was met with Christian's best effort to stay composed. Christian didn't feel like tiptoeing around the issue. "Ed, I've been evicted. I have exactly two weeks and three days to find a place to live."

Despite his gruff shell, Ed was concerned and eager to help. "That's going to be a tough one, Christian. It's mid-semester, and the university has grown so much that apartments are almost as rare as virgins around these parts."

Ed proceeded to gather all the real estate magazines and classifieds he had lying around the stand. He handed them to Christian. "How much do I owe you for this, Ed?"

"It's on the house; you've been a great customer for many years. Good luck with your search." Christian thanked Ed and was on his way.

Two shops down from Ed's was Christian's next destination. As he walked through the door, Thomas of Thomas's Computer Corner welcomed him. "Good day, Christian, how can I be of service on this brisk, snowy morning?"

"My laptop's been slowing down lately, and I wanted to get a thumb drive to back up my research. I have it backed up online, but nothing beats a nice hard copy in hand."

Thomas handed him a drive, saying, "It's on the house. One of the kids told me about your lecture yesterday. Way to give it to those pricks!"

Christian thought about insisting on paying, but he recalled something about a gift horse and its mouth. "Thank you, Thomas. You're a good man."

His tasks had distracted him briefly from the impending reality of his eviction, but it all flooded back as he opened the door to his familiar home. As he climbed the stairs, each step became more difficult than the previous. Something had to give. The weight of the world was getting a little too comfortable perched on his shoulders.

The pain of his wounded hip faded with the evening sun. He managed to fumble the cork out of the Johnny Walker bottle and grabbed the nearest rocks glass. The crackling of ice as he poured the amber liquid was music to his ears. He bypassed the normal cooling-down period and took a large sip, which proved painful yet invigorating as the warmth of the alcohol spread throughout his body. Feeling the weight of his coat and boots, Christian separated from his drink just long enough to shed these articles and light a fire.

Finally comfortable, he sat down and began scanning the apartment ads. Having lost track of both the drinks and time, Christian suddenly found the fire to be hotter than usual. The guides had proven to be a much better source of fuel for the fire than real estate. The closest apartments were several miles away and, quite frankly, too expensive.

Reluctantly giving up on his search for a new home, Christian embarked on his age-old quest for answers. As his laptop chimed, signaling a successful power-up, the pressing dilemmas began to recede one by one. Immersed in the ever-present thoughts that consumed him, Christian found solace in his quest to understand Collins' tragedy.

Chapter 20

Christian had spent two years searching for more proof of elusive inherited memories. Having exhausted every scholarly outlet possible, he was now reduced to trawling chatrooms, hoping to find someone who could bridge the gap.

Christian was desperate and frustrated, but quitting simply wasn't an option. The search for an answer seemed to be the only thing keeping the lightning-strike flashes of Collin's headless body from dominating his every waking thought and haunting his nightmares.

His trawls always began the same way. He would visit one of the countless chatrooms that were an endless source of potential subjects. On this occasion, after several hours, he had burned through all the possibilities, and the remainder of his Johnnie Walker Blue Label.

Ready to call it a night and pass out, he began X-ing out of the windows, only to see one last chatroom: Eastern Europeans who love their terriers. Christian chuckled to himself. "Why not?"

Once logged in, he saw his familiar screen name, MGBman23. Christian had always loved these cars. The MGB, a small British convertible, was a poor match for Christian's anything-but-compact build, yet he adored them nonetheless. He wasn't fond of the number after his name, but surprisingly enough, there were twenty-two people before him who shared the same passion!

With his courage gathered, he posed the question he had asked countless times before: "Do any of you have memories of a past life you cannot explain?"

The first response, from JackRusselMan12, was not very promising: "What on earth does this have to do with terriers?"

Ignoring JackRusselMan12's unhelpful remark, Christian continued, "I know it sounds strange, but I believe there is someone out there who is aware of memories from his or her ancestors that have been genetically passed down from generation to generation. I want to find that person."

Pupgirl69 then asked, "Why is it that my Wire-Haired Fox Terrier only relieves himself on my finest rugs?"

As Christian prepared to add this chatroom to the hundreds of other failed attempts, something unexpected blinked onto his screen. It was from RelicCollector1. "Do you have memories of the past?" they asked MGBman23.

Christian quickly replied, "I don't, but someone I once knew had them, and I've been searching ever since for more like him."

RelicCollector1 replied after a pause, "Were his memories like watching a movie?"

"Yes, they were."

"You'll probably think I'm crazy," RelicCollector1 said, "but I started having these flashes about a month ago. I was standing on a chair replacing a light bulb. Without warning, the seat collapsed. When I woke up, there was a massive lump on my head. A few minutes later, these flashes started. They only last a few seconds but are so real. It feels like déjà vu, except the memories are not my own."

A message appeared on the screen announcing Mozart3000's arrival in the chatroom. "If you're not here to discuss terriers, then I suggest you leave. Otherwise, I'll report you to the admin."

Christian ignored the threat, considering this promising lead. "Would it be possible for me to contact you, RelicCollector1?" Christian quickly asked.

"Sure," RelicCollector1 replied. "My email is…"

The computer screen flickered and turned blue. Despite his lack of computer expertise, even Christian recognized the Blue Screen of Death. "Are you kidding me?" he muttered as he glanced at the unopened thumb drive sitting on the entryway table. With a mixture of controlled anger and cautious optimism, he slowly powered his computer off and turned it back on again. This usually did the trick.

Terror and shock surged from deep within as he watched a message he had never seen before appear on the black screen, "Input/Output error: Cannot Access Hard Drive: Press Any Key to Continue." Christian pressed a key. The same message reappeared. Pressing the key over and over only filled the screen with this ominously taunting message.

The laptop mocked him, repeating the same message again and again. With a doctorate in psychology, he knew better than most that expecting a different outcome from the same repeated actions was not a promising behavior. Yet he kept pressing the button over and over, fully expecting a different result eventually.

A wave of heat washed over Christian as memories from the past few days flashed through his head, shaking him to the core—Dr. Jamison, Ian, his laptop, and finally, the ever-present image of Collin's headless body.

With a trance-like calmness, as if suddenly possessed, Christian froze for a moment. He then slowly closed the laptop, unplugged it, and casually walked over to the large bay window overlooking the street. Taking a deep, relaxing breath, he reared back and hurled the computer through the frost-covered window with all two hundred and thirty pounds of his force.

Like the Millennium Falcon escaping the Death Star, the laptop exploded through the window and soared over the street below. It struck the opposite sidewalk with the impact of a tranquilized buffalo mid-stampede. Christian watched as the laptop, in slow motion, bounced off the sidewalk and crashed against the stone pillar marking the university's northern entrance.

He stood in front of the shattered window as the dark, wintry night filled the room. A new kind of peace, one he had never experienced before, settled over him.

Chapter 21

Johnny and Brian, brothers and The Surgeon's two most trusted assistants, dove to either side as Allen's head came hurtling towards them.

The Surgeon beat Allen's headless body, muttering, "Motherfucking bastard. Why didn't it work?" His experiment had failed once again. "Put this head with the others and get rid of the body. Let's toss this one in the harbor by the Little Mermaid. That should keep them guessing so they don't come sniffing around here."

The Surgeon stewed in his anger as Johnny and Brian collected the head and cleaned up the mess.

"I'm getting really sick of this guy," Brian said as they made their way to a small chamber at the end of a long corridor, "If he didn't have that security camera footage of us robbing the jewelry store and stabbing the guard, I'd be out of here faster than you could say creepy psychopath."

Johnny filled a large glass jar with formaldehyde and dropped Allen's head in with a splash. "Fuck, some of that shit just went in my mouth," Johnny said, spitting and wiping, unable to get rid of the taste. "I understand The Surgeon not wanting anyone to discover the heads since he started placing those weird devices, like the one we got from Collin's brain, but it's so damn disgusting."

Johnny dry heaved and tried his best not to throw up as he placed a lid on the jar and then placed the jar on a long shelf holding twelve other heads. The first of which was Collin's.

This was the twelfth attempt in the past two years since Rhode Island. Something wasn't right. The Surgeon wondered why he couldn't repeat the success he had seen years ago with Collin. Everything had been replicated accurately.

His anger intensified as he reflected on the ancient relic that had been within his grasp, only to be lost.

None of this would have been necessary if he had that intact relic. His people would be ruling the planet by now if not for that miscalculation so long ago. The sudden and painful crack of a tooth in his lower left jaw was the icing on the cake.

"Brian, where's my mouthguard? I just broke another tooth. All this failure is really making me clench. Can you also call that dentist for me? I'm sorry for losing my temper again."

Both Johnny and Brian gratefully accepted the extremely rare apology.

The Surgeon's attention was diverted from his broken tooth by a rapidly beeping alarm. It was coming from an impressive array of computer equipment across the room. He quickly ran over to it and sat down.

In front of him, on the monitor, was a chatroom, and in it was his next victim. Johnny had discovered her several months ago. Since then, The Surgeon had been dividing his time between the acquisition of Allen and establishing the trust of this new, promising person.

As he logged in, a new but familiar person caught his attention: MGBman23. The Surgeon smiled, thinking, what are the odds? He reminisced about his time with Christian two years prior.

His fond, nostalgic smile quickly became a scowl as he saw who Christian was talking to and what questions he was asking.

He sent a message to MGBman23, asking him to leave the chat. When that didn't work, he knew what had to be done.

Unbeknownst to Christian, The Surgeon had discovered several of his subjects by following Christian's research. "Unfortunately," The Surgeon thought, "it's time to clean up this loose end."

Having hacked Christian's computer years ago to keep an eye on him, The Surgeon required little effort to unleash a virus that would not only destroy Christian's computer and all its data but also the online backups he knew Christian had made. In fact, it was the same virus he used on Collin's records years ago, with a few upgrades.

"Johnny and Brian, listen carefully; we have our work cut out for us. First, we need to prepare for my trip to Poland. It's time to pay a little visit to RelicCollector1. After that, I'll need your help dealing with Christian."

Chapter 22

Christian woke at the break of dawn. He peered over the duvet, engaging in a brief staring contest with the clock. After a few seconds, he triumphed, and the hazy green light transformed into numbers, indicating it was 5:45 AM. The events of the night before were nowhere to be found in his recollections.

Feeling invigorated, he glanced behind the bookcase to determine if the rays of light streaming in were an illusion or the real thing. Encouraged by what he saw, Christian rounded the corner and was greeted not only by the sun but also by a cool blast of fresh morning air. This wasn't the first time he'd forgotten to close the window.

As he silently chided himself for leaving it open, a sudden flood of memories overwhelmed him. His head began to pound from the excessive alcohol of the night before, and his crisp, beautiful daybreak transformed into a mottled, pain-ridden hell. Staggering to the broken window, he strained to see the remains of a black, crumpled plastic heap across the street.

This wasn't Christian's first rodeo when it came to hangovers. He staggered to the medicine cabinet, poured a glass of water, and dispensed two Alka Seltzers, which fizzed with a burst of bubbles. Next, he expertly took four 200-milligram Advil tablets from the bottle and chased them with the seltzer water. Taking a deep breath, Christian prepared for the final and most important step in curing his hangover. The two shots of vodka went down more smoothly than expected. Within five minutes, he was feeling almost eighty percent better.

Not bothering with a shower, Christian knew what he had to do next. On his way to the twenty-four-hour campus library, he scooped up the remains of his laptop. He made a beeline for the library computers immediately upon entering. Once logged in, he pulled up his Google Drive and his separate Amazon backup storage.

Christian felt the blood drain from his face as he realized that both databases had been wiped clean. There was no doubt that something nefarious had occurred. But there was only one person who could help fix the catastrophe: Felix.

Christian first met Felix during their freshman year in an Introduction to Data Coding class. It became painfully clear on day one that an IT profession was not in his future. Felix was a different story. He took to coding like a fish to water, eliciting words like 'genius' and 'prodigy' from the professor. After graduating, Felix became the head of IT for the university, a position he had now held for several years.

As Christian walked through the campus, he had to dodge the decomposing snow and ice from the trees, as the previous day's fall had already started to melt. By the time he arrived at his destination, it was already six o'clock in the morning, and the posted hours showed the office didn't open until 7 AM. Before he could berate himself for having walked all that way for nothing, he saw a faint light emanating from the corridor that led to Felix's technology den.

After a few minutes of furious banging on the door, Felix emerged, his eyes bloodshot. When Felix saw that Christian was not leaving, he gave in and said, "OK, OK, hold your horses."

A look of sadness washed over Felix's face as he sat down with Christian's computer. It was the expression of someone who had witnessed the destruction of something beautiful. Christian felt envious of Felix's job and the happiness it brought him. When Felix asked how this had occurred, Christian provided a truthful account of what had happened, omitting the contents of the chatroom conversation.

"I've heard enough," Felix declared as he disassembled the mangled laptop and retrieved the hard drive. Within seconds, it was linked to his computer, and he had access to it. "The good news, if there is any, is that your computer was dead before it ever took flight." Christian received no solace from this response. "Have you tried to access your backups on Amazon and Google? If not, don't bother as they've been erased as well."

"How did you know?" Christian inquired with amazement.

"Everything is documented in the virus code," Felix stated as he scrolled through thousands of lines of—to Christian—senseless symbols.

"A virus?"

"Yes," Felix reiterated. "And a stunningly tasteful one, at that. Whoever created and executed this was a coding mastermind."

Christian had a hunch about who had penned that virus, but he kept it to himself.

"Can I retain this drive?" Felix asked. "If I am given enough time and luck, I may be able to obtain some useful information."

"Of course," Christian answered as he jotted down his phone number and email address, offering it to Felix. "Please let me know what you come up with. Thank you so much for your assistance."

Christian knew that Felix had done everything he could. He rose to his feet and left the room as Felix delved further into the software code.

The snow was melting quickly as the sun advanced through the chilly blue sky. Small streams of water sparkled in the sun as they trickled down sidewalks and off the rooftops. On his way home, Christian stopped by Thomas's Computer Shop and purchased a new laptop, without any discounts or freebies this time.

After making some calls and cleaning up the loft, Christian could no longer ignore his rumbling stomach, having been too occupied to stop for breakfast.

The growling of Christian's empty and hungover stomach reminded him that lunchtime was quickly approaching. He decided that fish and chips were in order, and there was no better place than Ian's, especially now as he figured it would be on the house.

The mailman passed as he came out of his building exclaiming, "Beautiful morning, isn't it, Christian?"

"I love this time of year, except for the slick sidewalks," he added, recalling his aching hip.

"Amen, brother. Pickings are scarce today; just this one overnight express package from Denmark. Looks important!"

The mailman handed Christian the package, and he immediately tore it open. Inside was an impressive-looking envelope with a corporate letterhead embossed in gold ink, which read, "Norkap Pharmaceuticals: Making the World a Better Place One Pill at a Time."

Chapter 23

I an always reserved the back table by the fireplace for Christian. The fish and chips, accompanied by a room-temperature Guinness, really hit the spot.

With no expectations, Christian opened the letter using his lunch knife. "This has to be a joke," he said, louder than he meant to, catching the attention of nearby patrons who looked up from their meals.

Dear Christian,

At the Norkap Pharmaceuticals headquarters in Copenhagen, Denmark, we are pioneering new realms of mental health treatment. Our next-generation targeted psychotropic drugs are enabling therapists to achieve in days what used to take years.

Your work with Collin Trevor has uniquely qualified you for the position outlined below. We are developing proprietary blends of cutting-edge psychotropic medications that allow individuals to safely access memories and emotions that would otherwise remain repressed and unreachable.

As Christian scanned the room, he searched for any sign of suppressed laughter, unable to imagine this being a legitimate communication.

Our founder and CEO, Dr. Hans Rasmussen, came across a recording of your lecture on Facebook. He believes your theories hold merit and has authorized us to recruit your expertise with great enthusiasm. We would like to offer you a starting salary of US$250,000, with full vesting after five years. Health benefits are not offered in Denmark, as world-class healthcare is available to all citizens, visa workers, and students at no direct cost. Additionally, extra retirement contributions are provided; however, there are no benefits for college funds, maternity leave, or daycare, as these services are also supplied by the state at no direct cost.

Dr. Rasmussen has approved the payoff of your student loans over the next three years. We typically do not address this issue in Scandinavia because, again, university education is, of course, provided at no direct charge.

The only thing Christian really knew about Denmark was that it usually ranked number one in the best countries to live in the world. As he reflected on his massive student loan debt and the thousand-plus dollars a month he paid towards health insurance premiums, he started to see how it could rank so high.

The letter continued.

Enclosed, you will also find an approved work visa, a first-class ticket to Copenhagen International Airport, and a security card to access your fully furnished apartment.

Christian knew this was way too good to be true. He also knew exactly what his father would be saying if sitting there enjoying a Guinness with him, "Never forget, son, love makes the world go round... but money greases the wheel. And right now, your wheel is a-squeakin'. Take the job and the money."

The sound of Ian's voice brought Christian back to reality. "You OK there?

Did you get something in your eye?"

Christian instantly became aware of his right eye rapidly twitching. It hadn't been this bad since he was a kid.

"Yeah, I think an eyelash fell in there while I was inhaling your famous fish 'n' chips!"

He quickly leaped to his feet while rubbing his eye. "Think I'll run home and try to flush this out."

Who was he kidding? Christian knew exactly why his eye was twitching so bad as Ian watched him fumble his way out of the bar.

The letter from Norkap had triggered something in Christian that he hadn't felt since he was a kid.

Hope.

The most powerful and dangerous of all emotions. Not hope that he could pay his student loans or have a secure job. It was the hope that Norkap's new psychotropic drugs could allow him to finally remember what happened to him and his father on that horrific forgotten day.

Hope that Norkap's new drugs could achieve the thing that years of therapy, hypnosis, and traditional medication had not. Christian had long since given up all hope of ever knowing what happened to him and his father all those years ago. Now he hated himself for letting that hope return.

Chapter 24

The American Airlines Boeing 777, powered by Rolls-Royce engines, cut through the night sky as the three hundred and fifty souls on board eagerly anticipated their arrival in Denmark. The flight, which departed from Logan International Airport at 5:30 PM, was scheduled to arrive in Copenhagen at 7:20 AM, coinciding with sunrise.

Christian sank into the plush first-class seat, stretched out his legs in the ample space, and sipped his Absolut on the rocks. Anyone else would have been in seventh heaven, but he was anything but relaxed. Since reading the Norkap letter two days ago, his tic had only grown worse.

After leaving Ian's place, he had gone straight to a walk-in emergency clinic, where they reluctantly prescribed him Xanax. Although it offered some relief, the floodgates had opened. The only way to genuinely slow the tics was through intense focus, which exhausted him and could only be sustained for brief intervals.

Ironically, he found himself wearing the same dark sunglasses he had once deemed silly on Dr. Nilsson. Christian knew this was merely a stopgap measure and that he needed serious intervention before things worsened.

Immersing himself in literature about Denmark provided a welcome distraction from his tics. It quickly became evident how proud the Danes are of their country and culture. Denmark's geography consists of two main regions. One is Jutland, a small peninsula jutting out from Germany's northern border, primarily characterized by farmland and small coastal towns and villages. The other region is an archipelago of islands, located east of Jutland. Sjaelland, the largest of these islands, is home to Copenhagen.

In Danish, the city's name is København, which directly translates to "Køben—buying" and "havn—harbor," essentially meaning a harbor of commerce. To his delight, Christian discovered that one of his favorite childhood toys, Lego, was invented in Denmark. He also learned Denmark is famous for its cheese, high-end furniture, and electronics, among other things. These little cultural tidbits were very interesting to Christian.

The flight traveled eastward, deep into the Atlantic night, when Christian grew tired of his Danish studies. As with most flights on this schedule, the overhead illumination had been dimmed with the setting sun. Christian looked up and realized that his tiny overhead light was the only one remaining. Once his eyes adjusted, he discovered most of the other passengers were in a blissful, engine-induced slumber.

Just as Christian was about to turn off his light, he saw a Montblanc pen fall out of the pocket of the passenger across the aisle. While waiting for the man to notice his missing pen, Christian saw the foot of the passenger behind slowly reach forward and stealthily slide the pen toward himself. Someone else had obviously recognized its value.

Christian watched in shock as the passenger discreetly picked up the pen and slid it into his pocket. He hesitated but decided he couldn't stand by idly. "Excuse me, sir," Christian said, nudging the gentleman across the aisle, "I think your pen fell on the floor, and the kind gentleman behind you picked it up."

He turned to the man behind him, who had quickly retrieved the pen from his pocket. "Here you go," the man said, handing it to the rightful owner. "I thought you were asleep and wanted to wait for you to wake before returning the pen."

The man took his pen back, thanked the man behind him, and then turned to Christian. "Thank you so much! I've had this pen for almost forty years.

It was a gift from Mikhail Gorbachev."

Christian noticed a USSR logo with a hammer and sickle on the pen as the man showed it to him. "Wow, I imagine there's an interesting story there!" Christian exclaimed, admiring the piece of history.

"Yes, it was used to sign a historical accord between the USSR and Denmark. But please forgive my manners—my name is Dmitry Ivanov, the Russian Ambassador to Denmark," he said, extending his hand.

As he shook hands with Dmitry, Christian exclaimed, "Wow, I've never met an ambassador before. I didn't realize you guys flew commercial airlines?"

Dmitry replied, "Alas, state jets are reserved for ambassadors to countries like the United States and China."

Christian felt bad about his comment, and Dmitry could sense it. Picking up on Christian's feelings, Dmitry quickly added, "I can accomplish much more out of the spotlight and wouldn't have it any other way."

Although still feeling slightly self-conscious, Christian felt a bit better and introduced himself. "I'm Christian Yates, from Rhode Island."

Noticing Christian's pamphlets and books about Denmark, Dmitry inquired, "Is this your first time visiting Denmark?"

"Is it that obvious?" Christian said, tidying up his workspace.

Dmitry smiled and responded, "Be proud of your efforts to understand the culture you're entering. Many people come to Denmark and take advantage of all the social benefits without trying to learn and appreciate the culture, people, and language that define it. But that's a discussion for another time. So, what brings you to Denmark, if I may ask?"

Christian replied eagerly, "I'm starting a new job with a company called Norkap Pharmaceuticals."

"Congratulations, Christian, I hear jobs at Norkap Pharma are highly sought after."

Feeling relieved, Christian responded, "Thank you."

Suddenly, Christian noticed Dmitry staring at his right eye.

"I wasn't prepared for how dry the air gets during these flights! My right eye isn't happy," Christian complained.

Dmitry nodded in agreement and advised, "Happens to me all the time.

Try to get some sleep. That'll help." He leaned back in his seat and said, "It was great meeting you, Christian. I'll leave you alone to catch a few z's before we catch up to the sunrise."

Both men settled in for a peaceful hour of slumber.

As they made their uneventful descent, Dmitry handed Christian a card with his cell number and home address on the back, remarking, "I owe you for saving my pen. I know you must be very busy, but my wife Eva and I would love to invite you over for a traditional Danish dinner this evening after you've settled into your apartment."

Christian felt grateful but hesitant to accept the invitation. "Thank you, but you don't owe me anything," he said.

"Nonetheless, we're thrilled to welcome you to Denmark," Dmitry responded warmly.

Christian had no plans and always tried to embrace new adventures, so he finally conceded, "Well, then, I humbly accept your invitation."

"Wonderful!" Dmitry exclaimed. "How does 18:00 sound?"

Dmitry watched with patience as Christian tried to make the time conversion in his head. "It's OK, you'll get used to what you Americans call military time! It's 6:00 PM. See you then!"

They parted ways, and Christian headed towards baggage claim.

After discovering that ride-sharing services like Uber and Lyft were illegal in Denmark, Christian hailed a traditional taxi.

As the taxi navigated through the city's hub-and-spoke grid, it became obvious he was no longer in the United States. Gone were the towering skyscrapers, replaced by ancient buildings averaging five or six stories except for castles and other historic landmarks that could rise much higher. Most buildings had either red or dark gray terracotta roofs or tarnished green, brassy metal coverings.

As they drew ever closer to the center of Copenhagen, a symphony of urban wonders unfolded. The city revealed itself as a collage of historic elegance and modern flair. Cobblestone lanes followed ancient routes, leading the way through a captivating blend of Danish architectural marvels.

Ornate bourgeois palaces stood alongside contemporary proletariat structures-a homage to the country's bloodless transition to a land of people unafraid to prune the overarching branches of exploitation when necessary to preserve the delicate tree of social democracy. But, just below the surface, among the roots of this majestic tree lie the seeds of ones and zeros that threaten to claim the means of production all for itself-another bloodless transition?

Bicycles flew by, their riders exuding an air of effortless cool, as if in perfect sync with the city's vibrant pulse. The aroma of freshly baked pastries casting temptation from all directions. Parks and gardens whispered tales of respite and tranquility, inviting young and old souls alike to find solace in their meditative embrace. With each passing moment, Copenhagen's charm enveloped Christian's senses, leaving an unquestionable impression of a city where culture, history, and modern liveliness coexist in perfect harmony.

While waiting at a stoplight, Christian observed a crew of four workers—two women and two men—repairing a section of the cobblestone street. He was amazed by their expertise, pride, and precision in placing each stone as they poured sand and pounded the stones into place with rubber mallets.

Copenhagen's bike culture was a sight to behold. Cyclists clearly ruled the city and motorized vehicles understood their place and were just lucky to be there. He watched as a well-dressed man cycled past with a fine leather attaché case secured to the rack on the back of his bicycle.

Christian had read that Copenhagen was one of the cleanest and greenest cities in the world, and his experience affirmed that. As they drew even closer to the city's core, Christian noticed several massive castles including a round tower with a large C and the number 4 superimposed over it. The taxi driver noticed Christian observing the architecture and offered some background. "That's Christian IV, the Builder King. He ruled Denmark about 400 years ago and was responsible for many of the sights you will see throughout Copenhagen."

"Very impressive, and I especially like his name!" Christian exclaimed with pride.

"Yes, you chose a good country to visit. Christian is a popular name. Speaking of which, if you make it out to the harbor, you should check out the statue of the Little Mermaid. It's based on the writings of Hans Christian Andersen!"

"Sounds like I've got a head start with a name like Christian! By the way, is today a holiday?"

"None that I can recall," the taxi driver replied, wondering if he had missed something. "Why do you ask?"

Christian looked around and remarked, "It's just that there are Danish flags everywhere I look. We do this in the US for our Independence Day, July the Fourth."

"Oh, I see!" the driver said, with relief at not having forgotten a holiday. "We Danes have a lot of national pride, and we love our flag. You should get used to seeing that red background with a white cross wherever you go!" The driver faded off on his explanation as he slowed to a stop. "Looks like we're here. Wow, you said your company is providing this apartment? They must really like you. Not everyone gets a top floor apartment off of H.C. Andersen Boulevard overlooking Tivoli Gardens."

"I had no idea," Christian said as he tipped the driver and stared up at the fourth-floor penthouse.

Christian lugged his bags to the elevator and inserted the access card that had been included in the package. The elevator pinged and rose to the fourth floor. The opening of the elevator door unveiled a fully furnished, ultra-modern luxury apartment. From the elevator, he could see all the way across the apartment to a wall of floor-to-ceiling windows that provided a 180-degree view of Tivoli Gardens.

As Christian stood in his new apartment, looking down at Tivoli Gardens, he was amazed at the stunning scenery. From his position, he could see the park's many rides, rollercoasters, and carnival games. The colorful lights and sounds of the park seemed to call out to him and invite him to come and explore. Christian grinned with excitement as he battled the waves of sleepiness that washed over him.

Looking closer, Christian could see lush greenery, dotted with vibrant flowerbeds and leafy foliage. The gardens were landscaped carefully, creating a wonderful backdrop for the perfect park.

As he surveyed the view, Christian noticed the crowds of people milling about in the grounds, looking like tiny ants compared to the sprawling amusement park.

Christian felt incredibly privileged to be living in an apartment overlooking such a historic landmark. He began to let his guard down and accept the possibility that this might be a legitimate job. Maybe Karma had not forsaken him but was instead saving up for one big payoff for all his pain and suffering. "Rich or poor, it's good to have money!" his dad would often say. Christian chuckled to himself, "A luxury penthouse isn't that bad either."

Exhausted, Christian fell back into a modern Danish-looking leather sofa for a few minutes of shuteye. An hour before his appointment, an alert jolted Christian from his eight-hour 'nap.' It was 5:00 PM, and Christian was blinded by his west-facing view as the spring sun filled the skies over Tivoli.

After a quick shower and while brushing his teeth, Christian fumbled with Dmitry's card. He clumsily plugged the strange Danish phone number into his contacts, praying that texting and calling would seamlessly switch over, as Verizon had promised before his departure. With just ten minutes left until the hour, Christian quickly plugged Dmitry's address into Google Maps as he entered the elevator. He was delighted to see that he was just a few blocks away.

Chapter 25

Johnny and Brian could always tell when The Surgeon was stressed, especially when he tried to multitask. "Johnny!" he roared, "My Facebox, NOW."

Without hesitation, Johnny went to a shelf in the corner of their underground lair and lifted a large, lacquered wooden chest with considerable effort. As he lugged it across the room, the ceiling began to shake. They had felt and heard this minor disturbance so many times that it was barely noticeable anymore.

This was no ordinary subway annex, as Allen had suspected. It was an undiscovered World War II bunker built by the Germans deep below the city of Copenhagen. It had been constructed in extreme secrecy as a redundant operations hub and hideout for ranking officials of the Third Reich.

The Surgeon was delighted that the Germans had never used the bunker, and the secret of its existence died with the Führer. A combination of mid- and low-level lighting throughout, combined with furnishings and amenities taken from Holocaust victims throughout Europe made it both comfortable and sickening.

Johnny finally made it across the room with the chest and heaved it onto the table in front of The Surgeon with a thud. "Careful, Johnny," he said in an agitated but controlled voice. "This chest contains the secret to my success!"

"Sorry," Johnny murmured as he walked away, feeling his veins pulsate in frustration.

Humming an eerie tune, The Surgeon began opening the chest. The top flipped upward to reveal a mirror, and the front and sides swung open to reveal a network of drawers and compartments.

Sliding the lowest drawer out, The Surgeon lifted a stack of valid passports from around the world. He flipped through them until he found a Polish passport and several credit cards matching the name. Taking the open passport, he slid it underneath a clip located on the mirror so he could see the picture.

Then he began opening other compartments and pulling out the various components of his disguise. He moved the wig aside, which he had used when apprehending Allen, to reveal a long gray beard and some adhesive. Next, he opened a small drawer and took out matching thick eyebrows and lashes.

The disguise, he figured, didn't need to be too elaborate. There wasn't much chance that RelicCollector1 would recognize him anyway. Johnny and Brian were in a separate room, fighting and screaming their way through a Fortnite battle when The Surgeon breezed by.

"I must tie up a few loose ends before leaving for Poland. I should be back by tomorrow morning. In the meantime, I need one first-class ticket to the Warsaw Chopin Airport reserved under this name for tomorrow," he said, throwing them the passport and a credit card. "And I need two first-class return tickets. Also, I'll probably need some help with my ensemble before leaving tomorrow," he added, pointing to the gray beard and makeup sitting beside the wooden chest.

Brian shrugged. "Sure, no problem." He hated the fact that The Surgeon rarely said please or thank you.

Stopping at a bookshelf, The Surgeon took down a Kierkegaard philosophy book on existentialism. He threw it onto the plush leather sofa between Johnny and Brian, "I want both of you to read this. Maybe it'll reverse some of the damage this ultraviolet game must be causing."

Chapter 26

Christian arrived with only two minutes to spare. He didn't notice the door opening as he straightened his tie and surveyed the ornate stonework. A warm glow radiated out of every window and poured out of the door, filling the late afternoon with cheer. Dmitry greeted him with open arms and led him into the ornate foyer. An elegant woman was waiting, and Dmitry introduced his wife, Eva.

Dmitry's darker Russian features were contrasted and magnified by Eva's fair Scandinavian complexion. As he was led into the cheerful house, Christian could tell that Dmitry was the kind of man who enjoyed entertaining.

"So be it! Come, Christian, let us have a drink and get to know one another." Dmitry brought Christian to a dark-paneled library with a blazing fire and two opposing dark leather chairs. The highly reflective brass bouillotte lamps and sconces emitted a muted golden glow throughout the room that amplified the rich royal green walls above the dark wood paneling. The feel was that of an English country estate.

"This is my equivalent of what the Americans would call a man cave," Dmitry explained with glowing pride.

Christian surveyed the room approvingly. "I like what you've done. I think this is exactly how I would do it if the opportunity ever affords itself."

Dmitry filled two rocks glasses with ice. "Black Russian?" he said, half asking, half informing. Christian nodded with clear approval.

As they sat down, Christian caught a glimpse of the roaring fire through the amber Kahlua in his drink. The warmth of the day was fading with the sun, and he was thankful for the heat.

Classical music filled the room, but it reminded him of how little attention he paid in his classical music appreciation elective as a freshman. He vaguely remembered the teacher chiding him, "You should pay better attention. You never know when you'll be in the company of a president or ambassador at a stately function. Your knowledge of classical music could be the feather in your cap that saves the day."

As they settled into the plush, brass-studded Chippendale wingback leather chairs, Dmitry's expression quickly changed as he leaned forward and glanced around the room. Christian suddenly felt uncomfortable and wished Eva would walk in and announce dinner.

Dmitry explained in a hushed voice, "I didn't want to say anything on the plane or at the airport, Christian, but as soon as you mentioned Norkap Pharmaceuticals, I knew I had to intervene."

Dmitry lit a cigar and drained his glass like it was water, as Christian tried to make sense of his words. Before Christian could comment, Dmitry continued, "Hans Rasmussen. He is the founder, CEO, and top shareholder at Norkap Pharmaceuticals. Do you know who he is, Christian?"

"I know of him, but I have never met or spoken with him," Christian replied.

Dmitry leaned in even further, which drew Christian even closer. "This conversation must never leave these walls," Dmitry said hesitantly. Christian nodded in agreement, and Dmitry continued, "On the surface, Norkap Pharmaceuticals is your typical drug company, chasing the latest and most profitable niches."

Christian cautiously nodded and said, "But?"

Dmitry continued, "But since the late 90s, Norkap has been the world's leading distributor of untraceable 'Black Op' meds to all the major governments, terrorist groups, and any other organization able to pay the price."

Christian wasn't sure if Dmitry was joking or not. "Seriously?" he asked.

"Serious as a heart attack," Dmitry replied with regret in his tone. "Governments have been using drugs for everything from enhancing soldiers to interrogating prisoners. In World War II, soldiers were given amphetamines to keep them alert for days on end and fight with the strength of multiple men. In the 1960s, psychedelics were used to interrogate prisoners, and to enhance folks with psychic abilities so they could remotely view secret meetings and classified documents of enemy governments. The list goes on and on. But in today's climate, where plausible deniability is the standard, Norkap is the unofficial industry leader."

Trying to digest what Dmitry had just told him, Christian fought to lift his dropped jaw and physically lifted himself out of the shock. "Well, shit. This is just about par for the course when it comes to my luck."

Dmitry could see Christian's distress and tried to comfort him. "Listen, you have every right to be untrusting after everything you went through back in Rhode Island with Collin and the university. But Norkap is also a very successful and legitimate pharmaceutical company, and there's no reason for you to suspect they have any malicious intentions towards you. At least, as long as they never connect you with me."

Christian wasn't sure which part of Dmitry's last statement made him more lightheaded with shock, but he decided to address the Collin part first. "Hold on, rewind. How on earth did you know about Collin and the university?"

Dmitry casually stood up, collected their rocks glasses, and brought them over to the bar.

With his back to Christian, he began refilling their drinks. "Within thirty minutes of inviting you to my home, I not only knew why and how long you would be here in Copenhagen, but I also knew your criminal, medical, and social background right down to the nervous twitch in your right eye that you've had since childhood."

Christian's face quickly turned red, having been caught in a lie about his tic.

"Don't be embarrassed. I would have done the same thing. Your tic is nobody's business," Dmitry reassured him.

The red faded as quickly as it came. "Thank you for understanding."

"As far as the rest of the intel is concerned, when you're the ambassador from a former communist bloc country, especially Russia, it's a foregone assumption that at any given time and place, there is a US or Chinese operative looking to manipulate and/or do harm to you or one of your loved ones. Welcome to Statecraft 101! Sorry if you find this uncomfortable, but when it comes to the safety of my family, there is no trust, only verification."

Once again, Christian had to physically lift his dropped jaw. He regained his composure and continued as Dmitry handed him a fresh drink. "This still doesn't explain why you have such a problem with Hans Rasmussen?"

"By the late nineties," Dmitry began after a large gulp of his drink, "the USSR had fully dissolved, and the entire Eastern Bloc was finding its way. Hans had bribed and recruited one of my closest aides to his cause, and they were using my diplomatic credentials to supply all the FSRs—Former Soviet Republics—while cutting Mother Russia out of the loop. To make a long story short, I and my family were almost killed by a Russian death squad when one of Hans's deals went bad. My aide was killed, which was fitting for his treason. I was eventually exonerated but will never forgive or forget what Hans did to me."

"Wow!" was all Christian could muster.

"Ironically, we recently received some disturbing intel that Hans has been violating human rights standards and pushing the limits to develop some kind of mind-altering next-gen drug that gives its user almost superhuman control over their mind and body, which could have many scary possibilities if used maliciously. If you find yourself in over your head, or just need someone to confide in, please don't hesitate to reach out to me."

Before the conversation spiraled any deeper, Eva called everyone to dinner. As they sat down, Eva brought out a platter of meatballs, a large bowl of boiled potatoes, and a bowl of salad, accompanied by a ladle of brown sauce.

Eva proudly explained to Christian, "This plate is called *frikadelle*—you may know them as meatballs. The secret to good *frikadelle* outside the seasoning is a perfect balance of ground pig and cow meat fresh from the butcher. Both the potatoes and salad were grown in our backyard. This is actually very common in Denmark, even for city folk like us."

Christian thoroughly enjoyed the meal, despite the disturbing revelations from Dmitry. The conversation that accompanied the meal was delightfully simple and uncomplicated. After a nice espresso with a shot of Sambuca, Christian said his farewells to Eva, and then Dmitry walked him to the door.

"I know our conversation earlier probably shook you up a little, but please don't let it dampen your resolve. You should give this job your best, if only for yourself. Just promise me you won't compromise who you are or what you believe in. Also, you might not want to mention that you know me. It could prove to be what your American businessmen call a CLM!"

"A CLM?" Christian asked.

With a hearty laugh, Dmitry clarified, "A Career Limiting Move!" After a moment of laughter, they shook hands heartily, and Dmitry bellowed, "To your left!" as Christian reached the sidewalk with no clue as to which way was home.

Chapter 27

While admiring his latest disguise in the mirror, The Surgeon placed the remaining items in his travel bag. He gave Johnny and Brian one final reminder. "Remember, keep a close eye on Christian, but under no circumstances are you to make contact or give him any suspicion that he is being watched."

"Yes, sir," they both replied.

"With any luck," The Surgeon proclaimed with manic glee, "I'll be back tomorrow with a new little friend!"

Johnny and Brian risked a nervous glance at one another as The Surgeon's cheerful whistles echoed down the dark tunnel, long after he had vanished from sight.

Chapter 28

While reminiscing on the events of that evening, Christian forgot he was in an elevator. He was quickly reminded when the door opened to reveal the million-dollar panoramic view of Tivoli Gardens. He knew exactly what his dad would have said about this: "If it seems too good to be true, then it probably is." *The funny thing is*, Christian thought to himself, *knowing this is too good to be true is giving me some peace, as I feel less guilty about enjoying it while it lasts!*

In that spirit, Christian went to the galley bar, which was fully stocked, and made a straight Absolut on the rocks. From there, he simply sat back and enjoyed the view of all the people, lights, and amusements in the Tivoli Gardens below.

Having resolved himself to getting a good night's sleep, Christian ignored the fact that he wasn't at all tired and went to bed after finishing his drink. One and a half hours later, Christian found himself tapping his foot to the distant beat of a local discothèque and mulling Dmitry's warnings over and over in his head.

Did that really just happen?

He knew the eight-hour nap earlier had doomed any chances of curing his jet lag in this sleep cycle.

While wondering what to do until the morning, a group of gleeful yet inebriated Danes bellowed a drinking song from the street below. It drifted in along with the cool fragrant spring breeze through the open window by Christian's bed.

"Vi Skåler med vore venner og dem som vi kender, og dem som vi ikke kender, dem skåler vi med. Skåååål, Skåååål." Had Christian understood Danish, he would have known the song went something like, "We toast with our friends and those that we know. And those that we don't know, we toast with them as well. Cheeers, Cheeers." The group of merry Danes turned the corner, and the song began fading into the distance. Still feeling a rush from the earlier events and libations, Christian threw his shoes on and followed the song.

Before long, the singing Danes had led him down so many twists and turns that he couldn't remember the way back. After several more disorienting turns, the distant drinking song abruptly stopped and was replaced by the rhythmic thumping of what had to be a bar or discothèque. He followed the thumping bass, and had it not been for the rattling door frame, he would never have found the well-hidden bar. Ironically, the bar was named 'Godt Gemt' which roughly translated means well-hidden! As the door opened, he was bathed in music and the clamor of inebriated patrons. It was one of those unadvertised, best-kept-secret places that were devoid of tourists or giggling teenyboppers, and he fell in love with it immediately.

Christian claimed the only empty chair next to a group of rowdy Danes, making his Americanness obvious by ordering his double Absolut on the rocks in English. "Where are you from, and what's your name?" one of them asked bluntly.

"I'm from Rhode Island, and my name is Christian."

"Well, Christian from Rhode Island, my name is Henrik," the man declared gleefully.

"Pleased to meet you, Henrik," Christian replied, shaking his extended hand. "Can I offer you a drink?"

"Absolutely not, you're the guest, and I insist on buying. It looks like you need it more than me anyway, by the looks of your twitching eye. Are you

OK?" Henrik asked with a chuckle.

"Yes, just a little jet lagged, I guess," Christian lied.

Turning to Christian with a serious look, Henrik said, "Well, I think your *special* condition merits a *special* Danish drink! How does that sound?"

"Fine by me!" Christian replied.

Henrik ordered a round of shots. The bartender lined up five shot glasses and poured a black viscous liquid into each one. The bottle said Absolut, but Christian had never seen black Absolut vodka before. "This is one of our favorite drinks. It's called Sort Svine, or Black Pig in English. I can guarantee that this will cure your twitch if you have enough of them!"

"How is that?" Christian inquired.

"It's hard to twitch with both eyes closed?" Henrik said, grinning, as Christian began to understand why the Danes were known for their dark humor.

After a hearty laugh, Christian inspected the drink with sincere curiosity. "What's this made of?" he asked.

"You can make it at home," Henrik said with pride. "All you do is take a bottle of vodka and add Turkish Licorice which is a type of rock-hard licorice candy, and let it sit overnight. It'll dissolve, and after a little shaking, voilà! Sort Svine!"

The aroma of black licorice and vodka was more appealing than Christian had expected. He wondered if the taste would be as pleasing. With fluid grace and precision, Henrik and the others raised their shots and roared, "Skål!" Christian did his best to follow suit. The bittersweet sting caught him off guard, but the overall taste was quite pleasant. Christian bought the next round.

Several hours later, Christian had lost count of the shots and the time. After helping Christian master the drinking song from earlier, Henrik began pointing out some of the eligible women around the bar. As tempted as Christian was to stay and continue drinking until breakfast was served (and it really was served), he decided to face the journey home with the hope of a few hours' sleep before his first day of work.

After some heartfelt farewells and promises of meeting there again,

Christian left, trying his best to focus on the door and not the spinning room.

Christian surprised himself at how well he could bellow the Danish drinking song as he stumbled down the street. The wet cobblestones reflected the streetlights as steam rose from the recent rain. Christian had been forewarned of how dark and rainy it could be in Denmark, so much so that it made England look like a Caribbean resort. He had also learned that this grim climate helped evolve a Danish concept called "Hygge." The closest English translation for Hygge was "cozy," but this did not come close to encompassing the meaning. All the darkness and rain had forced the Danes to evolve and learn to create an atmosphere of bright joy and comfort in all aspects of their life. Whether it was through genius lighting in a house or mastering feng shui in a football stadium, Danes could science coziness anywhere and everywhere.

As he strolled down the street, Christian found himself bellowing the drinking song, not really knowing what he was saying. For some reason, it felt natural. After a few twists and turns, he quickly realized he had no idea where he was. On top of this, he was intoxicated, which made for a rapid climb to a panicked state as he reached for his phone to map the way back to his paradise. The panic grew when he realized his phone was dead.

All the roads and buildings looked the same in the foggy orange glow of the streetlights. Feeling all too sober now, Christian figured he could just walk down one of the small streets until he reached a more active area.

In his mind, he did not think there was much to worry about. One of the many facts that his Danish literature had boasted was an almost non-existent crime rate. As random as it was, he also found himself thinking about Collin and realized, apart from Dmitry's comment, he hadn't thought about him for several days, which was a first in the two-plus years since his death.

His thoughts were quickly drawn back to the totally desolate Copenhagen streets at 4:00 AM, and how the low crime rate was providing very little comfort at that moment. With each step, the feeling of being followed grew from a distant hunch to an almost certainty.

At first, he thought it was just good old-fashioned paranoia, but after a few blocks, he was sure he had a shadow. Every time he looked back, there was a painful emptiness and nobody to be found, but as soon as he started walking, he would hear footsteps echoing in the distance.

"Stop being so paranoid!" he demanded of himself. "You're just drunk and lost." Then, with a sigh of relief, he saw cars passing by on what appeared to be a larger road, about seven or eight blocks ahead of him. He welcomed the end of this narrow alley of a street and began joyfully strolling towards the exit.

It was then, as he passed a dark angled window of a corner butcher, that he saw the blurred reflection of a faceless figure, no more than three feet behind him, just standing there.

With his eyes locked on the reflection in the window, Christian surged forward to escape this ghostly pursuer. No sooner had he taken the first step forward, without looking ahead, did he run into the arms of someone else who had also appeared out of nowhere.

In a panic, Christian struggled to push this obstacle away, only to hear Henrik yelp, "What are you doing, man!"

Christian recognized the voice and halted his struggle. He instantly looked back where the dark figure had been only seconds before, to see only shadows and an empty, narrow street. He then turned to Henrik. "Was that some kind of joke? How long were you guys following me?"

Puzzled, Henrik replied, "It's just me, and I haven't been following you. I'm on my way home."

"But there was someone right behind me, you must have seen him?"

"Are you sure you didn't sneak a few shots of absinthe at the bar when I wasn't looking?" Henrik said, laughing. "There was no one behind you." Then, without warning, his smile turned to dread as he gasped in horror and pointed over Christian's shoulder. Once again, Christian was immobilized with fear at the thought of whatever it was Henrik saw behind him. Christian didn't have the courage to turn and face this terror. Unexpectedly, Henrik burst into laughter. "You're like the frightened little brother I always wanted!"

Relieved yet angry, Christian took a deep breath. "That's pretty sick, you know!" There was that dark Danish sense of humor again.

"Are you lost or something?" Henrik asked.

"If you must know, I am. You wouldn't happen to know where this is?" Christian held up the address he had pulled out of his wallet. Henrik chuckled a little as he provided surprisingly detailed directions to Christian's address.

They shared a few more laughs as they walked to the busy street ahead. Christian made the last stretch alone, as the earlier scare haunted his thoughts. He admitted to himself that it could have been a shadow that he saw in the window. On the other hand, it seemed so real. He finally decided to forget the whole episode and settled in for a few hours of alcohol-induced sleep before his first day of work.

Chapter 29

Norkap was only five blocks from his apartment. Adjusting his coat and tie in the early morning sun, Christian couldn't help but admire the impressive building that stood before him. Standing tall amidst the bustling heart of Copenhagen, the ultra-modern Norkap headquarters emerged as a dazzling testament to innovation and sleek design. Its facade, a magnificent display of shimmering glass panels, mirrored the dynamic cityscape around it, reflecting the ebb and flow of urban life. Four stories of architectural brilliance soared toward the heavens, their clean lines and geometric precision a harmonious blend of form and function. Within its first three transparent floors, a symphony of scientific discovery unfolded, as brilliant minds worked tirelessly to unlock the mysteries of health and wellbeing.

A friendly Norkap receptionist greeted Christian as he wandered into the lobby, head swiveling from one side to the other trying to take in all the architectural splendor. "Hi, you must be Dr. Yates. We've been expecting you!"

Christian had hoped to impress the receptionist by greeting her in Danish. But he found himself at a loss for words and embarrassed when he couldn't remember any. As the seconds and his right eye ticked away, Christian's anxiety grew. Mortified and speechless, he finally blurted out, "Well, it's nice to be expected!"

In response, the receptionist gave him a strange look, "Are you OK?"

"Sorry!" Christian apologized as he quietly chided himself for not heeding his father's advice: "Better to keep your mouth shut and let them wonder if you're an idiot, rather than opening it, and confirming their suspicion."

Thankfully, the receptionist seemed to take the awkwardness in stride and presented Christian with a cloth tote bag bearing an emblem of the planet Earth with a giant 'N' orbiting it.

The bag was packed with folders, pamphlets, pens, and various other Norkap-branded items that pharmaceutical reps could use during sales calls with doctors. "This bag has everything you'll ever need to know about Norkap Pharmaceuticals, and then some!" the receptionist explained.

Christian reflected on Dmitry's advice and wondered if the welcome packet contained a step-by-step guide to violating the Geneva Convention on torture while still upholding patient privacy.

The receptionist led Christian through the grand atrium, which was filled with fountains and greenery. "I'll introduce you to your orientation guide. He will show you the ins and outs of life at Norkap Pharma. If you have any questions, he can answer them," she explained.

They ascended an escalator to the second floor and entered a spacious conference room boasting floor-to-ceiling windows, like those in Christian's apartment. The room was consumed by a large light-wood conference table. At the far end of the table was an executive, high-back black-leather chair with its back to them.

As they walked towards the table, the chair slowly and ominously began to swivel, revealing the individual who would teach Christian the intricate survival techniques necessary to navigate the Norkap landscape. "I'd like you to meet Henrik," the receptionist said.

Christian's eyes widened with excitement and confusion as he looked upon his drinking buddy from the night before.

Henrik could only hold the serious expression for a few moments as a giant grin emerged. "Well, well, well, our paths cross again. Why didn't you tell me you were here to work for Norkap Pharma?"

Christian was about to ask the same question when the receptionist glared at Henrik and left in a huff.

Unperturbed, Henrik laughed, "Lesson number one. Don't sleep with your co-workers!" As if on cue, another woman walked by the window, giving him the finger. "Lesson number two. Don't sleep with the FedEx courier!" Henrik laughed nervously with a tinge of concern as she turned the corner.

"Maybe it would be easier to tell me the ones you haven't been with?" Christian said jokingly.

Henrik laughed, but the mirth faded as he seriously contemplated the question. "I like the way you think Christian!"

Christian was starting to feel comfortable with Henrik but held back from posing the question that had been nagging him since dinner with Dmitry.

"So, I'm sure you know all about Norkap Pharma," Henrik said in a professional tone. "You know we're a Fortune 10 company, and Hans Rasmussen, our CEO, is one of the wealthiest people in the world, even with the insane Scandinavian taxes..."

"I didn't actually know that." Christian admitted with a hint of embarrassment.

Henrik deviated from his usual script and asked, "Most people we hire have been scratching and clawing their entire lives to get a job here, so what gives?"

"I didn't apply for this job, to be honest. I had never even heard of Norkap Pharma outside of the occasional stock reports on CNBC and random drug commercials," Christian revealed.

Henrik was intrigued. "Well, that's interesting. But it's neither here nor there. We have much to do and little time to do it," he said, leading Christian out of the room and down the hallway. "As one of the largest pharmaceutical companies in the world, Norkap is involved in almost all families of medicine, from blood pressure and diabetes to cancer and erectile dysfunction. Not that I would know anything about that!" He nodded as an attractive pharmaceutical rep passed them in the hall. "You've been hired to work in the psychedelic research division. This is our newest and most exciting branch and the only division housed here at the Copenhagen facility."

Christian was intrigued. "One of my classmates completed his dissertation on psychedelic-assisted therapy," he shared.

Henrik nodded. "Yes," he said. "For years now, therapists have been using drugs like ketamine, cannabis, psilocybin, LSD, and ayahuasca to help people delve deeper into their subconscious and rapidly increase the process and success of therapy. We're working on a new generation of drugs, and that's where you come in! But let's not get ahead of ourselves. The next stop is Legal, where you'll sign more NDAs than a CIA operative!"

"NDA?" Christian asked innocently.

"Sorry, Non-Disclosure Agreement! I've already told you too much. Follow me," Henrik replied.

Five hours later, Christian and Henrik emerged from the Legal department feeling dazed. Christian attempted to ask Henrik a question, but he was quickly shushed.

"The only words I want to hear from you are 'Henrik, let's get high!'" Henrik declared, causing Christian's face to turn red. The receptionist, who was situated right beside them, rolled her eyes, and turned back to her computer. Henrik looked at Christian with a shrug, "What can I say, I have a problem." He winked at the receptionist, who responded by flipping him the middle finger when Christian wasn't looking.

Christian was perplexed. Henrik had violated every HR code there was, yet everyone looked the other way. Maybe a conversation for another time.

"It's too nice of a day to be cooped up inside," Henrik declared as they walked out of the front entrance and towards a bridge.

"Where are we going?" Christian inquired.

"As I'm sure you've noticed by now, Christian, your name is very popular in Denmark. Well, we're going to a special and unique place called Christiania," Henrik replied.

Christian gave him a puzzled look. "Is it like Tivoli Gardens? I haven't been there yet."

"Well," Henrik said, "both places are focused on growing things, but that's where the similarities end!"

"Huh," Christian said, trying to picture Christiania. After crossing several bridges and blocks, they passed under an archway bearing the inscription, "You are now leaving the European Union."

Christian watched as Henrik approached the first person he saw, gave them some money, and immediately lit up the joint that was given to him.

"Ahhhhh," Henrik sighed, exhaling a cloud of smoke. "This is the only way to undo the damage of five hours with Norkap lawyers."

"Is weed legal in Denmark?" Christian inquired as Henrik passed him the joint.

Henrik was relishing Christian's naïveté. "There are three parts to my answer. First, this is hash, not weed. Second, weed and hash are not legal in Denmark. And finally, we're not in Denmark!"

Henrik laughed at the puzzled look on Christian's face as he continued, "Christiania is a unique social project where the Danish government designated this area, an old military base, as a free town outside the realm of Danish control. The inhabitants of Christiania govern themselves, and the government mostly stays out. There have been clashes over the decades, but it's been a success overall."

Without hesitation, Christian took the hash cigarette and inspected the artfully wrapped organic mixture of cigarette tobacco and hash with white smoke dancing out one end.

Christian could count on one hand and one finger, how many times he had taken recreational drugs. Except for alcohol and sugar, of course. He had no moral objections; it was fear. It had taken a lifetime to build a wall that could contain whatever damage he couldn't remember from the day his father died when he was just nine years old. Deep inside he trembled at the thought of a mind-altering narcotic destroying that marvelous wall and releasing the horror contained within.

But something inside him had changed. The past few years had almost broken him, and the past few days had removed the *almost*. Christian was ready to face his demons. He seriously doubted a hash cigarette could rise to that occasion, but it was a hell of a good start.

Henrik watched with excitement as Christian inhaled way too deeply and held it in way too long.

"Holy shit, man!" Henrik exclaimed. "Now it's a party!"

As the drag from the hash cigarette set in, the background noises began to fade one by one. He became acutely aware of a world unlike any he had ever encountered before. He could suddenly feel a refreshing sense of freedom, as if the air itself whispered tales of rebellion and counterculture.

Vibrant graffiti adorned every available surface, splashes of color against the backdrop of industrial buildings and narrow cobblestone streets. A medley of scents wafted through the air, mingling the fragrance of freshly brewed coffee with the unfortunate scent of cannabis, a subtle declaration of the community's relaxed ethos.

People of all walks of life moved with an effortless coolness, their eclectic fashion choices and unapologetic individuality lending an air of bohemian charm to the scene. Everywhere he turned, there were signs of a community dedicated to creative expression, communal living, and an unwavering commitment to self-governance. For the first time, he began to feel a confidence that had till now eluded him. A confidence that he could handle whatever it was Norkap would throw at him.

Or maybe he was just really stoned.

Meanwhile, Henrik was walking around in circles chanting, "Ølstafet, Ølstafet, Ølstafet." Suddenly, a homeless-looking gentleman with dreadlocks appeared from a building with ten beers and two sticks. Henrik tweaked his eyebrows at Christian as the man laid the sticks down about 10 meters away and brought the beers to them.

"Here's what you do, Christian," Henrik instructed. "We're going to guzzle our beers, run to the sticks, bend over, and place our foreheads on the sticks while keeping them touching the ground. Then we'll run around the stick five times, run back, guzzle the second beer, run back to the stick, do five more turns, and come back to the next set of beers."

Christian looked at Henrik as if he had three heads when he opened the first two beers and said, "Go!" Christian made the first round and guzzled the second beer, then another round and a third beer. As he spun around the stick this time, everything became blurry. He somehow managed to stumble over to a bench before collapsing.

Two hours later, Christian woke up with a splitting headache. In the distance, he saw Henrik talking to what he assumed were some Christiania locals.

Henrik came running over when he saw Christian waking up, saying, "We were worried about you for a while. I told them to let you sleep since we had been up all-night drinking and you were jet-lagged."

"Thanks, I think?" Christian said, trying to suppress the urge to vomit.

"It's OK if you want to puke and rally! I can do this all day long," Henrik replied.

"I'm starving," Christian said, listening to his stomach rumble. He hadn't eaten since dinner at Dmitry's house the night before, and the hash didn't help.

"Follow me," Henrik exclaimed. "There are some places to eat in Christiania, but part of being a free state is that there are fewer health regulations and standards. No need to get sick twice in one day!"

As they made their way back into town, Christian decided it was time to better understand Henrik. "I have to ask," Christian said matter-of-factly, "how on earth do you get away with... well, to put it bluntly, being you?"

Henrik laughed out loud and turned to Christian. "I've been asked that question more times than I can count, but never quite in that format. I love it!"

Henrik walked in silence as if he had forgotten to answer and then suddenly spoke, "Here's the deal. I was raised by my uncle, who happens to be the richest person in Denmark and one of the richest people in the world. My uncle is Hans Rasmussen, your new boss!"

Christian stopped walking as he tried to digest what Henrik just told him. Henrik continued, "I don't officially work for Norkap, which is probably the reason none of the women have sued me, even though Uncle Hans begs me to stop screwing my way through his workforce. I just can't help it! Women in the pharmaceutical business are smoking hot, and I'm addicted."

"Well, if you don't work for Norkap," Christian asked as he continued to slowly digest the information, "what are you doing there, and with me?"

Henrik laughed again. "It's not like I'm stalking you! Remember, you found me in the bar that first night. But to answer your question, Uncle Hans has me do all the things he can only trust family to do, even though he pretty much keeps me in the dark about the really cool stuff."

"So, is he the reason you're with me?" Christian asked cautiously.

This time, Henrik was more serious. "I honestly have no idea what he has planned, but the short answer is yes. He told me to get you straight to Legal and make sure you signed all the non-disclosure paperwork. He also told me to introduce you to as few people as possible and keep you away from Norkap until he meets with you." There was a pause while Henrik stared into the sky. "Now that I think about it, I probably wasn't supposed to tell you that."

There was another pause as Henrik stamped his foot and then continued with a tone of frustration, "But what does he expect? He kicks me out of my apartment, tells me to do all this crazy stuff, but doesn't tell me why. Serves him right if I blow it."

"He kicked you out of your apartment? Why would he do that?" Christian asked.

"Your guess is as good as mine. You're the one living in it now!"

Everything was starting to make more sense to Christian. "So that explains the penthouse."

"He said you wouldn't be there long, but I have no idea what that means. Is he looking for another apartment for you? Will you be traveling? Who knows? That's Uncle Hans for you."

Now, Christian was both interested and concerned as they continued walking.

"So, when do I meet him?" Christian finally asked.

"Tomorrow morning," Henrik bluntly replied. "So, let's enjoy the evening!"

Chapter 30

For over thirty years, The Surgeon had been searching for a way to unlock the memories he knew were passed from generation to generation in humans. Two years ago, he met Collin and learned a great deal, but was unable to interact with and control his memories.

Since Collin's death, The Surgeon had been desperately trying to replicate the electronic device that gave Collin his abilities, but with no success. On top of that, Christian had managed to avoid the blame for Collin's death and was becoming a serious liability.

The Surgeon's trip to Poland had been a waste. RelicCollector1 had failed, just like Allen before her and all the others. The Surgeon knew it was time for him to call it quits. He probably should have stopped years ago, but he had developed a perverse taste for the hunt that he had not expected. On top of that, there was always the hope of an unimaginable reward hidden deep within humanity's collective memory.

"Thirty years," he said to himself. "Thirty years, and nothing to show for it."

He had come close several times, but he knew that close meant nothing in this game. Even before Collin, The Surgeon had proof of the existence of genetic memories and an astonishing secret embedded deep within those memories that could change the world. This was why his resolve would never waver.

He carefully watched Christian and Henrik walk past him outside a cafe where he was hiding behind an open newspaper. "Christian, Christian, Christian. What to do with Christian?" he murmured to himself through one of his thick, fake beards.

Chapter 31

They walked in silence as Christian tried to make sense of everything, and Henrik tried to figure out how to explain to Hans why he had spilled his guts to Christian. Before he realized it, they were back at Tivoli. Henrik looked up at his penthouse with longing, "I know it's only been a day, but I miss my place." Christian wanted to feel sorry for Henrik, but empathy eluded him. "I thought we'd go to one of my favorite restaurants. It's a little touristy, but the food is great, and the staff will literally carry me home when I've had too much because I live so close!"

"What's it called?" Christian asked.

"Groften," Henrik replied as they approached the entrance to Tivoli Gardens. Henrik nonchalantly walked past the long line of anxious tourists waiting for admission. He was oblivious to all the angry comments and agitated groans as he winked at a girl manning the admissions gate. She just bit her lower lip and waved them through as he gestured that he'd call her later.

A thought occurred to Christian as Henrik walked backwards, now making lewd gestures to the girl, who was returning them with equal enthusiasm. "Henrik, did anyone wash the sheets and clean the furniture in your penthouse before I arrived?"

Christian was envisioning a blacklight and the dome of a planetarium star show when Henrik responded, "Of course, I had new linens and towels delivered along with a good cleaning."

Christian breathed a sigh of relief as a flood of colors and fragrances hit him while trying to keep up with Henrik, who was also feeling the hunger pains from the hash. "I've never seen anything like this," Christian said as he swiveled from side to side, trying to take in all the beauty.

"You couldn't have picked a better time to come," Henrik said, "it's mid-spring, and all the plants are in full bloom."

They finally arrived at Groften, and once again, Henrik broke the lengthy line, almost enjoying the protests of all the patrons. The host immediately recognized him and turned away from the customer she was assisting mid-sentence to take Henrik's hand and lead them to the best table in the house, with stunning panoramic views of the park. Christian exclaimed, "You're a superstar, Henrik!"

Henrik immediately shushed Christian, "Please, don't talk like that."

"Like what?" Christian didn't understand.

"We Danes live by an unofficial set of rules we call *Jente Law*. Many say it's the reason Denmark is almost always voted the best country in the world to live." Christian's research had already confirmed that Henrik wasn't kidding about that, so he nodded in agreement.

Henrik continued explaining the *Jente Laws*, "I can't remember how many laws there are, but their essence is as follows—you should not think that you're special, you're not better than anyone else, you're not smarter than anyone else, you don't know more than anyone else, you're not more important than anyone else, you're not good at anything, you don't laugh at anyone else, there's nothing you can teach anyone else, and nobody cares about you."

Christian was too busy guzzling glass after glass of water and gobbling down the bread to react appropriately. After swallowing a particularly large mouthful and contemplating Henrik's words, Christian finally exclaimed, "Is that a joke?"

"No, not really." Henrik responded after swallowing his own mouthful of food.

"It sounds like a suicide note!" Christian blurted out, realizing he was starting to embrace the Danish dark humor.

Henrik laughed. "That's good! You have a way with words, Christian. And yes, these laws were originally part of a satirical fictional novel written by a Danish Norwegian author named Aksel Sandemose. He was attempting to capture the unspoken rules that govern Scandinavian society. Believe it or not, we really do live by many of these rules, for better or worse.

"For example, there are no academically gifted classes or rewards for the students with the highest grades in any of our schools. If someone in a class has a birthday party, everyone in the class is invited. If someone is struggling, the rest of the class unites around them, and helps in any way they can."

As Christian prepared to take another bite of the amazing bread, he stopped and looked at Henrik, "You're really serious about this Jente Law, aren't you?"

Henrik nodded his head with an affirmative up and down as he took two consecutive shots of Sort Svine and then gulped down a bottle of Carlsberg beer, all while maintaining constant eye contact with Christian.

"By the way," Henrik said when he caught his breath, "that's called Smørrebrød, or butter bread. There are several Danish words you must learn, and one of them is 'Tandsmør.' It literally translates to 'tooth butter,' meaning butter that is so thick it captures an impression of your teeth when you take a bite of the bread!"

With a full mouth, Christian broke decorum as three muffled words escaped, "I love Smørrebrød!"

The bar TV interrupted Christian and the scheduled handball game playing on a Danish station with a special report. Christian didn't understand it, but the headline mentioned 'The Surgeon.'

Henrik began to protest the interruption, but was cut short by Christian, "Hush!" Christian blurted to Henrik, holding his hand over Henrik's mouth as he tried to understand what was happening on the television.

"OK, OK!" Henrik said. "I know it's not baseball or basketball, but we love our handball."

"It's not that," Christian said, desperately trying to understand the report. "Can you tell me what that reporter is saying?"

"No problem," Henrik said, "Looks like that serial killer, The Surgeon, has struck again." He paused to listen to more of the report. "Apparently, they found the headless body of a woman who went missing the other day in Poland." Another pause as he listened. "They're just saying her name, but I can't pronounce it! Now they are saying she was a well-known antiques dealer known worldwide by her eBay name, 'RelicCollector1'."

Christian suddenly felt sick as he recalled that night back in Rhode Island where he met RelicCollector1 in that chatroom while looking for people with genetic memories. He would never forget that night. *Is her blood on my hands too?*

Henrik snapped Christian out of his spiral with a firm pat on the back, and another shot of Sort Svine, but the thought of RelicCollector1 would join Collin in haunting Christian's thoughts moving forward. He pushed these feelings out of his head and tried his best to enjoy the rest of the evening.

They proceeded to work their way through a variety of amazing traditional Danish dishes, and by the end of the evening, they had the entire restaurant singing the "Vi Skåler" drinking song.

As they strolled out of the park with the midnight sun peeking over their shoulders from the horizon, Henrik stopped and addressed Christian in a very uncharacteristic serious manner, "I like you a lot, Christian, and I love my Uncle Hans, but at the end of the day, he's a real bastard. Technically, I'm the real bastard, and my uncle is a metaphorical bastard. I have no idea what he has planned for you, but whatever it is, be careful. Uncle Hans only sees people for what they can do for him, and he's quick to disregard them once they've outlived their usefulness."

"Is this your Danish dark humor, or are you serious?" Christian asked, waiting for Henrik to break into wild laughter at any moment.

"According to my grandparents," Henrik said with sincerity, "Uncle Hans used to be the most loving, warm, and kind person you could imagine. Then, thirty years ago, his brother, my father, sabotaged an archaeological dig in Greenland, killing himself and everyone else except Uncle Hans. They say

125

Uncle Hans lost his heart in Greenland and returned with ice in it's place."

"Thank you," Christian said with a sincere hand on Henrik's shoulder. "I appreciate the heads-up, and I'm sorry you've had to spend a lifetime carrying the shame of what your father did in Greenland. Believe it or not, I know how you feel, and understand what living with something like that can do to a person."

Christian saw a split second of pain flicker in Henrik's eyes. It vanished just as quickly. "OK, Dr. Yates, how much for that little session?"

Christian laughed, "It's on the house. Actually, it never happened, as the last thing I need is to be arrested for practicing without a license!"

They both had a good laugh as Henrik began walking backwards towards the entrance to Tivoli, "OK, well, I'm off to find that girl from the ticket booth. Meet me at the entrance to Norkap at 10 AM tomorrow morning, and I'll take you to meet Uncle Hans. Goodnight and sleep well."

With that, Henrik disappeared into the crowd, and Christian went straight home and passed out.

Chapter 32

As promised, Henrik was waiting in front of the massive four-story cube of glass that was Norkap. "You look well-rested," Henrik said as Christian drew closer. "Are you ready?"

"As ready as I can be," Christian said with an undercurrent of tension and excitement.

Henrik led Christian through the building and past the regular elevators to a smaller hidden elevator door with a large plaque that read, "4th floor only." There was no button, just a slot to insert a card. Before Henrik could insert his security card, the door hissed open. Henrik began walking into the elevator, not waiting to see if anyone was exiting.

Christian stopped him as they watched one of the most stunningly beautiful women he had ever seen walk out. Her attention was focused on a document, and she started walking past Christian and Henrik without noticing them. This was obviously unacceptable to Henrik, as he blocked her path. "Christian, this is Britt. Britt, this is Christian, our newest hire."

Christian's eyes met hers. Neither blinked and after a longer-than-normal pause she simply said with a very warm and welcoming grin, "Guten tag."

Christian was starting to feel embarrassed, but he couldn't look away. Finally, he forced the only word that was coming to mind, "Skål."

Britt's smile got even bigger as Henrik stared in disbelief.

The elevator door began swiftly hissing closed. Christian caught it moments before it would have hit Britt. By the time he regained his balance and looked back up, Britt had vanished down the corridor.

"What the hell was that?" Henrik exclaimed. "I've been trying to get with her for the past three years with zero success, and then she eye-bangs you within two seconds of meeting you!"

"Eye-bang?" Christian asked with a confused look.

"You know," Henrik continued, "when a girl makes love to you with her eyes."

"You're crazy," Christian bellowed as the supercharged elevator door almost crushed them both. He and Henrik quickly entered the elevator and Henrik inserted his security card.

On the way up, Henrik continued, "Anyway, Uncle Hans hired Britt about three years ago. She's an archaeologist. He sends her all over the world looking for all the weird herbs and drugs that he no longer has time to search for himself anymore. I'm not exactly sure where she's from, maybe Germany or Switzerland? Like I said, she's never given me the time of day."

The elevator door opened to a large, dimly lit room that looked more like a museum than a pharmaceutical company. Throughout the room, there were glass-encased artifacts on pedestals with focused spotlights shining down on them from the ceiling. Henrik explained as they traversed the massive room, "Uncle Hans, or Dr. Rasmussen, as everyone else refers to him, is also an archaeologist. He's spent the better part of his life traveling the world and investigating indigenous peoples, their cultures, and most importantly, their secret native drugs. That's how Norkap got its start. Decades ago, he discovered some kind of crazy herbal drugs that the indigenous Pygmy people of the Congo had known about for centuries. He made a fortune with it as a painkiller and the rest was history!"

"Was he looking for something specific?" Christian asked.

"Nobody really knows. Like I said last night, he came back from that dig in Greenland a different person. Ever since then, he just disappears for weeks or months at a time and comes back with these things you see in the cases. He's been doing this for almost thirty years. There are Mayan statues, Native American pipes, Aboriginal boomerangs, Amazon dart shooter things, Eskimo beads, and on and on and on."

By the time Henrik had finished his tour, they had arrived at Dr. Rasmussen's door. Henrik knocked on it loudly, there was a buzzing sound, and the door opened. Across the dimly lit room was a huge desk with a shadowy figure motioning them to enter. This room was equally as large as the previous one had been, and as they walked across, Christian noted recessed cubbies in the walls on either side with even more ornate artifacts, each imprisoned under a dome of focused light.

They finally reached the desk. "Greetings, Dr. Yates. I'm so happy you accepted my invitation, and I trust my nephew has taken good care of you?"

"Yes, sir," Christian replied. "Henrik has given me a crash course in Danish culture and customs."

"Please, call me Hans. I figured Henrik was on his best behavior as I didn't see any articles in the local tabloids or arrest reports."

Henrik laughed, but Christian immediately picked up on a hint of embarrassment and pain accompanying the laugh.

Hans continued, "Thank you for your help, Henrik. I trust you went to Legal and had Dr. Yates sign all the appropriate non-disclosures and whatnots?"

"Yes," Henrik replied, "we are all set."

"Excellent. That will be all for now. Thank you." With that, Henrik turned, gave Christian a nod and a wink, and disappeared into the shadows.

Christian watched him depart, wishing he could have stayed. When he turned back to the desk, Hans had swiveled his computer monitor toward Christian and begun playing a YouTube video. Christian immediately recognized it. "Hey, that's the lecture I gave the other day."

Hans suddenly became even more serious and intense. "I'm only going to ask this once, Christian. Did anyone from my company or anywhere else give you any material for that lecture?"

"I don't understand," Christian said, more as a question than a statement.

Hans continued, "Your theory on indigenous people and their retained ability to access memories more easily than others is truer than you know."

"Seriously?" Christian exclaimed. "In what way?"

"First, answer my question, and don't lie. I'll know if you're lying to me. It's a gift I've had since childhood, and it's served me very well over a lifetime, with only a few exceptions." Christian noticed a brief pause in Hans's confidence and wondered what those few exceptions could have been.

"No, nobody gave me any material. I developed those theories over the past two years with blood, sweat, and tears ever since Collin was murdered."

"Yes, I know all about the Collin incident. Truth be told, now, the whole world knows about the lecture and the Collin incident." Hans pointed to the number of views below the video.

"Is that ten thousand?" Christian asked as he leaned in for a closer look.

"No," Hans said matter-of-factly. "It's ten million."

Christian gasped.

"The whole world is talking about your now-famous lecture. It's been both a curse and a blessing for me," Hans said with hesitant optimism.

"How so?" Christian asked.

"As you know, you are bound by law to never mention anything we talk about to anyone ever. If you do, we will lock you in a deep dark dungeon and throw away the dungeon!"

"Understood," Christian said, trying not to visualize this dungeon.

"I've spent a lifetime secretly working on a drug that truly unlocks the human mind. With Britt's help, who you may have met on your way up, I've finally obtained the final components to make this drug. We've also discovered that indigenous peoples, such as Inuits and Native Americans, are less prone to experience the drug's main side effect."

"What side effect is that?" Christian quickly asked.

"For whatever reason, most people experience a dramatic decrease in heart rate and respiration when taking the medication. It's almost like it puts them in a state of hibernation. We have not seen that side effect in Native American and Inuit peoples, and I need to figure out what it is that makes them immune to those adverse reactions.

"Ever since the breakthrough, I've been doing everything in my power to get approval from the Danish equivalent of your Food and Drug Administration—FDA—to start human trials, but they have categorically denied my attempts."

Christian interrupted, "I have so many questions."

"Please, ask away," Hans said encouragingly.

"First, does Denmark have indigenous peoples? Second, what exactly do you mean by unlocking the mind, and finally, what do I have to do with all this?"

"All good questions," Hans conceded. "First, most people think of Denmark as one of the smallest countries in the world when, in fact, the Kingdom of Denmark is one of the largest countries in the world." Christian raised his eyebrows as Hans continued, "Greenland is not only the largest island in the world, but it is also a territory of Denmark."

Before Christian could object, Hans cut him off. "Australia is a continent!"

Christian reluctantly nodded in agreement.

"Fun fact," Hans continued, "within twenty years at the present almost exponential rate of global warming and glacial melt-off, Southern Greenland will have more desirable ocean-front property with a Caribbean-like climate than any other country in the world."

"Wow!" Christian exclaimed, "I should buy some land in Greenland with all that money you're paying me!"

"That was my exact thought over twenty years ago." Hans gloated, "Alas, you can't buy land in Greenland, but that hasn't stopped me from finding some very creative workarounds. I currently possess more land-rights in Greenland than any other individual or corporation on the plant!"

"No grass grows under your feet, does it?" Christian said, trying to acknowledge Hans's business acumen with one of his father's old sayings.

"Global warming," Hans sneered with a mocking tone, "If you can't stop it, might as well make an ass-load of money off it!"

"Now back to your original questions. First, the Inuit are the primary indigenous peoples of Greenland which you now know is a part of the Danish realm. To answer your second question, my psychoactive drug allows a person to go into a state of trance where they can travel to any point in their life memories from their first consciousness to real-time present day. They can view the memories like they're watching a movie, and they also have some form of heightened awareness of their physiology. There is so much to discover, but my hands are tied. I need the DKMA, Danish Medicines Agency, to approve my human trials. Unfortunately, up until a few days ago, they have completely denied me access to the Inuit for human trials. This all changed with your lecture. They are now willing to give me a provisional permit."

"That's great news!" Christian exclaimed.

"Problem is, they will only do it on one condition," Hans continued.

"What's that?"

Hans looked Christian directly in the eyes. "They will only approve if you are the lead investigator on the trial."

"Wow!" Christian said, feeling very special. "But wait, if they haven't given you permission for human trials, how do you know about the side effects and the fact that the Inuits and Native Americans are immune?"

Hans donned a Machiavellian sneer. "Some situations call for permission, others call for forgiveness."

Christian remembered his dad using that expression on more than a few occasions. He then reflected on Dmitry's suspicions of Hans illegally experimenting on people, but now wasn't the time for confrontation.

"What about past memories from their ancestors?" Christian asked, trying to conceal his eagerness.

"Sorry, I know how much that means to you, but no signs of ancestral memories. Then again, who knows what could happen during human trials? I hope you understand the potential of this drug—the ability to go back and view every detail of every memory. This has applications in every aspect of life, from psychotherapy to education to criminal justice and countless others. It's literally worth billions, and I'm not going to miss the opportunity!"

Christian understood the potential of this drug better than anyone else on the planet.

"So, what's the next step?" Christian asked as he began to imagine the possibilities.

"Like I said before, the Danish DKMA is a regulatory agency like your American FDA, but at the end of the day, they are Danish and want Denmark to win this prize. Your now-famous lecture is going to get a lot of people digging, and it has become a race! First to publish and first to patent."

Hans lifted a small silver briefcase with a solid green LED light shining by the handle. "This temperature-regulated, satellite-uplinked briefcase contains two hundred edible doses of ReminEssence. That's what we're calling it for now, but that may change. When you arrive at the Inuit camp in Greenland, and are ready to administer the first dose, I will unlock the case via the satellite uplink."

"Greenland?" Christian asked, afraid of what the answer would be.

"There is a limo out front waiting to take you to the airport, where one of the company jets is prepped and ready to take you to Qaanaaq, Greenland."

"Hold on!" Christian exclaimed as his right eye twitched more intensely, "I never agreed to any of this!"

"I'm almost one hundred percent certain you will accept this offer," Hans said with confidence. "This is quite simply the best and only lead you have right now to potentially understanding how Collin became the way he was. For all we know, ReminEssence could have helped him."

Despite his objections, Christian knew Hans was right, and, furthermore, he had no intention of turning this opportunity down.

"But I need to pack and get my passport," Christian said, trying to maintain some control over the situation.

"We've already retrieved your clothes from Henrik's penthouse, and you won't need your passport as you're not leaving Denmark. In fact, we will be holding onto your passport as an added security measure. Not that we need it. This briefcase can be tracked anywhere on the planet if you decide to run with it, and even if you escape with it, we can trigger a self-destruct at any time."

"Yikes!" Christian exclaimed. "What if it malfunctions and blows me up? And that's crazy about keeping my passport. Why would I run?"

"Don't worry, there's no bomb, just a concentrated UV burst within the case that will completely neutralize and denature the ReminEssence so it would be useless in the hands of my competitors.

"They all knew I was up to something big when Norkap passed on creating a COVID vaccine. I promise you, they are working night and day to discover my secrets. As far as your passport is concerned, well, it's my way or the highway. You can take it or leave it. But I hope you take it! My way, not the passport!"

Christian felt he had displayed a convincing amount of resistance. He knew that if he had too anxiously agreed to all of Hans's demands, there would be less trust. Christian wanted as much trust and goodwill as possible so when the time was right, he could take his dose of ReminEssence safely under the radar.

It took all his concentration to control his twitching right eye as he pondered the possibility of ReminEssence helping him access the repressed memory of his father's death and gaining more insight into genetic memories.

"Okay, I'm in. What's next?"

Hans stood up and extended his hand, "We shake on it."

After walking to the elevator, Hans swiped his card and handed another card to Christian. "This will cover any of your expenses. Keep your wits about you, your mouth shut, and your eyes and ears open and you should be just fine! Jesper, one of my most trusted human trials folks, will be waiting in Qaanaaq and will help you get to the Inuit camp."

With his other hand, Hans handed Christian the silver case. Christian stepped into the elevator, but Hans stopped the door as it was closing. "By the way, I think we have a medication that could help with that twitch in your right eye. Just swing by the pharmacy on your way out."

Christian mused at the irony as the door closed between him and Hans. He then looked at the card Hans had handed him. It was an American Express that simply said Norkap, but it was black. He'd seen green and gold Amex cards, but never black. *Maybe a chemical or dye spilled on it*, Christian thought to himself.

Henrik met him as he exited the elevator. "Holy shit, I was just briefed on the plan. Uncle Hans won't let me go with you, that sucks!"

"That's a bummer. I assumed you were going with me," Christian said with disappointment as they walked out of the building.

"Well, I'll be here when you get back and we'll pick up where we left off!" Henrik said as Christian got into the limo and shut the door.

Christian received a text from Dmitry as the limo sped towards the airport. "Hi, Christian, just checking in. Everything OK?"

"All good," Christian responded, "On way to airport."

"Where to?" Dmitry texted.

"Greenland."

"Too bad, we were hoping to have you for dinner again tonight."

"Maybe I can get a raincheck! BTW, I think you were right about what we discussed the other night. But don't worry, everything is OK so far." Christian felt an extra eye twitch with that last text.

"Just be careful and text if you need anything."

"Will do, we're pulling up to the airport now. Take care."

The limo made multiple turns after arriving at the airport, and eventually drove into a hangar where a large jet with a Norkap Pharma logo was ready for takeoff with its engines roaring. The driver screeched to a halt and rushed Christian onto the plane.

Chapter 33

For as long as he could remember, Christian had always fallen asleep during takeoffs. There was something about the traumatic vibration and hum of the engines combined with the steep ascent and pressure from the g-forces sinking him deep into the embrace of his seat.

This flight was no exception.

As the plane rocketed towards the heavens, the last thing Christian remembered was the mechanical thump of the landing gear as it folded into the underbelly of the jet.

However, what made this flight different was the scene that greeted him upon waking.

The small oval window kept fogging as Christian leaned closer and closer, trying to capture the icy vastness of Greenland from the comfort of his warm jet cabin forty-thousand feet above. It was a landscape of ethereal beauty and raw power sprawled out beneath him, a scene that spoke of the Arctic's ancient majesty.

The glacier, like a colossal beast of frozen hibernating grandeur, was lying in wait. Its glistening surface shimmered under the gentle beams of sunlight, each ice crystal refracting the rays, transforming the landscape into a rainbow of hues. Shades of pristine white mingled with the faintest hints of celestial blue, painting a landscape that seemed to defy the boundaries of his imagination.

The glacier's expanse revealed towering peaks and jagged ridges, their icy summits reaching skyward like frozen soldiers guarding the secrets of this icy realm. Deep fissures, as dark as the abyss, carved intricate patterns into the glacier's surface, like ancient runes etched by the hands of time itself.

From the vantage point of the jet, the grandeur of Greenland was especially captivating; evoking a profound sense of humility and wonder. It was a scene where time stood still, where the enormity of the natural world unfolded in all its splendor, leaving an indelible imprint that Christian knew he would never forget.

He was surprised as the pilot announced they were about to land at the Thule US military base. Most flights went directly to the new Qaanaaq airport according to his earlier internet search.

The touchdown was uneventful, and he was promptly rushed from the Norkap jet to a Norkap helicopter. As the door closed, Christian caught a brief glance of the jet pilot handing a silver case, much like his own, to a very official-looking military person with a blurry line of brass stars on his shoulder.

Dmitry's warning was a stone in Christian's boot that refused to let him fully embrace the hike.

The copilot of the helicopter reached back and handed Christian a headset. The pilot's voice mingled with the rhythmic centripetal roar of the rotor, "Welcome to Greenland! The flight to Qaanaaq should last about forty minutes. The glacial winds are rough today, so hold onto your head, Fred!"

Christian was counting the seconds as they swooped in for a choppy landing in Qaanaaq. Before removing the headset and stumbling to solid ground, he asked the pilot, "It's almost midnight and the sun is still shining—do you ever get used to it?"

The pilot responded without hesitation, "Never! It's a real shit-show when it comes to getting a good nights sleep. It takes a certain kind of person to handle the constant daylight, and I'm not that kind of person."

"Yikes!" Christian replied, wondering how long his stay would last.

"Just pray your work wraps up before the winter," the pilot continued, "The constant darkness makes this look like a walk in Tivoli."

Stepping out of the chopper, Christian realized this was no ordinary daylight; there was something about the alien angle of the sun and the barren surroundings that made him feel like he was literally on top of the world.

By the stroke of 1 AM, he had checked into his hotel room. The sun was at its lowest point on the horizon. He knew it would only get brighter from there as he closed the special blackout blinds in his room. However, sleep was slow to come as visions of hiking the glacier and meeting the Inuit people consumed his thoughts.

The following day, Christian woke with renewed energy and surveyed the town as he exited the hotel. Nestled among the Arctic expanse, Qaanaaq revealed itself as a resilient outpost in the remote embrace of Greenland. It stood as a testament to the human spirit's unquenchable desire to connect with nature.

As the biting Arctic winds danced through the streets, the humble dwellings of Qaanaaq clung to the rugged terrain. Colorful houses, decorated in eclectic hues, stood in defiance of the icy surroundings, creating a vibrant mosaic against the snowcapped backdrop. Each home seemed to tell its own story; a reflection of the unique journeys undertaken by its inhabitants in this far-flung corner of the world.

The Arctic light bathed the town in immortal light, casting long shadows upon the frozen earth. The Arctic air carried the scent of brine and untouched wilderness, invigorating the senses and inoculating each breath with a virgin pureness that somehow cleansed the soul.

Qaanaaq teamed with the warm camaraderie of its residents, their footsteps one with the crunch of freshly fallen snow. A tight-knit community, united by generations of shared history and a deep reverence for their Arctic home, overcoming the isolation of their surroundings.

Along the way, one of these residents caught Christian's attention. He was a burly man in a thick wool fisherman's sweater. The man was slumped against a building in a way that made Christian wonder if he was even alive.

Approaching the man, Christian asked what had happened. There was no response. He cautiously drew closer and began to shake him, hoping to elicit a response. The man's eyes slowly opened, and upon seeing Christian, he pulled out a long, razor-sharp knife and held it to Christian's throat within a split second.

The man spoke something in Danish as Christian apologized in English. The knife immediately dropped as the man realized his folly. In an apologetic voice, he addressed Christian saying, "I am so sorry. You surprised me, and I thought you were trying to rob me."

Confused and not understanding why the man tried to attack him, Christian asked, "First of all, why would you carry a weapon like that, and secondly, why were you passed out on the street? I thought you were dead."

Grinning, the man sat up and explained, "This must be your first time in Greenland. Up here, we work very hard and have little to do with our money but save it. As you can see, there aren't supermarkets or liquor shops on every corner. Instead, we get large shipments each month, and by the time they arrive, everyone has long since depleted the prior month's supply. You can imagine how ecstatic people are when a new shipment comes. There are usually several nights of heavy drinking, feasting, and anything else you can imagine before the good stuff once again runs out."

Christian couldn't tell if he was being serious, but nodded as the man continued. "These warm months are the best time to stock up on fish, so that's what we do. I'll go out and fish for 14 hours straight and then rest for a few hours before starting again. The constant daylight is great for this. Now you know me—what brings you to our little icy corner of the world?"

Christian began explaining, but stopped just as quickly as he remembered all those NDAs he had signed back at Norkap. "The details aren't that important, but I'm here on work. Do you know a man named Jesper? I was told to meet him here at a bar and grill called the Ice Tavern."

The man pointed out a sturdy, two-story building constructed from local stones about two hundred meters down the street, "Just down that way. You can't miss it and you certainly won't miss Jesper!"

"Thank you," Christian said, noticing the police lettering across the front of the man's sweater for the first time as he stumbled to his feet.

"Any time!" the man said. "At your service!" He staggered down the hill to the docks where his weathered fishing boat was gently swaying in the cool glacial breeze.

Continuing down the rough, unplanned street, Christian's gaze drifted to the icy cliffs in the distance as they plunged into the even icier ocean. He quickly reached the crude yet well-built stone structure, only to find it dark and locked.

Christian tried to envision the Ice Tavern during the dark, frozen winter months. He imagined villagers being drawn out of the darkness from all directions by its warm, inviting glow, as the sounds of jolly patrons and the smells of delicious food enchanted the arctic night air.

His attention was then drawn to a man effortlessly splitting wood up the hill from the tavern. If someone had asked Christian what a Viking looked like, this would surely be his example. The man noticed Christian at the same time and motioned for him to come up the hill with the ax, waving it with the ease of a child waving a sparkler.

As Christian drew nearer, he heard the man's deep voice cutting through the clean breeze. "By the looks of it, I'd have to guess that you're Christian. I'm Jesper."

Jesper then turned back to his last log and split it with such force that one of the cleaved pieces came hurtling toward Christian. He quickly ducked and heard a booming, "Sorry about that!"

Once Christian was upon him, he realized that Jesper was a good four inches taller than he, and his rippling muscles were impressive by any standard.

Wasting little time, Jesper spoke. "I hope your travels went smoothly. We were all shocked when the news trickled down that the DKMA had suddenly reversed their stance and were allowing *official* human trials."

Jesper fell silent as his gaze drifted to Christian's twitching right eye. Before Jesper could comment, Christian quickly put his dark glasses on. "Sorry, I have some kind of light sensitivity in my right eye. The doctors are trying to figure it out." *Why do I keep lying to everyone about this?*

Jesper just shrugged,"OK, then, let's go inside and finish this discussion."

"It's good to meet you," Christian said as they walked down the hill.

Jesper replied, "By the way, did Hans tell you about the two other men he was sending? They arrived last night, shortly after you."

Christian was a little confused. "No, he just sent me a message during the flight on where to meet you today. He said you were his best human trials guy and to follow your lead." They finally reached the tavern, and Christian tried to fight a growing suspicion that something just was not right.

Jesper unlocked the door to the tavern, and as it slowly crept shut behind them, his calm controlled demeanor melted away. With a surging sense of urgency in his voice, he grabbed Christian's arm and slammed him against the wall. "Just listen and say nothing. I need you to do exactly what I tell you. I'm a friend, and you're in great danger!"

"What on earth are you talking about?" Christian demanded as he struggled to escape. Jesper slammed him even harder against the wall this time and punched him in the stomach. Doubled over and trying to catch his breath, Christian realized Jesper was profoundly serious.

"You must forget everything you know and trust me with your life. You're in danger. Can you do that?" Christian hesitated, and Jesper backhanded him across the face, knocking his dark sunglasses to the floor. He asked again, "Can you do that?"

This time, Christian nodded as he wiped the blood from his nose. "There's a saddled horse behind this building; her name is Gidget. I want you to take the back exit behind that bar. You will see a trail that leads straight up the mountain slope behind this town. You do know how to ride, don't you?"

This time, Christian quickly nodded in agreement. "Yes, but..."

Jesper cut him off. "Once you're up the hill, you must ride several kilometers inland until you reach the glacier. If all is arranged, there will be a snowmobile waiting at the top of the glacier, behind a large stone that's shaped like a pear."

There was a distant noise down the street, and Jesper frantically looked towards the door, then back to Christian. "The two men Hans sent are planning something very bad. Last night, they arrived at the bar and

141

introduced themselves saying Norkap had sent them. Later on, I went outside to get some firewood, and they were on the other side of the woodpile, talking. One of them was on a satellite phone, and I overheard him confirming plans to kill you and dispose of your body."

"Why didn't you call the police?" Christian demanded.

"There's only one policeman here!" Jesper said. "And he's a drunken sociopath!"

Christian didn't argue, realizing one hundred percent of the people he met that day had assaulted him.

He then remembered Henrik's sick sense of humor back in Copenhagen. He briefly wondered if this could be some kind of dark prank, an initiation of sorts to the Greenland crew.

Looking at the smeared blood on his hand, he quickly dismissed that idea and knew this was no joke. He had little doubt that Jesper was telling the truth, or at least thought he was. Jesper backed away and peered out the window. His sense of urgency increased.

"Once you've climbed the glacier and found the snowmobile, go eastward along the edge of the ravine for about five kilometers, and you'll reach the Inuit camp. God willing, you'll find…"

There was a knock on the door, followed by a crash as whoever was on the other side tried to kick it down.

Christian hesitated for a moment, and Jesper violently motioned for him to go. He wanted to do exactly what Jesper had ordered, but something in him was frozen. "Run, for God's sake, Christian!" Jesper exclaimed as the hinges cracked with another blow from the other side.

An overpowering sense of déjà vu consumed Christian as he stood there, frozen, with death just inches away, knocking on the door. Where the sense came from, he knew not.

"Sometimes, it's better to be a live coward than a dead hero. You'll know what to do when the time comes." For whatever reason that saying of his dad's came to mind, and it was just enough to tip the scale.

Like a flash, Christian flew into action, as if he were obeying his father's dying request.

He caught a brief glimpse of Jesper leaning into the door with all his weight as he turned the corner and dashed outside to Gidget.

Chapter 34

Having grown up working their mountainside horse farm with his dad, Christian felt right at home leaping onto the horse and setting her afoot.

Of course, he'd never run for his life across the glaciers of Greenland before.

Microscopic pieces of ice felt like razors in the arctic wind as he galloped up the steep green hillside. Far below, gunshots and a crash echoed from the Ice Tavern. He had only been acquainted with Jesper for a few stressful minutes, yet Jesper may have just sacrificed his life for Christian.

Would he be joining Collin and RelicCollector1 in my nightmares?

He felt a familiar pressure in his ears as Gidget ascended the mountainous grade with effortless speed and grace. Once at the top, Christian risked a peek over his shoulder only to see a shrinking dot where the village once stood. Without hesitation or stopping to catch her breath, Gidget galloped down the trail as if she could sense the peril hunting them.

After ten minutes of vigorous riding, Christian saw the unimaginably large icecap that encompassed most of Greenland. The oceans of flowing green fields halted at the base of the icecap, which resembled a giant sloppy pancake that had been carelessly poured over the landscape.

As they drew closer, Christian panicked at the sheer size of this ancient ice blanket. The hill at the village was one thing, but there was no way they could scale this rock-hard ice cliff.

His fear of the climb was quickly replaced by concern at a revving sound emerging behind him. Christian looked back and saw two men in an old Range Rover approaching quickly. Neither of them was Jesper.

By the time he reached the base of the icecap, his pursuers were one hundred meters behind and closing fast.

Christian worried the horse would stop at any minute and send him flying into the wall of the glacier, but instead, she sped up, and with a smooth yet forceful transition, they were suddenly heading up the slope as though it was an open field.

As they neared the top of the icy cliff, Christian saw the large, pear-shaped stone Jesper had mentioned. It really did look just like a pear. There was even a wild plant growing out of the top that made for a perfect leaf and stem.

The moment he breathed a sigh of relief, there was a jolt, and the smooth upward climb turned into a slippery descent. He should have known not to let his guard down and jinx himself. With the loss of momentum, Gidget had no choice but to back down the ice face.

Christian wasn't ready to confront the looming fate that lurked below, so he leaped from the horse and grabbed hold of a rock jutting out of the ice. After checking that his faithful steed had made it down, he fumbled for a foothold. Two feet from reaching the top, all he needed was one good crevice to pull himself up. After a few failed attempts, Christian finally got a grip and thrust himself onto the flat, barren surface above.

Diminished from the struggle, Christian lay paralyzed on his stomach and unable to budge. After a few minutes, the severity of the situation recharged his resolve. His adrenaline rushed again, and he struggled to his feet. Before limping over to the stone, he turned his head to see the progress of his pursuers, only to find a silent, majestic view over the plains and distant ocean. They must have taken an alternate route.

Clueless about his location, Christian quickly made his way to the stone.

Turning the corner, he was sickened to see no snowmobile. But, before panic set in, a metallic glimmer behind a pile of ice near the rock caught his eye. With apprehension, he drew closer and recognized the outline of a snowmobile. Christian thanked God for all the winter weekends in Vermont snowmobiling with his freshman-year roommate.

The vehicle started instantly, reassuring Christian that it had been well maintained. He took off with a jolt as he squeezed the throttle on the right handle.

Before long, he was approaching the great ravine in the barren, icy distance. He remembered Jesper's frantic instruction and hurtled towards it at full throttle. Although his assailants were still nowhere to be seen, this made Christian's apprehension increase rather than decrease.

After traveling a few kilometers, Christian started to relax, feeling that he had eluded his pursuers for good. But suddenly, a faint echo in the distance caught his attention, and a few moments of focusing revealed two tiny dots on the horizon that were growing larger with each passing second.

The ravine to his right was involuntarily corralling him towards his pursuers. His only hope was to get ahead of them before the two paths merged.

With renewed motivation, Christian pushed the throttle even harder and brought the already roaring vehicle to its full potential, enabling him to outrun his pursuers before their vectors merged. With a decent gap between them, Christian had the luxury to relax and contemplate other issues. It was then that the revelation hit him. Even if he reached the Inuit camp safely, what would he do then?

And if that wasn't enough, he began to wonder if this was merely a setup to lure him out into the middle of nowhere with no witnesses. Christian had to consider the possibility that he was driving into the wild to meet a fate that would forever stay between him and his attackers. At this point, he was in a full-blown panic. His hands became so sweaty that the handles became oiled bars, almost impossible to grip.

He glanced into the rearview mirror just in time to see one of his attackers closing the gap. To his disbelief, the man pulled out a handgun and aimed it straight at Christian's back. Reacting instinctively, Christian swerved towards his attacker, causing the rear treads of his snowmobile to collide with the pursuer's front skis. He then heard a shot ring out, as his left rearview mirror exploded.

The attacker's front ski was damaged in the collision, and Christian watched in horror and relief as the snowmobile behind him swerved, wobbled, and ultimately plunged end over end into the seemingly bottomless ravine. Seconds later, an explosion echoed up from the depths of the chasm.

Christian knew no one could have survived that fall. Despite this, the second attacker was still a fair distance away but closing fast. Christian prayed for the first time in years and pushed the throttle even harder, if that was possible.

Chapter 35

The Surgeon answered Johnny's call on his satellite phone with urgency. "What's the update?"

"He's dead," came the voice from the other end of the line, mingled with the roar of a snowmobile and gusts of wind in the background.

"Excellent work! You're ahead of schedule!" replied The Surgeon with an unusual sense of appreciation.

But that praise was short-lived as Johnny continued, "No, Brian... Brian is dead!"

The Surgeon, with a sinking feeling in his chest, realized the gravity of the situation. "You must forget about that right now. The only thing that matters is Christian," he said hurriedly, trying to maintain control of the situation.

Johnny's response was immediate and resolute. "Fuck you, you goddamn sick twisted bastard, and fuck your plan. I'm going to kill Christian, and then I'm going to find you and rip your throat out."

The Surgeon regretted his earlier insensitivity as he tried to reason with Johnny, "I'm sorry..." But all he heard was a thud, followed by the sound of a snowmobile quickly fading away in the distance.

Chapter 36

As he zigzagged, attempting to outrun this monster, Christian began to feel like a gazelle being pursued on the Serengeti by a helicopter. He knew that dwelling on such thoughts wasn't going to help, so he shook his head and focused on the task at hand.

The constant vibration and rough terrain were beginning to take their toll, causing his arms to feel like jelly. The rattling had become so intense that his joints were at risk of dislocation, and the pain in his buttocks was so severe that he had to partially stand up to relieve the pain.

His already precarious situation grew worse as he heard the engine begin to sputter. He was running out of fuel.

Christian was too preoccupied with the fuel gauge pointing to the red 'E' to notice the enormous valley he was approaching. Suddenly, he looked up to realize that the path ended a few feet ahead of him, and past that was a steep drop into a massive rift valley.

With very little time to prepare for the descent, Christian braced himself and adjusted his posture. The snowmobile flew over the edge, and just before the impact, he stood up even more in hopes of absorbing more of the forces with his legs. As he plummeted down the slope, the Inuit camp far below came into focus.

The camp consisted of a few huts and igloos backing up to the cliffs at the opposite end of the valley. He rejoiced at the sight all the same and prayed that he had enough momentum to make it to the camp as he tightened his grip and leaned into the descent.

Out of fuel with no brakes, the snowmobile had become a giant bobsled as he reached the bottom of the slope and careened towards the deserted camp.

As the huts and igloos flew by in a blur, he knew there was no stopping the snowmobile. Like a rag doll cast from a child's stroller, Christian heaved his body off the snowmobile moments before it collided with the cliff. The collision reduced the snowmobile to a mangled pile of metal. Fortunately, there was no explosion as the fuel had long since been depleted.

He felt his fingernails ripping off and his hands shredding as he desperately grappled the rough icy ground trying to slow his slide towards a jagged metal remnant of the snowmobile. He finally came to a stop, just inches from the projectile impaling his head.

There was no time to celebrate the survival of this most recent brush with death as he heard the other snowmobile rapidly approaching in the distance.

Ignoring the pain coursing through his body and hands, Christian quickly stumbled to his feet and painfully limped to the entrance of a large cave at the foot of the cliff. He darted inside, praying that his pursuer hadn't seen him enter.

He scanned the sparsely decorated single-chamber interior, noting a few furs on the walls and a well-used fire pit at the center. There were some small carvings and unidentified Inuit gadgets, none of which could serve as weapons.

At this point, the chase had weakened Christian to the verge of collapse. He turned towards the entrance, just in time to see his death step inside.

Christian felt a moment of relief as the stranger holstered his gun, but this sense of solace quickly disappeared as the man uttered with an enraged voice, "The man lying dead back in the ravine was my brother. I'm going to slice your neck like a beast and watch the blood course out with each diminishing heartbeat until you're dead."

Johnny was growling with rage, not just towards Christian but also towards The Surgeon and the world.

Christian braced himself as Johnny produced a machete-sized hunting knife with brutal serrations on one side and a razor-sharp blade on the other. He knew very well that he had neither the skill nor the energy to fight this man, with or without a knife.

Johnny took a quick fake stab to both assess Christian's skill and toy with him. This was enough to make Christian jump back and gouge his head on a pointed rock protruding from the cave wall.

With his consciousness fading, Christian held his lacerated scalp as he fell to his knees and helplessly watched Johnny raise the knife for the fatal blow.

Just as the knife began its downward swing, a figure emerged from the shadows, grabbed Johnny's knife hand, and effortlessly snapped his neck with one fluid motion.

Johnny crumbled to the ground, with an almost peaceful look on his face.

With warm blood coursing through his hair and a throbbing headache, Christian slowly lifted his head and squinted.

Everything began to blur, but not before recognizing the mysterious Interpol agent who had now saved him twice.

Chapter 37

The loss of Johnny and Brian was regrettable but acceptable considering the circumstances. As far as The Surgeon was concerned, they had brought it on themselves by getting sloppy.

He wasn't complaining though. Pursuing Christian over the glacier had led to the discovery of something far more significant than he could have ever imagined.

Like a child in a candy shop, The Surgeon watched the live footage stream from dead Johnny's body camera as Christian was scooped up and carried out of the cave by someone very unexpected. Someone he thought had died decades ago. Someone who had taken a priceless discovery with him to a deep icy grave.

The Surgeon prided himself on being one of the greatest manipulators to ever live, but even he could not have planned or predicted this stroke of good luck. The best part was, now all he had to do was sit back, let Christian solve the puzzle and bring the prize to him.

Chapter 38

The attempt to focus was futile as the strong morning sun shone through the window, pinning Christian's eyes shut. He eventually gave up and dozed off for a few more hours, waking up to a late afternoon breeze that carried the cool fragrance of mountain wildflowers. The sun was no longer overpowering his vision.

Despite his severe headache, he mustered the energy to turn over and saw someone sitting on the other side of the bed. Christian instantly recognized the woman in the chair, despite only seeing her for a moment with Henrik at the elevator in Norkap. He would never forget her face or voice. "Try not to move too much. You sustained a bad injury to your head," she said.

Christian slowly and cautiously moved his hand to the back of his head, where he felt about three inches of stitches and a lot of swelling. "Who did this?"

"You smashed your head in the cave at the Inuit camp when that guy tried to kill you. Don't you remember?" Britt replied.

Flashes of the attack surged through his body as he relieved each moment—from the drunken sheriff to the brush with death in the cave.

"You're lucky my grandfather is good at stitching, or you'd be in a hospital answering a lot of questions."

"Your grandfather?" Christian asked, perplexed.

"You'll find out soon enough," she replied. "In the meantime, you need to rest."

"But…" Every muscle in his body surged with pain when he tried to turn to Britt, "Where am I, and where is Soren?"

"You're in Switzerland, and Soren is downstairs. There is much to be explained, but for now, you need rest."

As she left the room, Christian's attempts to call out fell on deaf ears as the last remnants of his coherence vanished into the void.

This time, Christian woke up in a cold sweat. In his dream, he had been neck-deep in icy water, with people pursuing him. The more he struggled, the slower he moved. The water not only hindered his running, but it also numbed his legs. He wasn't even certain if he had legs. The dream ended when a snarling polar bear reached the water's edge and clubbed him in the head as if he were a seal.

Lying in bed, Christian reached down to verify that it was just a nightmare. No lights were on, and the air was fresh and chilly. Fortunately, the moonlight was so bright that he could see easily. Ravaged by hunger, Christian ventured out in search of food.

After two tries, he stabilized himself enough to stand on his own. The thick wooden door to the bedroom opened into an enormous hallway that led to an even more luxurious staircase. At the base of the stairs stood a towering grandfather clock, basking in the white moonlight that streamed through the oversized French windows. Christian could see that it was just past midnight.

He discovered the vast kitchen after searching around. There was a half-eaten ham in the industrial stainless-steel refrigerator. Christian ate till he was stuffed, and then ate some more. The gluttonous feast triggered a spell of nausea as he backtracked his way to the bedroom, falling into the bed just in time for another deep sleep.

The following day, Christian woke up to sunshine beaming in, but this time, it was a welcome sight. He gradually rose from the bed, muscles not so stiff, and made his way downstairs. In the light, Christian realized he wasn't residing in an ordinary home. It was a magnificent mansion, and judging by the rugged peaks and steep ledges he could see out the windows, the mansion was nestled deep in the Alps.

As Christian regained his balance, determined to complete the last two steps of the ornate stone spiral staircase, Soren breezed out of the kitchen with two cups of hot tea.

"Good morning, I was about to come up and check on you. Feeling any better this morning?"

Christian nodded as he lightly touched his stitches.

Soren went on, "you must have many questions, and so do I. Let's sit on the veranda, and I'll tell you what I know."

Soren led Christian through a grand living room with a fireplace as tall as him, and then towards two nine-foot-high French doors.

Christian's footsteps echoed softly as he emerged from the baroque mansion, nestled on a cliff deep in the Swiss Alps. Dewdrops clung to the exquisite stonework of the expansive veranda, reflecting the first gentle glimmers of sunlight as dawn cast its vibrant hue to the horizon.

Dizzying peaks loomed like ancient titans, proud yet serene, as they stood watch over the valleys and slopes unraveled below.

A crisp cool breeze brushed through Christian's hair, carrying with it the scent of fresh snow and alpine flora. The head trauma and stitches became a distant memory as his heart swelled with a sense of wonderment and exhilarating dread when he approached the precipice of the veranda, observing the abyss of a two-hundred-meter drop and jagged rocks spanning below him.

He stood there, spellbound by the beauty that commanded his very soul, until Soren broke his trance with an invitation to sit and enjoy their tea.

Chapter 39

Soren's typically stoic and composed demeanor contorted into a rare scowl as he pivoted toward Christian, his voice laced with urgency. "How did you become entangled with the likes of Hans Rasmussen?"

A hint of defensiveness colored Christian's response. "Norkap Pharmaceuticals offered me a dream job, and in the blink of an eye, I found myself the frontrunner for the Ironman Arctic Triathlon. But what about you? How did you know about me and locate me in Greenland?"

Soren's eyes locked onto Christian's as he explained, "I was tracking The Surgeon, more specifically, his henchmen, Johnny and Brian. Your input two years ago put us on the trail of a black-market jeweler crafting mysterious golden cubes for a shady clientele. We traced Johnny and Brian through this jeweler and unearthed their link to a Polish antiques dealer known as RelicCollector1, though, as always, it was too late."

Christian couldn't help but cringe at the mere mention of RelicCollector1. Soren pressed on, "Ever since then, both we and the Danish authorities have been tailing them, hoping they would lead us to The Surgeon."

Christian was taken aback. "But how did you know I was in Denmark?"

"Johnny and Brian have been shadowing you since your arrival, and we've been shadowing them," Soren explained. "Incidentally, both the American

State Department and the Danish government are rather intrigued by your peculiar relationship with a Russian ambassador."

Christian hastily clarified, "Oh, that's Dmitry. He's just a friend I met on the flight over."

Soren leveled a stern gaze at Christian. "When all of this is behind us, you'll have some explaining to do. Mingling with Russian officials, brushing shoulders with Hans Rasmussen, and becoming an overnight internet sensation have drawn far more attention than you might realize."

Christian hadn't had the chance to step back and assess the broader scope of recent events, but Soren's words forced him to reckon with it. A warm rush surged through his head as he reflected on the whirlwind of the past few days.

Before they continued, Christian took a moment to express his gratitude. "Before anything else, I want to thank you for saving my life... again."

Soren regarded Christian and replied with gravity, "Don't thank me. We're part of something far larger than ourselves, a saga that has unfolded over decades, leaving countless lives in ruins." His concern deepened as he continued, "By the way, is your right eye all right? It's been twitching since this morning."

Christian felt a twinge of embarrassment. "I'm not sure. Maybe I took a harder knock to the head than I thought."

Soren's voice remained steady as he advised, "Let's keep an eye on that, no pun intended, and ensure it's not a symptom of something more serious."

Christian laughed and felt guilty about lying, but it was equally stressful trying to explain that he had been scarred for life by an ultra-violent event, of which he had no memory, when he was just nine years old. "If you happen to find an extra pair of dark sunglasses, that would be great. The bright sun is giving me a killer headache."

"Of course, we must have a pair lying around here somewhere," Soren said, his expression conveying concern. He took his own deep breath before continuing. "You must have a million questions, so let's start with me. My original name is not Soren Müller. It was Lars Rasmussen, and I'm not Swiss. I'm Danish."

Christian was surprised but not shocked. After all, the events of the past few weeks had been nothing but strange. "Rasmussen must be a common name, considering that both Hans and Henrik share it," he said.

Soren winced as if a phantom assailant had knocked the wind out of him, "Hans is my brother, and Henrik was—I mean, is—my son."

Christian's eye twitched. "Are you kidding me!" he exclaimed, the echo of his outburst reverberating through the mountain peaks. He lowered his voice, feeling embarrassed for losing his cool. "I'm sorry, but how is that possible?"

Christian's heart went out to Soren as he watched this powerful apex male struggle to tell the story, "Hans and I grew up in a traditional Danish family and were always competitive with each other. We both studied archaeology at the University of Copenhagen and both fell in love with the same woman, Ingrid. For better or for worse, she chose me. We got married and had a beautiful baby boy, Henrik."

Christian was fighting to believe the story Soren was telling him, but his rational mind was not accepting it.

"On the drive home from the hospital, we were hit by what they assume was a drunk driver who fled the scene. Ingrid was killed, while Henrik emerged without a scratch. Some might not call what happened to me surviving, but I did live — albeit spending the next year in a coma, nursing countless broken bones and other injuries. No one thought I'd make it. Henrik was cared for by my parents. This all happened over thirty years ago."

A butler materialized from the depths of the sprawling estate, silently refilling their tea. He then placed a tray with bottled water and aspirin in front of Christian. "We're still working on the sunglasses," he announced with exaggerated formality.

Soren's voice snapped him back to the history. "To everyone's amazement, I came out of the coma. But I wasn't the same — I was a shadow of my former self. Every movement was agony, and my heart ached with the loss of Ingrid. This led me to a vicious cycle of opioid addiction, which soon spiraled into heroin.

The courts, along with my family, kept Henrik away from me. My life became a blur of crimes – stealing from both kin and strangers to fuel my addiction, punctuated by stints in jail or the hospital."

Christian struggled to reconcile the image of the Soren he knew — a paragon of strength and intelligence — with the broken man now being described.

"The most haunting memory," Soren began, his voice introspective, "was waking up each day, assuming it would be my last. But death never came. I felt I deserved an end by my own vices and despised myself for being to cowardly to do it myself."

Listening intently, Christian asked, "What about Hans? Where was he? Why didn't he step in?"

"Hans had embarked on an archaeological quest in Greenland just weeks after my accident. My coma followed by the descent into addiction spanned three years, and during that time, he was absent. I never heard from him."

After chasing four aspirin with water, Christian focused as Soren went on, "It was a snowy Christmas Eve in Copenhagen. The brief daylight of winter had already faded when I found myself looking for shelter. Out of the blue, I saw my parents with Henrik, who was sipping hot chocolate. He had grown so much — looking healthy and well-loved. Yet, there was an unmistakable sadness in his eyes. The only other time he saw me was when I was being hauled away by the police after breaking into my parents' house for drug money. He stood at his bedroom door, watching, unaware that the man being arrested was his father."

Christian empathized deeply for both Soren and Henrik, knowing all too well the pain from a childhood devoid of parents.

Soren's voice wavered, "Earlier that evening, I'd taken a few shots of Absinthe and a huge dose of heroin from a new dealer. As the overdose took hold, my last memory was of collapsing into the snow while watching my son disappear around the corner."

Tears welled up in Soren's eyes, just a blink away from freedom.

Chapter 40

I t would have taken more than ten fingers to count the times he had overdosed and wound up in a dark hospital room; Narcan coursing through his veins, and no recollection of how he came to be there.

Shit, Lars thought to himself as every surface of his body burned with an itch that he knew scratching wouldn't help.

It's Christmas Eve, the hospital's probably running on a skeleton crew, just my luck.

"Can someone PLEASE get me some fucking antihistamines," Lars demanded, "or God forbid a little methadone?"

He knew all to well how bad things could go if they didn't get ahead of the withdrawal.

Even if scratching would help, he knew it would be impossible, as every hospital in town had learned long ago to immobilize his body with double the necessary restraints.

Reaching deep into his bag of tricks, Lars feigned an urgent distress call, "Help, I can't breath, my throat is closing!"

This usually did the trick, but not tonight.

160

Where's the normal procession of nurses, doctors, and social workers?

And why am I naked in the pitch-black on this hard bed with no pillow or sheet?

The Narcan had consumed the last remnants of opioids in his system as Lars became painfully aware that he was not in a hospital.

At that same moment, in the dark periphery, the echoing clang of an electrical lever being thrown ignited a blinding overhead surgical light. Fully restrained, Lars fought to move his eyes just enough to see there was only darkness outside the confining shell of the light.

Then a voice emerged from the shadows. Had he not been detoxing in some kind of make-shift dungeon, Lars would have laughed at the melodramatic Dracula accent that drifted in through the black vale surrounding him, "You should make yourself at home," The voice said cheerfully, "You're going to be here for a while."

Lars half-expected to hear, "I vant to drink your blood."

The comical voice combined with the circumstances triggered a spark of hope in Lars, as he remembered the hallucinogenic properties of the absinthe he had consumed earlier.

Of course, this is just a really bad trip.

That hope was purged from his thoughts by a crushing blast of firehose water as it washed away all the vomit, urine, and feces that so often accompanies a heroin overdose.

As Lars choked on the water and began to pass out, his final thoughts were of little Henrik disappearing around that snowy corner.

...

Lars had endured numerous cycles of detoxification and withdrawal over the last two years, but none like this, and all ending the same...relapse.

He awoke dry and clean, but still naked and restrained as his captor stared down upon him. This stranger's look matched his accent, with blacked-out round glasses, a well-groomed black beard, and waist length hair running down his back in a tight pony tail.

"My name is Lucas and I'm from Romania," He announced in his ridiculous accent, "That's all you need to know for now." Lars's attempted response was met with a needle in the arm as he faded back into oblivion.

He woke the next day consumed with a fever and the violent throes of withdrawal. Absent were the compassionate nurses and concerned doctors to ease his suffering, just another blast from the firehose to clear away the vomit, urine and feces that had once again accumulated at some point in his delirium.

Lars retained consciousness this time after the hose-down and ravenously gobbled down the single piece of Danish rugbrød bread Lucas dangled over his mouth. This was followed by another sedative injection upon swallowing the last bite.

This pattern continued day after day as Lars's mind and body were slowly purged of the toxins.

Lars was trying to calculate the duration of his captivity when Lucas came strolling through the dark chamber and leaned into blinding surgical light that was burned into his retina.

Without a word, Lucas slowly raised a photograph that triggered a blood curdling rage as Lars violently tested the boundaries of his restraints.

"If you lay a finger on that boy, I'll rip my arms and legs off to escape and tear your throat out with my teeth."

"I believe you," Lucas said with admiration and respect as he backed away nervously, "That's the parental instinct I was hoping to see."

He then held up a picture of Lars's parents, which further fueled the flames.

Lucas patiently waited for Lars to calm down, "Don't think for one second that I've expended my valuable time and resources saving you out of the goodness of my heart."

Lars's rage continued to subside as he responded with sarcasm, "You call this saving me?"

"Actually," Lucas said in a reflective tone with a slight break in his Transylvania accent, "Yes... Yes I do...You're welcome."

Lars immediately picked up on the accent slip as Lucas continued, clearly annoyed, "I'm going to show you two more pictures, and you had better think long and hard as you answer the questions that follow."

Lucas slowly raised a picture of Lars's brother, Hans, "Can you tell me who this is?"

"That's my brother Hans," Lars said, devoid of emotion, "He's been on an archaeological dig in Greenland for the past three years."

"You're half right," Lucas said in a congratulatory tone, "He's actually been right here in Copenhagen for the past week or so and will be returning to Greenland in two days to continue his little dig."

"OK," Lars said, "So what does that have to do with me?"

"I'm glad you asked that question," Lucas continued, slightly distracted as he casually strolled around the table admiring Lars's stunning physique, that years of addiction had barely blemished, "You're going to convince Han's to let you join his dig in Greenland."

"The Hell I will!" Lars exclaimed as he began thrashing again.

Lucas held up the final picture in his stack. It had been taken by someone else on the streets of Copenhagen, and it was of Lucas squatting down to Henrik's level handing him a piece of candy right in front of Lars's parents, "I have virtually unlimited resources and can get to anyone at anytime. Part of this last week was meant to give you a small taste of what I'm capable of, and, of course, to get you sober."

Lars knew Lucas was right. His dormant parental instincts were back, and stronger than ever, "What do I do?" Lars asked, clearly broken and resigned to his fate.

"For now, all you need to do is convince Hans to take you back to Greenland with him. After that, just stay clean, and report all progress to me in a timely fashion."

"I can't make any promises," Lars said, "but I'll give it my best shot."

Lucas's final words drifted through the air as Lars felt the familiar prick in his arm and began slipping into the abyss, "Your kid, your parents, and your brother all die a horrible death if you fail."

Chapter 41

~*~ Present Day ~*~

Christian didn't even try to suppress his twitching eye as Soren paused to regroup, "My next memory was one of waking on the same street where I had overdosed the week before. Only now, I was clad in the most advanced arctic gear money could buy. Beside me was a rucksack packed with twenty-thousand kroner and a portable shortwave radio. Accompanying it was a note advising me to broadcast daily updates to a certain frequency."

Christian wasn't sure what to say, so he asked the first question that came to mind, "That's why you got so upset at Ian's pub two years ago when I described Dr. Nilsson. He was using the same ridiculous accent trick that your Dracula guy used."

"Yes," Soren said confirming Christian's theory, "I think Lucas and Dr. Nilsson are the same person. I didn't make the connection until that day in Ian's Pub."

"By the way," Christian asked while surveying his surroundings, "where are we, and what is this place?"

"We're in the northern Swiss Alps, near the German border," Soren explained, "This estate belongs to Andre, who *was* my father-in-law and *is* Britt's grandfather."

It took Christian a few moments to work out the genealogy, followed by a gasp of surprise, "Wait, you're Britt's father?"

"My life must seem like one of your American Soap Operas, and I apologize for that," Soren offered, unable to imagine what Christian must have been thinking, "And yes, Britt is my daughter."

Christian prepared himself as Soren picked up where he left off almost thirty years ago, "As agreed, I approached Hans the next day, clean and sober, all decked out in my fancy arctic gear, begging him for a chance to prove myself on the expedition."

Chapter 42

~*~ Three Decades Earlier ~*~

Hans replied to his brother with palpable contempt and condemnation. "The only reason I'm even considering letting you join the team is because Leif lost half his foot to frostbite. But make no mistake, I'd still prefer his crippled contributions over listening to your delusional heroin promises. Unfortunately, he's ready to throw in the towel, and I'm left with no other choice."

Lars swallowed his pride and pledged loyalty to Hans. "Send me on the first flight back to Denmark if I let you down."

When they disembarked from the helicopter at the end of their long journey to Qaanaaq, Hans and Lars grabbed their backpacks. The biting needles of the frozen Arctic night welcomed them with a sharp sting. The departing helicopter whipped up a blinding storm of ice and snow, momentarily clouding their view.

Out of habit, Hans immediately began jogging toward the warm embrace of the Ice Tavern bar and grill, where the other eight team members awaited.

The solitary crunch of just one set of boots alerted Hans that Lars was no longer by his side. Turning around, there was something about the sight of his brother in the distance that suddenly and unexpectedly softened his heart. The emotional barrier Hans had constructed over the years crumbled in an instant, and he felt the weight of the pain from his brother's past three years of suffering.

As the helicopter's sound faded into the night, the slowly settling snow and ice revealed Lars's silhouette, gazing up at the magical Arctic sky.

Mesmerized by the legendary Northern Lights, Lars couldn't look away from the shimmering dance of emerald and jade. Even Hans, having braved three grueling Arctic years, remained in awe of the ethereal river of green, purple, and pink ribbons unfurling across the star-laden horizon.

The photographs and videos Lars had seen of the aurora borealis paled in comparison to the real-time celestial splendor unfolding before him. It floated overhead like a procession of angels. An ancient power that cured his soul of all its damage, just as the harrowing week of captivity and torment had cleansed his mind and body of all their toxins.

Hope…

A single frozen tear on Lars's cheek served as a stark reminder of the lethal cold, eager to bestow frostbite in just a few short minutes. He hurried to rejoin his brother, who had already turned back towards the Ice Tavern, discreetly wiping away his own crystalline tears.

The thick wooden door of the tavern swung open, releasing a frigid Arctic gust that heralded the brothers' arrival. The warm, inviting glow from candles and a roaring fire momentarily dimmed under the cold assault.

The bustling tavern, a blend of locals, tourists, and their eight team members, fell silent. All eyes were on Hans and Lars as they struggled to close the door against the wind.

"Apologies," Hans said, catching his breath and brushing off the accumulated snow.

The warmth and cheerful ambiance returned as they navigated past the shining bar and occupied tables, making their way to a large table near an expansive fireplace at the back. Their eager teammates greeted them with a tray of vodka shots.

Raising his glass, Hans ignited the toast, "Everyone, meet our newest recruit and my brother, Lars."

"Skål!"

Before they could drink, Anya, one of the four female team members, locked eyes with Lars. A spark passed between them, warming his recently mended soul. She felt it too, quickly turning away in a blush to a weathered man with a sizeable cast on his right foot. "And to Leif – may he enjoy many adventures on his remaining one and a half feet!"

"Skål!"

Another team member interjected, his arm wavering from holding up the drink for so long, "And to Hans, for sharing the best news ever!"

"Skål!"

At last, everyone downed their eagerly anticipated shots.

Each team member warmly greeted Lars, but it was the electrifying tension during Anya's welcome that was particularly memorable for him.

Once introductions were made and another round of shots had been poured, Lars pulled up a chair beside Hans. "What's this incredible news everyone's talking about?" he inquired with piqued curiosity.

Leaning in, Hans began, "For the past three years, we've been on the hunt for an ancient civilization believed to have existed over one hundred and fifty thousand years ago."

"Unbelievable," Lars remarked, "but there were no known civilizations from that era, only small nomadic tribes."

"Exactly," Hans responded in a hushed tone, cautious of the nearby tourists. "According to a trustworthy but anonymous source, this supposed civilization of advanced early humans possessed a sacred relic which was the source of their knowledge and power. Our initial two years were dedicated to pinpointing the exact location of this elusive society."

Understanding the implications, Lars noted, "Given the timescale, this part of the world would have been completely different."

"You couldn't be more right," Hans said, a tinge of frustration in his voice. "About a year ago, utilizing advanced Ground Penetrating Radar (GPR) and geographic triangulation techniques, we identified a buried mountain—over two and a half kilometers tall. The civilization we are seeking lies at the base of this lone mountain."

"That's staggering," Lars commented.

"It is," Hans agreed. "We've spent the past year digging and have only managed to penetrate a quarter of a kilometer. The excavation is painfully slow and meticulous. Morale has plummeted recently, prompting our current hiatus. Leif's unfortunate frostbite was another blow."

As a classically trained archaeologist, the conversation deeply intrigued Lars. He was determined to make the most of this unexpected journey, despite the adverse events that had led him here.

Hans continued, "This past week, my anonymous source informed me that this civilization had transformed the entire peak of this two and a half kilometer high mountain into a temple of unimaginable proportions. The relic we are looking for should be located within this mountaintop temple. I just informed the group of this yesterday before we departed from Denmark. This means we only have to burrow another quarter of a kilometer to reach this temple at the summit of the buried mountain. Moral is at an all time high now that we don't have to spend the next decade bludgeoning through the remaining two and a half kilometers of ice to reach the city."

"That is wonderful news!" Lars exclaimed as he surveyed the team, their faces aglow with excitement over the good news. Yet, a heavy cloud of guilt hung over him as he remembered his pledge to Lucas and the dire consequences if he failed.

They all slept well at the Qaanaaq Inn that night after an excess of drinks and a satisfying dinner, knowing it would be their last taste of civilization for a while.

The following morning—or what passed for morning—they loaded their supplies into the two snowcats and embarked on the eighty-kilometer journey eastward to their base camp. "Technically speaking," Lars mused, "it's more of a summit camp."

The tank treads of the snowcats produced an awkward, repetitive mechanical roar reminiscent of a WWII tank battalion as they crawled across the treacherous glacial terrain. Lars tried to take in the surroundings, but it was a futile effort. Everywhere he looked was an unending expanse of eternal winter darkness.

"Welcome to northern Greenland in December!" Anya announced, seated next to Lars in the dimly lit, constantly rocking cabin of their snowcat. Lars tried to keep to himself, but the undeniable chemistry between them was palpable.

They spent the next ten hours of the glacial crossing getting to know one another. By the end of the drive to the summit camp, Lars was struggling with the feelings he was already developing towards Anya.

This was beyond unacceptable, he thought to himself. The last thing he wanted to do was put another person he cared for in harm's way. Not to mention he had never properly mourned the death of Ingrid between the coma and subsequent heroin nightmare.

Over the next few months of hard labor and perpetual darkness, Lars made a valiant attempt to work diligently and keep his distance. He didn't want to draw attention to his secret updates to Lucas via the small hand-cranked shortwave radio.

However, the round-the-clock darkness left little to do when not working or sending clandestine radio communications. Lars eventually succumbed to his feeling for Anya as their relationship provided a source of warmth that kept the relentless assault of the arctic at bay.

"Lucas, are you there?" Lars muttered into the radio as he prepared to give his nightly update.

"I'm here." the vamperic voice whispered over the radio.

"Nothing new to report here," Lars noted in a low voice, "It's been about two months now, and we're still averaging roughly a meter or two a day. the bottleneck is the wooden timbers we need to reinforce the tunnel as we dig. Turns out, trees are a rare commodity in these parts."

With no acknowledgment of Christian's update, Lucas's voice came through with chilling new instructions, "Once you find the relic, you are to take it by any means necessary, and eliminate everyone in a cave-in, except your brother. Spare his life, but he must believe the cave-in was an accident."

"I didn't sign up for this!" Lars growled into the handpiece, struggling to keep his voice down.

"Earlier today," Lucas casually continued through the radio static, "I was relaxing at my favorite café, watching your parents and son. Henrik seemed happier than I've ever seen him, and I could see the relief on your parents' faces, knowing you're staying clean and working hard with your brother. You have no idea how easily and painfully I could end their lives... or maybe you do. More details will be forthcoming."

As Lars sat there in dark disbelief, listening to the static, he noticed a shadow outside his tent. He had no idea how long it had been standing there. "Who's there?" Lars asked, his voice trembling.

"It's me, Lars," came Anya's voice as she quickly unzipped his tent and slipped in.

"How much did you hear?" Lars asked, panic in his voice.

"Enough," she replied, unable to hide the sadness and disappointment in her voice, "Why didn't you share this with me? You know I love you, and I believe you feel the same way."

"I'm so sorry," Lars explained, "I didn't want to drag you into this terrible mess."

"Well... that ship has sailed," Anya declared frankly, trying to hide a nervous grin. There was a brief and uncomfortable silence as Lars awaited the two words he suspected were coming, "I'm late," she finally confided as the shy grin emerged.

Without hesitation, Lars pulled her into his arms as tears rolled down both their cheeks. "I love you. We'll figure this out together."

Anya was speechless as Lars recapped in painful guilt-ridden detail, the three years leading up to their meeting. Lars watched her in silence as the reality set in. Then, without hesitation, she looked deep into Lars's eyes and vowed, "You'll never be alone again. I don't know how, but we will figure this out together."

A lone tear rolled down Lars's cheek as he looked into the loving eyes of his salvation.

Regaining his composure, Lars said with a deep trembling breath and resolution in his voice, "One thing is non-negotiable, Lucas can NEVER find out about you or our potential baby."

Anya agreed with another shy smile, "I have no argument there," Lars listened as Anya began thinking out loud, a plan clearly begging to form as she spoke, "How does this sound? Next week, when we travel back to Qaanaaq for supplies, I'll tell Hans that I received word of a death in my family and need to return to Switzerland right away. My father is a wise man with many resources. He'll know what to do."

Lars was clearly delighted at the thought of Anya getting off that glacier and as far away from Lucas as possible, "That sounds absolutely wonderful!"

"In the meantime," she said, glancing over to the shortwave radio, "Think you can teach me how to use that thing? My father's place in the Swiss Alps is north-facing, so I should be able to get a good signal from there to here."

Lars was taken aback by Anya's unconditional commitment and fearless nature as he taught her everything he knew about using the radio. He knew he didn't deserve this, and he hated himself for involving her, but the love was pure and unconditional.

The first week without Anya was miserable, but Lars knew he couldn't let anyone suspect his relationship with her or their possible child. Then, several months passed with no word. His mind became consumed with doubt and fear. Could Lucas have somehow found out about her and done something horrible? Maybe *she* was now locked in his dungeon-*The ultimate leverage to ensure I follow through with his horrific plan.*

Each day, Lars became more convinced that Lucas had Anya. Images of her strapped to that monstrous table under the spotlight dominated his every waking moment.

Then, late one night, like a message from heaven, Anya's angelic voice emerged from the static of his shortwave radio, "Lars, are you there?"

He desperately grappled for the receiver, replying, "Yes! Yes I'm here."

"Please forgive my absence," She said with sincere emotion, "this was the first chance I've had to reach out to you."

Trying to control his tears and trembling voice, Lars exclaimed, "My God, it's so good to hear your voice. Are you OK?"

There was a pause followed by an emotional response, "I just had a doctor's visit," another pause that felt like an eternity, "I'm about to start my second trimester with our healthy baby girl."

Lars was speechless as the tears rolled down his face.

Before he could respond, a powerful male voice with a strong German accent boomed over the handset, "Hello Lars, this is Anya's father, Andre."

This was not how Lars envisioned meeting the father of the woman he had impregnated and placed in grave danger, "Hello, sir, I'm so sorry..." Lars began, but Andre interrupted.

"The day will come for us to discuss this properly, but this is not that day. My daughter loves you, and you are the father of her child, my grandchild. We've discreetly investigated your situation. My people believe you are dealing with a highly dangerous operative who operates with zero footprint."

Lars's heart sank at the thought of Lucas finding out and harming his family. But Anya had entrusted her life to him, and now it was his turn to reciprocate that faith.

Andre continued, "We suspect a major nation-state is behind this, possibly China or the United States."

"How could you know that?" Lars asked.

Andre explained, "My analysts found security footage of the sidewalk in Copenhagen where you overdosed. We have footage of the day you were taken, and of the day you were returned all dressed up in your arctic gear. On both days, the footage was doctored to remove the moment of them taking you and returning you. When viewing the feed, you literally vanished like magic, and then reappeared like magic a week later. It's the same story throughout the city with any traffic or security footage that involved your kidnappers."

"He's not joking," Anya exclaimed, "and that's not all. My father's people found video footage from an Israeli spy satellite that happened to be over Copenhagen the day you were taken, and that footage had also been hacked and edited."

"How can your dad possibly know all this stuff?" Christian asked, "Who is he?"

Andre spoke up before Anya could answer, "That's also a conversation for another day, right now, we need to focus on the problem at hand."

"OK, so how do we stand up to a superpower?" Lars asked with a defeated tone.

"That's the million dollar question," Andre said bluntly, "And the answer is, we don't. We have to beat them at their own game, not that this is a game."

"I'm all ears." Lars said, hints of hope returning to his voice.

"Trust me when I say this," Andre proclaimed with confidence, "The moment these people obtain that relic, all witnesses will be eliminated, including you and Hans, I don't care what promises they made to you or anyone else."

"So, we were all doomed from the start, no matter what I did?" Lars said with a question as he fought to wrap his head around the words Andre was saying.

"Yes and no," Andre said bluntly, "You were all doomed right up until the moment Anya overheard your conversation with Lucas, and you made the very smart decision to trust her."

"I don't understand," Lars admitted.

"Had you not been recruited by Lucas and fallen in love with Anya, we would have had no idea what was happening, yet the outcome would have most certainly been the same. They would have simply found another way to infiltrate the dig and my precious Anya and everyone else would have died in a way that would surely have looked like an accident. We would never have suspected a thing."

This made sense to Lars as Andre continued, his voice becoming broken with emotion, "It is I who owe you my undying gratitude, and I will forever be in your debt."

Lars was not expecting that as he said the first words that came to mind, "So what do we do now?"

Anya spoke matter-of-factly, "You and I have to stage our deaths in a cave-in, and we must take the relic with us. The beauty of dealing with an entity as powerful as this one, according to my dad, is that they will immediately begin withdrawing if they believe you are dead and there is no chance of acquiring the relic."

"That makes sense," Lars exclaimed, "If we fake our deaths and take the artifact, whatever it may be, there will be no need for them to eliminate any loose ends."

Anya continued, "Remember the underground stream we have to cross about twenty meters down the tunnel?"

Lars responded. "Yes, the makeshift bridge over it actually washed out the other day and we had to rebuild it, set us back a week."

"We originally came across it before you joined the team," Anya explained. "We traced its course by floating an extra emergency tracking beacon down it on a borrowed kayak from Qaanaaq. It runs underneath the ice for roughly two kilometers east and then empties into a large ravine that turns into a river during the summer. That river flows into the ocean and could provide the perfect undetectable escape route for us. We know a kayak can fit through it, so with any luck, one with two people can as well!"

Chapter 43

~*~ Present Day ~*~

J udging by the anguish etched on Soren's face, Christian began to fear the ending of this tale.

"Anya and I spent an entire year engaged in covert communication and clandestine planning, all while solidifying my scheme with Lucas to orchestrate a cave-in, sparing only Hans.

"Anya, her father, and I worked tirelessly to establish entirely new identities, not just for ourselves but also for Britt, who had been born into this tumultuous world as our perfect little baby girl."

Christian braced himself as the story unfolded and became clearer with each passing moment.

"The time we had long awaited finally arrived when the last vestiges of ice crumbled away, unveiling an ancient temple that could rival the grandeur of both the pyramids and the Great Wall of China combined. The temple was a Herculean marvel, featuring hundreds of two-hundred-foot-high columns that would give most Redwoods a run for their money. These towering pillars were meticulously arranged throughout the temple, bearing the weight of the mountain above. At the heart of this mind bending space that was equivalent to ten football stadiums in size, stood a solitary one-meter-high column, forged entirely of solid gold. Perched atop it rested the elusive relic that had been the epicenter of our quest. The relic turned out to be an ancient stone tablet with a map of the world on the top half and unrecognizable writing on the bottom half."

Soren paused, his gaze distant, as if he were reliving each moment.

"Anya had returned several months earlier. Remarkably, no one suspected a thing, as far as we could tell. Her father and I had pleaded with her to stay away, urging her to let me stage my own death. But Anya was resolute; she insisted on us both having a fresh start, a life free from the perpetual fear of being pursued.

"Our plan was uncomplicated: we placed a two-person kayak out of sight, ten meters down the tunnel created by the underground stream. The stream's languid flow allowed us to crouch down and traverse the waist deep flow without difficulty, until we reached the kayak.

"Lucas had dispatched a sizable care package, ostensibly from my parents. Concealed within were ten powerful C4 explosives, accompanied by a remote detonator to control them all. We had to bide our time, allowing everyone to safely reach the surface. Then, in a daring move, Anya and I would seize the relic and sprint into the cave's depths, triggering the first explosive at the entrance before any pursuers could follow. Once we were safely aboard the kayak, heading toward the open ocean, we'd activate the remaining explosives.

"Everything was in place and ready to proceed; we just needed to get everyone safely to the surface. Hans, however, realized he had forgotten his camera and insisted on making the treacherous journey back to retrieve it. Hans had sprained his ankle a few days before, so I offered to go in his stead."

Soren's voice trembled with intensity as he recounted the harrowing events that unfolded after exiting the tunnel. "I emerged from the tunnel into blinding sunlight, our entire day had been spent underground. My eyes took time to adjust, and it took a half-hour of rummaging through crates to find the camera.

"Just as I placed it on the table, a deafening gunshot rang out behind me. In an instant, agony shot through my head as a bullet grazed my skull. The last thing I recall was collapsing to the ground, losing consciousness," Soren continued. "It's nothing short of a miracle that I survived; the bullet had glanced off my skull. Anya always said I had a thick head, and she was right." Soren's pain was infused in every word.

"Upon regaining my senses and struggling to my feet, I rushed to the tunnel entrance only to witness something beyond belief. Hans was standing there, tending to several sticks of burning dynamite embedded in the cave wall. There was a gun holstered at his side, and the coveted tablet was beside him on the ground. No one else was in sight." Soren's rage was palpable at this point.

"I saw red. That traitor shot me, and who knew what he'd done to the others. Without hesitation, I tackled him, and we both crashed to the ground, landing on the tablet and breaking it in half. After a frantic scuffle, we both glimpsed the dwindling fuse on the explosives, realizing time was running out.

"We lunged for the tablet fragments. Hans grabbed the top part, and I seized the bottom. He made a desperate dash toward our camp. I tried to pursue him but lost my footing and tumbled. By the time I regained my stance, it was too late."

Soren painted a vivid picture of the treacherous tunnel layout. "The tunnel descended at a steep angle, with narrow steps carved into the path for traversing. A gutter designed to channel runoff water ran parallel to these steps. With time slipping away, clutching the lower piece of the tablet, I hurled myself down the gutter just as the explosives detonated. The cave crumbled behind me as I slid down, finally coming to a stop at the makeshift bridge that spanned the underground stream, our concealed kayak still safely anchored just around the bend with a heavy stone."

"The cave-in halted just short of the underground stream, leaving our planted C4 explosives untouched. The cave was emitting random ominous cracking sounds from all directions, but I didn't care. I sprinted as fast as I could along the nearly half-kilometer tunnel, heart pounding with fear for what I would encounter below." Soren paused briefly to collect himself.

Tears welled up in Soren's eyes as Christian watched him gather his strength to conclude the story.

"Lying lifeless where they had fallen were the team, including Anya. Hans had mercilessly gunned them down. I rushed to Anya and cradled her lifeless form as the cracking sounds intensified. Part of me yearned to detonate our explosives and join Anya in that icy grave, but I had to survive for Henrik and Britt. I cast one last glance at the Arctic tomb that would forever hold Anya along with the others, and found the strength to sprint back to the stream.

"The cave walls were crumbling around me. I released the anchor on the kayak. Two kilometers later, I shot out of the ice tunnel into the open river. I gave one final glance back and clicked all the buttons on the C4 remote detonator. A huge explosion rang out and the narrow tunnel where the stream emptied into the river collapsed.

"The rest of the day was spent paddling to the ocean where a ship awaited to transport us to Northern Italy. From there, we would assume our new identities and continue to Switzerland. However, there was no longer any us, we or our."

Soren attempted a trembling sip from his empty teacup.

Chapter 44

The appearance of a giant figure emerging from the shadows of the mansion brought Soren out of his trance. Within seconds, he had leapt from his seat and wrapped his arms around the behemoth of a man. "Jesper, my friend, I'm so glad you're OK!" The bone-crushing hug elicited a whimper of pain from Jesper. Soren immediately released him, revealing a sling and bandages on his shoulder.

Christian stood up too quickly in his eagerness to greet Jesper and became lightheaded. Jesper steadied him back into his seat with his good arm. "I'm glad to see you're OK," Christian exclaimed once he regained his composure. "I heard a crash and several gunshots as Gidget spirited me to the glacier."

"Yes!" Jesper recalled, wincing and rubbing his wounded shoulder. "They fired a clip of bullets through that door and got a lucky hit before disappearing to pursue you. Fortunately, they didn't stop to smell the roses."

Jesper proudly displayed the silver Norkap briefcase. Christian was about to interject with a warning about it's tracking capabilities, but Jesper was one step ahead, "No worries, I've been using these cases for years. All you have to do is tape a little aluminum foil over this spot here—" he pointed to a small dot near the handle covered with silver foil, "—and voilà, no more sat link."

Before Christian could ask his next question, Jesper continued, as if he were reading Christian's mind, "My dad worked with Soren and Hans on that dig in Greenland thirty years ago. He was suspicious of Hans's corruption and was subsequently murdered by Hans along with the rest of the crew. I wasn't much younger than Soren at the time. He found me and risked everything to share the truth with me. Not a day goes by when I don't want to choke the life out of Hans, but Soren refused to let me throw my life away. We've been secretly working together ever since."

Soren picked up where Jesper left off, "I was presumed dead with the others, and Hans had pinned the cave-in on me, saying I tried to kill everyone and steal the relic for drug money.

"For years, all I wanted to do was kill Hans for what he did, but there was too much at stake with Lucas somewhere in the background and Henrik and Britt to think about."

Soren's story was cut short again by the arrival of the butler, pushing a cart carrying several ice buckets filled with frosted bottles of beer. Behind him, another butler delivered several platters of sandwiches, ranging from ham and turkey to roast beef and swiss. The cold beers and food were a welcome distraction from the penetrating spring sun.

The sun's relentless glare reminded Jesper of something as he reached into his vest pocket with his good hand. Out came Christian's dark sunglasses, "You dropped these in the Ice Tavern. I'm glad I found them, because it looks like that twitch from your light sensitivity problem is still happening."

Soren raised an eyebrow at Christian, who bashfully covered his twitching eye with the sunglasses.

Chapter 45

The sudden halt in conversation made it clear that the sandwiches and beer were well received. Christian was grateful for the break as he tried to assimilate all the new information.

After taking a hearty bite of his roast beef sandwich and washing it down with his Heineken, Christian broke the silence. "The archaeological dig in Greenland seems to have been the catalyst that set all of this in motion. Could there be something we're overlooking? Something that might clarify things?"

Before Soren or Jesper could chime in, Britt gracefully glided across the veranda and fixed Christian with her piercing blue eyes. "May I offer my perspective on that, Dr. Yates?"

Christian couldn't help but notice Soren's concerned look at Britt's sudden interest in the conversation. It was clear, however, that he had long since learned to pick his battles with her.

Impressed at how quickly Britt tackled his attempt to turn this into a family therapy session, Christian responded, "I'd appreciate your input, and please, call me Christian."

As Britt delved into her story, Christian thought he detected a subtle wink from her and hoped Soren had missed it.

Britt began, "We've never been able to identify Hans's *anonymous source*, but that's just one of a hundred questions that need answering."

Soren interrupted, "I forbade her from applying for that job at Norkap but was quickly reminded just how headstrong she can be, just like her mother, God rest her soul."

Britt continued, "I have a theory and everyone thinks I'm crazy for even thinking it."

Soren immediately interjected, "Don't say what I think you're about to say, Britt."

Despite Soren's warning, Britt leaned in and whispered, "I think Hans is The Surgeon."

Christian gasped…

Jesper nodded in agreement…

And Soren exploded with anger and frustration, "I warned you," he exclaimed as the tea cup exploded. The archaeologist in him immediately regretted crushing the valuable antique like it were Styrofoam.

Undeterred by Soren's reaction, Britt continued, "It makes sense. Hans is obsessed with creating a drug that allows people to access past memories. Whenever another Surgeon victim appears, he always happens to be on one of his top-secret expeditions. You told us Hans was in Copenhagen at the same time Lucas kidnapped you with his fake Dracula accent and ridiculous disguise."

"Don't say it!" Soren warned her again.

Britt persisted, "I believe the top half of the tablet contained a map detailing the locations, around the world, of significant relics of power. The last two trips that I completed for Hans were to Australia to investigate the aboriginals, and to the Amazon rainforest to investigate the Yanomami indigenous peoples. He was primarily interested in their use of psychotropic natural drugs in their ceremonies. We know what the bottom half of the tablet says because I translated it decades ago."

"You can't help yourself," Soren growled to Britt as tossed the fragments of the crushed tea cup over the cliff and stormed back to the mansion, knocking his chair over in the process.

A hissing beer bottle interrupted the ensuing silence as Jesper turned the cap as if it were a twist-off.

After watching Soren disappear, Christian turned to Britt. "So, that would mean Dr. Nilsson, who I spent a solid month working with, was Hans in disguise? There's no way. I would have made the connection when I met Hans the other day."

Britt took a deep breath before replying, "It's hard to believe, but I think Hans is so talented with disguises and accents that he was able to pose as Lucas and fool his own brother."

"Holy shit!" Christian exclaimed. "That's so outlandish that it almost makes sense."

"You saw it firsthand with Dr. Nilsson. His key to success was making the disguise and accent over the top. It throws people off guard and all they can remember are the ridiculous details, like his Swedish Chef accent and crazy beard."

Christian had to admit, it made sense. Britt continued, "Lucas had a similar over-the-top disguise and silly Romanian accent."

"Remind me how this all ties to Hans?" Christian said, becoming more perplexed.

"I believe that map on the tablet details the locations of various psychotropic drugs around the world. When combined, they form a mind-altering super drug. I believe Hans has been traveling the world discovering these ingredients since he obtained the top half of the tablet twenty-five years ago. I also believe he has been performing secret and awful experiments on people under the guise of The Surgeon to develop this super drug."

"You think ReminEssence is a combination of all the drugs he's been scouring the earth to find over the past twenty-five years?" Christian asked, making sure he understood.

She paused for a moment before continuing, "Yes! I think he found all the ingredients listed on the map on his half of the tablet. I believe ReminEssence is powerful, but it is still incomplete."

Christian leaned in; his curiosity piqued. "How can you be certain that it's incomplete? Maybe he guessed the remaining ingredients."

"My dad's bottom half of the tablet contains a single ingredient, and I know what it is. I can guarantee you there is no way he will find it, no matter how hard he looks, or how many people he kills in his experiments," Britt explained.

Christian was thrilled. "This is incredible news! We have samples of ReminEssence here in this case, and you know the final ingredient! What is it? We can put an end to this right here and right now!"

"I wish it were that simple," Britt responded. "The hypothesis is that ReminEssence is a precise mixture of the other ingredients, which it may, or may not be. The bigger problem is the final ingredient."

"We're all relatively smart people, we can figure this out," Christian urged, his excitement growing.

"OK," Britt explained, "I can't disclose exactly what the final ingredient is, but it can only be found in a few places on the planet, and Greenland is the most convenient."

As Britt spoke, Christian gulped and began to feel the anxiety mount as he slowly reached back and felt the stitches in his scalp. "That's literally the last place on Earth I want to visit again," he said, trying to suppress his twitching eye.

The table grew silent as a distinguished older gentleman approached. Ignoring Andre's objections, Christian stood up and turned around. "You must be Andre. I'm Christian. I can't thank you enough for saving my life and helping me recover."

Without hesitation, Andre inspected Christian's and Jesper's stitches before opening a beer and taking a large drink. "Both your wounds are healing quickly, and there are no signs of infection. Excellent."

He turned back to Christian. "It is a pleasure to meet you. I have learned so much about you from Soren and Britt these past few years. You must have many questions, and we're happy to help answer them."

Andre continued, "For now, you must take it easy, since you are still recovering from a severe concussion. Britt could take you for a stroll around the grounds, if you are game?"

Chapter 46

Britt observed Christian's reaction to their surroundings as they strolled through an ornate garden, "I can only imagine how overwhelming this must feel," she commented. "I've known about this my whole adult life, and it still catches me off guard sometimes."

Christian leaned in and confided, "It just doesn't seem real. How could Soren walk away from his life and his son?"

Britt was quick to defend her father, "He had to make an impossible choice. Lucas, who we assume was The Surgeon and I believe was Hans, basically had his parents and son held hostage."

Christian continued to struggle with the concept, "I still can't believe Soren wouldn't have recognized his brother, no matter how elaborate and silly the costume and accent were?"

Britt rebuked him, "Again, you spent a month with Dr. Nilsson. Can you say with one-hundred-percent certainty that he was not Hans, now that you've met him?"

Christian reluctantly agreed, "It pains me to say it, but I can't. I always thought elaborate disguises were a cliche perpetuated by Hollywood, but The Surgeon truly is a master manipulator and master of disguises."

Britt continued, "Dad had just lost the second love of his life, and I was a baby being looked after by Andre, who had just lost his daughter. Andre couldn't stop my mom, Anya, from returning to the excavation site to carry out their plan to fake their deaths and start a new life, just like my dad can't stop me from working for Norkap and trying to find the evidence that will finally show Hans for the murderer and psychopath he is."

Christian reflected, "Okay, I guess I can understand why Soren did what he did, and I'm glad he did. Otherwise, we may have never met!"

"I have to admit," Britt said with a subtle blush that was only noticeable against the snowy alpine backdrop, "I've felt guilty at times keeping track of you over the past two years, especially this past week since you arrived in Copenhagen. There were several times when I just wanted to pull you aside and tell you everything."

Christian couldn't help but blush in response. They had both stopped walking at some point, but neither was sure when.

Their moment was short-lived as the butler cleared his throat while standing on the terrace above them, "Dinner will be served at 19:00 sharp in the main dining room"

Christian was certain he noticed a brief glare from the butler.

Britt explained to Christian, "Edmund is just a little protective of me. He's worked for my family since Papa was a child."

"Papa?" Christian sought clarification.

"Yes, that's what I call my grandfather," Britt replied as they resumed their walk.

Christian was overwhelmed, and he apologized for being awestruck. "I'm walking through the grounds of an estate that rivals Versailles with one of the most beautiful and intelligent women I've ever met. However, I just can't shake this dark cloud that's constantly looming in the background. With everything that's happened and continues to happen since before we were even born, how does your family find peace?"

Britt wiped away a tear from her smiling face and sighed, saddened by Christian's words. "It's all I've ever known," she said. "When I was a little girl, my father was constantly traveling the world, solving crimes that nobody else in Interpol could figure out. Despite everything, he's an exceptional agent and detective, but that's a story for another time. When he was away, it was just me, my grandfather, and our staff. They were more like family than employees. But even as a child, I sensed that something was off. My father would sometimes slip and say words in Danish, or I'd overhear them talking about Hans or the dig. It wasn't until I was in my late teens that my dad and papa finally told me the truth. I'm sure that factored into my choice to study archaeology. They both tried so hard to keep me away from it, but they eventually realized that nothing could stop me from helping. And now here we are."

Britt turned to Christian, "There's not a day that goes by where I wouldn't give up all the wealth and comforts in the world for one moment with the mother I never knew," she said, her voice laced with emotion. "And I know Papa and Dad feel the same way."

As they continued their walk, Christian couldn't help but ask more questions. "Who is Andre in the larger scheme of things, and where did his wealth come from?"

Britt chuckled. "I don't know how to say this, but there is 'old money,' and then there is 'when the Pharaohs ruled the earth old money.' That's exactly what Papa tells Dad or me when we ask where his wealth comes from. He doesn't have any family that we know of, and his wife died long before my dad met him."

Christian couldn't help but laugh. "Of course, because you don't have enough mysteries to solve!" Britt joined in his laughter, enjoying the lightened mood.

Chapter 47

As they strolled back to the mansion, Christian glanced at Britt. "Won't they miss you at Norkap Pharma?" he asked, as reality continued creeping in.

Britt grinned. "Hopefully not. I called in sick and used some of my accrued personal leave. Remember, nobody is looking for me or my dad."

There was a flicker of ambivalence in Christian's expression as he considered Britt's words. On the one hand, he was relieved that Britt was safe and away from the prying eyes of Norkap, but on the other hand, his own situation weighed heavily on his mind. "It would make me sick if you blew your cover saving me."

Suddenly, a thought occurred to him, and he turned to Britt. "What about your dad?" he asked. "He risked everything to save me."

Britt's eyes narrowed as she filled Christian in on the latest developments. "Interpol still thinks he's in Copenhagen, deep undercover, trying to infiltrate Johnny and Brian's network to find The Surgeon," she said, her voice hushed with urgency.

Christian's heart skipped a beat as he realized how isolated he had become. "Won't people start asking questions about me?"

"If our theory is right and Hans sent you to Greenland to get rid of you, then I'm guessing nobody will be concerned because technically, you never left Denmark," Britt said, her tone reassuring. "I checked all the records, and there was nothing about the approval of human trials on ReminEssence based on you leading the team."

Christian felt relieved, but Britt saw the haunted look in his eyes and hurried on, trying to distract him. "But look at the bright side," she said, pulling out her smartphone and showing him his lecture video. "You're still famous!"

Christian's expression was vacant as he stared at the now fifteen million views and thousands of comments. "Don't worry, it's a burner phone," Britt said, noticing the confusion on Christian's face. "Dad always makes me use one when I'm here. It's pay-as-you-go and usually untraceable."

Christian took a deep breath, his mind racing with new questions. "I still have more questions than you can imagine," he said finally. "But I think the most important one is, what do we do now?"

"That's going to be up to you. We can drop you off at the nearest US embassy, but there will be many questions, first of which will be, how did you get to Switzerland without a passport, and the next will be, who tried to kill you? Both bodies are several kilometers below the glacier in a bottomless ice tomb. After that, the questions will get increasingly difficult to answer."

"That's not an option!" Christian said with slightly more defiance than he had intended. "If there is any chance Hans is the person who killed Collin, then I want to see him pay."

Britt tried to suppress her joy at Christian's resolve.

Christian continued, "So it sounds like going back to Greenland is inevitable, but first, we have to confirm the other ingredients."

Both fell silent for a few seconds before they exclaimed in unison, "We need Hans's part of the tablet!"

Christian couldn't help but smile at the coincidence. "Jinx!" he exclaimed instinctively.

Britt looked at him quizzically. "Bless you?" she asked, confused.

Christian realized that his reference to the childhood game might not be a universal thing. "Sorry," he said, feeling slightly embarrassed. "It means that if two people say the same thing at the same time, the first person to say 'jinx' prevents the other person from speaking until they are 'released' by the jinxer." There was a brief silence, "I release you!" Christian exclaimed, laughing.

Britt just smiled, "Fun game!"

"We've been looking at this situation all wrong!" he insisted passionately, his eyes flashing with determination. "We're so obsessed with finding evidence against Hans, the potential Surgeon, that we've lost sight of what's truly important. We need to figure out what the tablet is telling us to do, see if it works and then share it with all the world! We can take the power away from The Surgeon and Hans, regardless of whether they're one and the same. And who knows, maybe we'll raise humanity to new levels of enlightenment in the process."

The excitement of Christian's revelation was extinguished by Britt's phone, which pinged with a message from Edmund. Her expression slowly morphed to one of fear as she read the message.

"It's Edmund," she said, her voice shaking. "He overheard my dad, papa, and Jesper. They're planning to put us under house arrest after dinner and deal with Hans once and for all."

Christian's panic was palpable. "Can they really do that?" he asked, his heart racing.

"Papa has a small army of staff and security guards," Britt explained, her voice barely above a whisper. "We're kilometers from the nearest roads. They could easily detain us on the estate."

"We have to get out of here!" Christian exclaimed, feeling the adrenaline pumping through his veins. Britt nodded her agreement.

"If you can get us off the estate," Christian said, his eyes shining with excitement, "I may have a plan that will get us back to Denmark!"

"Consider it done!" Britt declared, grabbing Christian by the arm and leading him towards the garage. The massive automatic door clanked open the moment she pressed the last digit on the keypad, revealing an incredible array of exotic cars. Britt strode confidently up to another keypad and punched in another code, revealing a wall of gleaming key fobs. "I think the Range Rover should do the trick," she said, clicking the fob with a quick beep.

Within moments, they were tearing down a winding road, several kilometers away from the mansion and quickly approaching the looming security gates of the estate. As they slowly drove through, Britt flashed a wink at the guard, "Hi, Marc, just heading into town for a little shopping."

He opened the gate without hesitation. "Have fun."

Britt explained to Christian, "Marc's family has worked for Papa since he was a kid. We basically grew up together! I hope this doesn't get him in trouble."

They were silent as Britt focused on navigating the precipitous road down the mountain. Once they reached the base and an intersection, she broke the silence. "OK," Britt exclaimed, returning her attention to Christian and grinning with excitement. "Where are we going? I can't wait to hear your master plan!"

Christian didn't reply at first as he rummaged through his wallet frantically muttering, "The enemy of my enemy is my friend, the enemy of my enemy is..."

Britt repeated her question with growing concern.

Finally, he mumbled, "We need to go to the nearest embassy!" as his calm search became a frantic cloud of flying debris from his wallet.

Britt nervously pushed the navigation button, plugged in a few words, and there was a ping, "It looks like the nearest United States Embassy is..."

Christian interrupted her as he victoriously pulled a card from his wallet and held it high. "No... the nearest Russian Embassy!"

Britt slowly turned to Christian. "Seriously?"

Chapter 48

Christian nodded to himself, taking a deep breath and remembering his father's words of wisdom. "My boy, never be afraid to ask. The worst they can say is no, and you'd be surprised how often they say yes."

The phone rang once, twice, three times— "Please pick up, please pick up!" Christian prayed silently—the call going straight to voicemail. He cursed under his breath, just as the phone beeped with an incoming call.

"Dmitry, is that you?" Christian answered urgently.

"Who is this?" The voice on the other end had a strong Russian accent.

"This is Christian," he replied. There was a pause, followed by the sound of a door opening and closing.

"My God, Christian, the whole world is looking for you," Dmitry whispered urgently. "They say you and another Norkap employee disappeared in Greenland, and they suspect foul play. Hans Rasmussen thinks a competing pharmaceutical company kidnapped you and stole a miracle drug that he was developing. Is that true? Where are you?"

Christian could feel the adrenaline pumping through his veins as he confirmed everything Dmitry had warned him about that night by firelight and Black Russians. Everything he had suspected about Hans and the new drug was true, and he had unwittingly landed himself in the middle of a dangerous game of espionage and international intrigue. But just as he was about to reveal more, Britt's harsh gaze and pointed gestures cut him off.

Sensing the urgency, Dmitry broke in with a whispered question. "Are you still there, Christian?"

Christian took a moment to collect himself before replying, "Sorry, we must have lost reception. He didn't tell me what it was, just that he wanted me to go to Greenland to help with human trials."

As Dmitry pressed for more information, Christian realized the gravity of his situation. He knew that the Russians, like everyone else, would be desperate to get their hands on Hans's miracle drug. And while Dmitry was a friend, there were no guarantees where his loyalties ultimately lay.

"We're in Switzerland and need help getting back to Denmark. I have no passport, and even if I did, you yourself said the world is looking for me," Christian said, trying to keep his voice steady.

Dmitry's response was reassuring, but also ominous. "Can you get to the Russian Embassy?"

"We're already on our way," Christian replied.

"Who is *we*?" Dmitry quickly returned, renewed concern in his voice.

"My friend Britt is with me, but I promise, you can trust her," Christian said, trying his best to convince him.

Christian's heart skipped a beat as he realized the full extent of the danger they were facing. But Dmitry's tone was calm and reassuring as he replied, "Don't worry, we'll take care of you both. Just go to the embassy and a diplomatic liaison will be waiting for you. I'll find a reason to commandeer one of those state aircraft that I normally don't get to use!"

Chapter 49

U pon arriving at the Copenhagen airport, the attaché effortlessly guided Christian and Britt through each security checkpoint unquestioned, enjoying the full protection of Russian diplomatic immunity. A sleek limousine with diplomatic plates awaited them outside the airport, and the attaché motioned for them to get in.

Half an hour later, the limo stopped a block away from Dmitry's house. As they exited the vehicle, Christian craned his neck to peer through the inky blackness of the night. The almost non-existent fingernail moon provided little illumination, and he felt the darkness closing in around them.

Suddenly, Britt tugged at his sleeve, and he turned to see a shadowy figure approaching from behind. The figure halted just short of the streetlight's meager protection, and Christian could feel his heart racing.

As the figure cautiously stepped into the light, Christian gasped with joy and relief, recognizing the familiar contours of Dmitry's round Eastern European face. He rushed towards Dmitry, pulling him into a bear hug. "You saved us," Christian said, his voice choking with emotion. "How can we ever repay you?"

Dmitry scanned his surroundings before turning back to Christian. "Alas, I've used up all my favors getting you here, and I just wish there was more I could do," he said, a hint of concern in his voice.

"Don't be silly," Christian replied, "you've done so much for us already, and we are forever in your debt."

Dmitry surveyed their surroundings with a heightened sense of situational awareness, honed by a lifetime of well-founded paranoia. "It's not safe out here in the open. Do you have a plan?"

"Yes," Christian said with enthusiasm, "We're going to…"

Dmitry cut him off mid-sentence, "Don't tell me. Plausible deniability is the most valuable currency in my line of work. Good luck, my friend."

Christian extended his hand for a farewell shake and felt the cold, heavy metal of a pistol cross his palm instead of Dmitry's hand.

"Take this," Dmitry insisted, handing him the gun. "Hans may need a little coaxing if he's as stubborn as I remember."

As quickly as he appeared, Dmitry vanished into the shadows, leaving Christian and Britt exchanging concerned glances. Christian quickly stowed the gun in his backpack, hoping he would not have to use it.

***

Henrik paced back and forth in his living room, pleading into his speaker-phone, trying to convince the ticket booth girl from Tivoli that she was the love of his life. This embarrassing display was interrupted by the sound of his elevator door closing. He turned and leapt back in shock at the sight of Christian and Britt standing in his foyer.

"I see your old key-card still works!" Henrik said as he tried to act calm, but quickly gave up and rushed over to embrace Christian. "Everyone thinks you've been kidnapped by Pfizer or murdered by Moderna for our latest wonder drug. What happened? How are you here?"

Christian hesitated before beginning, "I wish it were that simple, but the truth is—"

Britt interrupted him, "The truth is that Hans has a very dark secret. We know he's your uncle, but we're hoping you can help us."

Henrik turned to Britt with a look of revelation and awe. "Do you realize what's happening?" he exclaimed. Christian and Britt were brimming with anticipation, hoping Henrik was about to reveal Hans's true secrets.

"Those are the most words Britt has ever said to me in the past three years!"

Christian and Britt were clearly disappointed as Henrik made his way to the bar and began pouring shots for everyone. "I'm way too sober to have this conversation. I hope you all like Gammel Dansk. It's one of my favorite national drinks!" They each grabbed a shot and held them high. "Skål!"

After two more shots, they took a seat on the sofas, overlooking the lights of Tivoli Gardens. Henrik leaned back and crossed his legs, eager to hear what they had to say. "So tell me, what has my diabolically evil uncle done now?"

Christian and Britt exchanged glances before Christian started, "We think he has an ancient stone artifact with a map of the world on it."

Britt continued, "We believe he's been performing illegal human experiments and developing a super drug based on that map."

"And I think he tried to have me killed in Greenland!" Christian added as a side note.

Henrik briefly raised an eyebrow at Christian's last statement. "All those things sound like Uncle Hans, except the killing part... As far as the artifact goes, I've never seen a stone with a map of the world on it."

Christian and Britt breathed a sigh of disappointment as Henrik continued, "But I have seen a picture of it. Would that help?"

"Seriously?" Britt blurted out incredulously.

Henrik's sarcastic tone made Britt bristle with annoyance. "There you go again, talking to me!" He warned her, "If you keep this up, people may start to think you like me!"

Britt's response was filled with sympathy and compassion. "Believe it or not, Henrik, we have a connection that is deeper than you've ever had with any other girl. I hope that one day we can explore that further."

Her words hung in the air as Christian interjected, deftly redirecting the conversation. "But right now, we need to get that photo."

Henrik's response was nonchalant, as if retrieving the photo was as simple as grabbing a beer. "I can get it, no problem."

Christian and Britt were both intrigued and skeptical. "How?" they asked in unison.

Henrik's playful retort silenced them both. "Jinx! Neither of you can talk till I release you!" They all laughed, grateful for the momentary relief from the tension, then took a few more shots of Gammel Dansk.

Henrik's next statement made believers out of them. "Uncle Hans keeps it in the safe in his office. He thinks he's the only one that knows the code, but I figured it out."

Britt's enthusiasm was growing. "Of course you did! What is it?"

Henrik's cavalier demeanor returned. "I may be an alcoholic, pothead, womanizing playboy, but I'm not an idiot!"

Britt raised one eyebrow with an inquisitive look towards Henrik. "OK, OK, I can sometimes also be an idiot," he admitted.

The trio looked at each other, knowing the risks ahead. Henrik continued, "How's this? Let's all go there right now and have a look at it."

Christian nodded in agreement, nervous but optimistic. "Sounds like a plan!" he exclaimed.

Chapter 50

The Surgeon's contorted delight was illuminated by the glow of his computer monitor, casting shadows that writhed and twisted around him. Each key he struck sent shivers of dark delight running through him. "My dear friends," he murmured, his voice low and menacing, "the reckoning draws near."

He paused, his fingers flexing over the keyboard, his lips curling into a wicked smile. "Our decades of sacrifice and waiting will soon be over," he continued, "and when the time comes, we will be ready. We will strike with the force of a thousand blades, and our enemies will fall. The governments we have so faithfully served and who have forsaken us will have no choice but to bow down to us. Begin preparing your cubes."

As he spoke, The Surgeon's eyes flicked to an image that flashed onto his screen from one of his many remote spy cameras. His expression turned feral.

With a hiss, he leaned closer to the screen, gently touching it with one finger, "Excellent," he murmured, his voice thick with malice. "We have a new player on the board. Let the games begin."

Chapter 51

Norkap was an entirely different world at night without its artistic lighting and sun filled corridors. Henrik moved like a shadow, silent and efficient, as he navigated the intricate fourth floor maze with only the display lighting of the random artifacts to guide them.

Christian couldn't help but wonder how many times Henrik had pulled off a stunt like this, how many ladies he had seduced, late at night, within these walls.

But there was no time for idle thoughts. Henrik was focused, and Christian could practically feel the intensity radiating off him as he approached the bookshelf in the darkness. The faux panel swung open with a barely audible creak, revealing the safe within.

With a deftness born of long practice, Henrik entered the eight-digit code, and the safe clicked open. "The code was my drug addict, murderous father's birthday. That's the last date anyone would suspect Uncle Hans would hold sacred, but I guess that's what makes for a good code."

Christian watched Britt quickly brush a tear from her cheek just as Henrik turned around with a faded and worn photo from the safe. It had clearly been handled many times before.

Britt's eyes were filled with emotion, and Christian couldn't help but feel a sense of foreboding. The photo was the key to unlocking Hans's secrets, but what were those secrets? Christian didn't know what to expect and braced himself for what was to come.

As he slowly placed it on the desk, the three of them leaned in, their eyes wide with reverence and awe. Britt could feel her heart racing as she looked upon the ancient quartz tablet captured in the photo, covered in a mysterious, otherworldly map of the world that was more accurate than anyone could have imagined.

She knew instantly that it was authentic—she'd spent countless late nights studying her father's half of the tablet, and her PhD dissertation had been focused on a similar language that was believed to have emerged fifty thousand years after this one.

Britt efficiently swiveled the desk lamp head and focused the beam of light on the photo. Giddy as a schoolgirl she exclaimed, "This is shocking! See these six locators spanning the world?"

Henrik and Christian both nodded in awe as she continued.

"Here's Australia, and that mark is directly over the oldest Aboriginal settlement on the continent. They use pituri, also known as mingkulpa, as the primary psychoactive stimulant in their ceremonies and communing with ancient ancestors."

"This one," she said, pointing to China, "must be Langdang. Very popular hallucinogenic in ancient Chinese culture. Well known for conjuring devils and spirits for its users."

"And here." She pointed to Norway. "These are the indigenous Sami people. They utilize the fly agaric mushroom to access their ancestral plains."

Christian gave a puzzled look as Britt clarified, "You know, the red and white Super Mario Brothers mushroom!"

Christian and Henrik both grinned with boyish recognition as she moved her finger from Norway to the Congo region of Africa. "This is the exact location where Hans discovered the breakthrough pain killer from which he founded Norkap almost twenty-five years ago. The oldest Pygmy tribe in Africa is located here. They utilize a sacred hallucinogen called ibogaine."

"What's this down here?" Henrik asked, pointing to the locator in the

Amazon rainforests of South America.

"This was the last place Hans sent me. There are numerous Amazonian native tribes. They primarily utilize ayahuasca to open their minds for ceremonies and relaxation," Britt explained with enthusiasm.

Christian chimed in on the sixth and final marker as he pointed to North America roughly where Arizona would one day be. "I know this one from that Coachella kid in my class. That's the Navajo and they use peyote!"

"Yes!" Britt exclaimed, clearly impressed with Christian's contribution. "It's one of the most powerful psychotropics used by indigenous peoples and comes from a tiny spineless cactus."

So taken were they by the discovery and discussion, that none of them noticed the shadowy figure slowly emerging from the darkness.

Hans must have used an even more secret entrance. "I felt the same way twenty-five years ago when I first sat down to study that map," came his voice, low and menacing. "Tell me, what exactly brings the three of you here?"

Christian felt a mix of emotions growing inside him as his twitching right eye betrayed his unease. "We're all here because of this," he said, holding up the old photograph.

Hans's response was immediate, as he bellowed with righteous indignation. "You have no idea what that is!" he exclaimed.

"I know there are a number of good people buried in Greenland because of it, including your brother," Christian continued firmly. "And I know it wasn't really his fault."

"You know nothing about what happened on that day," Hans spat, but there was a hint of doubt in his voice.

"I know Lars tried to stop you from detonating the explosives on the cave wall," Christian pressed on.

Hans shook an accusing finger, his eyes flashing with anger. "Only Henry could have known that which means you're a goddamn American spy!" he snarled. "I'm one of the richest and most powerful men in the world now. You people can't bully me like you did back then. This conversation is over. I'm calling security!"

Hans glanced down, searching for his phone. When he looked up, he found himself staring down the barrel of Christian's gun. "Nobody is calling anybody until we get to the truth," Christian said, his voice hard and cold.

Henrik was the first to react. "Holy shit man, what are you doing with a gun? This is Denmark," he exclaimed.

Hans put the phone down and raised his hands. "Please don't hurt us. Henrik knows nothing about what really happened that day."

Britt was furious. "You bastard! How could you let Henrik grow up thinking his father was a traitor and murderer?" she spat.

"What do you mean, Britt?" Henrik asked, his eyes wide with confusion and hurt. "What does she mean, Uncle Hans?" he pleaded.

Everyone jumped a little, including Christian, at the clicking sound of him pulling the hammer back on the gun. "You're going to set the record straight right here and now for Henrik and for us, or I swear to God you'll be joining all these relics you've so carefully preserved," he said in a low growl.

He motioned with the gun for Hans to sit down at his desk. "OK, OK," Hans said with acquiescence. "But where do I start?"

"From the beginning," Christian said firmly. "How did you know where and what to dig for in Greenland?"

"OK, so Lars, Henrik's father, and I both studied archaeology at the University of Copenhagen, even though our parents wanted us to study business. We competed over everything, but at the end of the day, we were inseparable. Unfortunately, we both fell in love with the same girl, Ingrid. Of course, she fell for Lars because he was better than me in pretty much every way. Before we knew it, they were married and about to have a baby," Hans recounted.

Christian was surprised by the similarities between Hans's and Soren's histories. "Go on," he said.

"One day, around that time, I met a very strange American while having coffee at a café not far from here," Hans continued.

"Why do you say 'strange'?" Britt asked.

"Well, he always wore these blacked out round sunglasses, and had this thick beard with bushy eyebrows."

Neither Britt nor Christian could hide their surprise as Hans took notice, "Is there something I should know?" He asked.

"No," Christian replied, "He just sounds like someone we used to know."

"Did this person you used to know speak with a clearly fake melodramatic John Wayne accent?" Hans asked.

"No," Christian said, trying to hide his shock at the similarities to Lucas and Dr. Nilsson, "Please carry on. Sorry for the interruption."

Hans gave them both a suspicious look from the corner of his eye as he continued, "So anyway, at first I thought it was a joke and half expected him to say, 'Whoa, take 'er easy there, pilgrim,' but he was dead serious. His name was Henry, and he said he could make me rich. He then told me he was with the CIA and that they had discovered a scroll in Lithuania that detailed the location of a buried temple that housed a source of unimaginable power."

Christian and Britt both fought to maintain their objectivity despite the fact that Hans's story was articulating perfectly with Soren's recount.

"Henry explained that the buried temple was in Greenland, and Denmark would never give them permission to dig for it. Even if they did, they would confiscate any findings,"

Christian leaned forward in his chair; his eyes fixed on Hans. "So, what did you do next?" he asked.

"I thanked him for the entertaining story and suggested he spend a little less time at Christiania," Hans said with a rueful smile. "As I was about to get up and walk away, he slid a duffel bag across the table to me and walked away."

Britt raised her eyebrows in surprise. "What was in the bag?"

Hans paused for effect, a grimace on his face. "It was 400,000 kroner and a translation from the Lithuanian scroll. There was also a note that read, 'Hold onto this and study the translation. Don't try to contact the authorities, as I will know, and I suspect you know what we're capable of.'"

Henrik, who had been silent up to this point, finally spoke up. "So, what did the translation say?" he asked eagerly.

"The translation outlined an ancient oral myth about the city of Neith, situated in the northwestern corner of Greenland. The scroll, translated from the oral legend, had been passed down for over a hundred thousand years, through countless generations.

"The intriguing aspect was that the myth was perpetuated by just a single-family line that had escaped from Neith. The family patriarch, a holy man exiled from Neith, initiated the line. He regarded the myth as so critical that he taught his son the unique spoken language known only to the people of Neith.

"The humans outside their family line would not evolve to develop organized speech for roughly another fifty thousand years. This family line lived among their fellow people at that time passing the myth from one generation to the next by secretly teaching their children the language and memorizing the story. Each father passed on the myth as a birthright to his son in this family. It was extraordinary that this mythological narrative had survived for so long."

Christian reminisced about the icebreaker game they played in one of his psychology classes. The game involved sitting in a circle and whispering a short story to the next person who shared it with their neighbor, and so on. When the story returned to the original teller, it was vastly different. The descendants of the holy man also played this game, but Hans noted that they did so with incredible accuracy.

Hans continued, "The last descendant of the family passed away almost a thousand years ago. In his old age and with no children, the holy man recorded the story in written form. The manuscript disappeared, and was found fifty years ago during an excavation in Lithuania. The CIA acquired it shortly there after. The document provided a detailed description of the ancient city and its location. It also recounted the holy man's story in incredible detail.

"According to the legend, the holy man's people had discovered an elixir made of seven unique and powerful ingredients that unlocked the human mind and provided access to an unimaginable power source. This source of power caused them to transform from a nomadic animal-like band of cave people into a prosperous, highly sophisticated city in a time long before modern *Homo sapiens* ruled the planet.

"The holy man tried to stop his people from using this source of power, as he feared it would lead to their demise. The leaders of Neith did not like his warnings but agreed to send six of the seven ingredients to the most distant corners of the world, and store the tablet under great security in their sacred temple that sat atop the mountain.

"Each of the six initial ingredients had some power on their own and could unlock the mind to a lesser extent. However, they could only access the full power when the six ingredients were combined with the final seventh ingredient that happened to be on the lost bottom half of the tablet. It wasn't lost on me that seven is a cosmically significant number and represents the journey to a divine life path among other meanings."

Hans took a deep breath. "Is the gun really necessary?"

"That's up to you," Christian said, lowering the weapon.

Hans continued, "The city elders eventually exiled the holy man, as their society began to decline without constant use of the elixir. The story continued by describing how the holy man risked his life years later by returning to the city he was banished from, as he couldn't give up on them. Though the journey lasted five years, he came back to something unimaginable.

"The city was obliterated, and only a barren crater remained. The holy man believed that the gods retaliated from the heavens and destroyed the city. The writing in the manuscript was incredibly poetic, and it also recounted the holy man's journey through the ruins. According to the text, a magnificent mountain dominated the region, and Neith rested at its base. They crafted the top of the mountain into a grand temple that housed their sacred tablet with the ingredients. Henry concluded, as did I, based on the description, that a meteor had destroyed the city and part of the mountain, which explained the crater.

"The holy man was determined to retrieve the tablet from the temple, but when he arrived at the mountain's base, he found that 'the gods' had destroyed all the trails leading to the top. Though this was a setback for the holy man, it turned out to be beneficial for us—the story revealed that the city was in northwestern Greenland. With this information, combined with some advanced radar equipment, we eventually located the mountain peak, which now sits half a kilometer below the Arctic glacier."

Hans's expression turned remorseful as he continued, "I didn't hear from Henry for a week, and then Lars, Ingrid, and Henrik were in a catastrophic car crash. Henrik somehow emerged unscathed. Ingrid died and we assumed Lars wouldn't survive his injuries.

"After the accident, Henry found me walking home through Copenhagen. He offered his condolences, and then he said something that struck fear into my heart. He promised me that if I retrieved his relic in Greenland, he would ensure that nothing else like that would happen to my family again."

Henrik's eyes widened in disbelief. "Are you saying that my mother's death was a murder?"

Hans hesitated before responding, "Let's just say that I left that conversation with the realization that the lives of the rest of my family, including yours and your father's, would be in grave danger if I didn't go on this expedition. I agreed, and Henry gave me one million additional kroner. I secured all the permits, and the government was more than happy to grant them, since they didn't have to fund the dig."

Britt leaned forward in anticipation. "What happened next?" she asked, her heart racing with emotion.

Hans proudly recounted, "I handpicked a diverse multinational team, as mandated by the government, and set off on our quest to find the dig site. During the first three years of the expedition Lars woke up from his coma and spiraled into an opioid and heroin addiction. It broke my heart to not be there for him. However, he made a miraculous recovery and asked to join the dig."

Britt and Christian exchanged a quick glance.

"Unfortunately, Lars wasn't the same person I remembered. He was distant and distracted, but there was a glimmer in his eyes whenever he was around Anya, one of our team members. We continued on like that for two more years until we finally reached the temple and unearthed the tablet. However, I always knew that Henry would come looking for the artifact, and what happened next was beyond my wildest imagination."

"Go on," Henrik encouraged him.

"After unearthing the tablet, there were only nine team members left at the dig including myself. I suggested taking pictures of the excavation, only to realize I had left the camera up in the base camp. I had sprained my ankle earlier that week and was in no shape to make the half-kilometer hike up the tunnel to get the camera. Lars volunteered to retrieve it.

"After about an hour of waiting for Lars's return, we heard footsteps clamoring down the tunnel. We felt relieved knowing he had made it down safely, given how slippery the path was. Anya had brought champagne to celebrate.

"As the footsteps drew closer, we heard a pop and assumed Anya had opened the champagne. We quickly realized this was not the case, as Anya let out a piercing scream, clutching her stomach. It wasn't Lars who turned the corner; it was a man dressed in black wearing a ski mask. He demanded the tablet from me at gunpoint, with a John Wayne accent that I recognized instantly," recounted Hans.

Christian was overwhelmed with grief as he listened to the story, with Britt and Henrik sharing the same emotion.

"When I refused, Henry shot me, and then he executed the rest of the team without hesitation or remorse," Hans continued, his face darkening as he relived the memories.

"That should have been the end of my story, but the bullet meant for me hit the tablet and was deflected. It knocked me to the ground while Henry was focused on the team, shooting them one by one.

"Amidst the chaos and screams of horror, I crawled to my backpack and found my pistol. When he came to retrieve the tablet, I held the pistol to his head and pulled the trigger. There was a click, but no bang. I then remembered always keeping the first chamber empty as a safety. Henry instantly raised his gun to my head and there was another click. He was out of ammo. As I fumbled to cock my revolver for another shot, Henry took off around the corner and up the tunnel."

"With no one left to help, I pushed my body up the tunnel, disregarding the pain from my bad ankle. I raced to the surface, hoping to catch Henry, but he had fled the scene. As my eyes adjusted to the daylight after being underground all day, I heard a crackling, burning sound coming from the cave wall. Looking closer, I saw explosives with a burning fuse. I was trying to disarm them, but was tackled by Lars, with blood streaming down his head."

Christian screamed in denial, "No! Lars was trying to stop you from detonating the explosives!"

Hans looked Christian straight in the eye. "That is a lie!"

Henrik implored his uncle, "Please, tell us what happened next."

"Lars and I fought, and the tablet broke in half, probably weakened from the earlier gunshot. The fuse had disappeared into the explosives, and we both knew we were on borrowed time.

"Lars grabbed the bottom half of the tablet and dove into the cave through the runoff gutter. I barely escaped with the top half of the tablet, diving out of the entrance just as a massive explosion collapsed the tunnel.

"With no time to waste, I sprinted towards the basecamp tents to make a distress call. While radioing the Qaanaaq police, the camera on the counter caught my eye. As an afterthought, I clicked a quick picture of my half of the tablet. The last thing I remember after hanging up with the police was a crushing blow to the back of my head, by Henry, I assumed.

"When I regained consciousness, the top part of the tablet was missing, and Henry was nowhere to be found. Despite several months of rescue efforts, digging proved futile, and the team remained lost till this day. I never spoke of Henry or his heinous act of violence against the team.

"Instead, I placed the blame for the cave-in on poor Lars, a man who had suffered more than the rest of us combined. The investigators never questioned my allegations against Lars, accusing him of trying to steal the relic to fund his drug habit, especially given his well-documented history of addiction and theft. I had been very frugal with Henry's money during the dig and had a quarter of a million kroner remaining. I used that money to start searching for the relics of power and eventually founded Norkap."

Christian looked pensively at Britt, weighing his options. "His story makes sense, but we can't ignore the fact that The Surgeon is a master manipulator."

Hans interrupted Christian, looking stunned. "You think I'm The Surgeon?"

"Well, think about it," Christian said, his voice heavy with suspicion. "The Surgeon seems to strike when you are out on your adventures, and all the victims are found with various mixtures of psychedelics and other drugs, many unidentifiable. You yourself admitted you had illegally experimented on people to formulate ReminEssence."

Hans shook his head feverishly, denying the accusation. "This is insane. I know I've done some questionable things and crossed some serious boundaries developing ReminEssence, but I've NEVER killed anyone. Tell them, Henrik."

Everyone turned to look at Henrik, who seemed lost in thought. "I honestly don't know what to think," he finally said. "Up until a few minutes ago, I thought my biological father was the Antichrist. Now I just don't know."

Hans chimed in, his voice rising with anger. "Since we're pointing fingers, Christian, how do we know you're not The Surgeon? You've been obsessed with genetic memories for years, and the only reason the police didn't convict you for Collin's death was the testimony of some random Interpol agent. Now you suddenly know things from my past that nobody, but an American spy and eight dead people should know. Sorry to speak that way of your father, Henrik."

"No problem, Uncle, that's probably why I've drunk and whored my way through half of Copenhagen."

Britt interrupted, her voice rising above the fray. "This isn't helping us figure out who The Surgeon is. We need to focus on the evidence, not baseless accusations."

The room fell silent as everyone took a deep breath and tried to regroup. But the tension remained, like a thin wire stretched taut, ready to break at any moment.

Christian gulped, feeling suddenly parched. Britt jumped in, realizing that Christian hadn't considered the idea that others might think he was The Surgeon. "Let's assume that nobody in this room is The Surgeon. Let's also assume that your new wonder drug, ReminEssence, is derived from the first six ingredients on your part of the tablet photo," Britt said, looking around the room as she slowly nodded her head. "Yes?"

Hans, Christian, and Henrik all looked at each other and nodded in agreement.

"Good!" Britt exclaimed, sounding like she was praising a child for good behavior, "Now that we're all on the same page, can I assume that everyone in this room would like to learn the identity of The Surgeon and see him or her brought to justice?"

This time, everyone nodded their heads in agreement.

"Great!" Britt said with enthusiasm. "Well, it just so happens that I know the exact identity of the seventh ingredient! I think the best way to find the truth is to complete this elixir for the first time in over a hundred and fifty thousand years and see what all the fuss is about."

Hans stuttered as he tried to form a question, "W-who are you? How could you possibly know the final ingredient? What are you even doing here? I hired you to meet with indigenous peoples and find their secret ceremonial psychedelics to complete the map from the tablet!"

Britt smiled. "And I did just that, and discovered more than we bargained for. Let's leave it there for now."

Hans seemed OK with that answer. "I'm up for your plan, Britt. What is the final ingredient? We can finish this downstairs in the lab."

"I wish it were that simple," Britt said with a sigh as Christian rubbed his twitching eye, knowing what was next. "We have to hunt the final ingredient, and the best place to find it is Greenland!"

Christian shivered at the thought of returning to Greenland, but he pulled himself together for the greater good, putting the gun away in his backpack. "What do you say, Hans? Should we fire up the old company jet and make what might be the greatest discovery in human history?"

Henrik clapped his hands. "How exciting! I left a bottle of vodka on the plane last week. Let's hope it's still there!"

Hans looked around the room. "Surgeon or not, I started all this. The least I can do is help end it."

Chapter 52

The jet was fueled and ready, just like last time, but unlike last time, Christian wasn't alone. So much had changed since his first trip. He feared it was too much to believe that Hans was not The Surgeon, but maybe he wasn't.

He looked at Britt and Henrik and thought about Soren and all the other lives destroyed by this thing, this idea. Henrik had already lined up some shots of vodka, but he was clearly disappointed at the lack of Sort Svine.

Hans was on his smartphone, hopefully not arranging a death squad to meet them when they landed. The accelerating engine reminded Christian of how little sleep he had had as he fought the urge to close his eyes. As the jet left the runway and began its steep climb through the sky, Christian couldn't resist any longer and was lulled into oblivion, as always, by the rhythmic hypnotic roar of the jet engines.

An eruption of muffled noises in the background woke Christian from his deep slumber. He opened and closed his jaw in an unsuccessful attempt to relieve the pressure in his ears from the altitude change.

Slowly, he tried to open and focus his eyes to figure out the situation unfolding around him. The adrenaline burst that came with understanding the situation more than cleared his ears and eyes as he stared down the barrel of his own gun, while hearing Henrik and Britt pleading with Hans to put the gun down.

"You should have kept your backpack close," Hans said with a calm voice as he inspected the gun he was pointing at Christian. "Interesting, an American spy with a Russian gun. Here I was thinking you were just a very lucky victim of circumstance, having stumbled into the Collin situation, then giving your famous lecture that put me at your mercy."

"Mercy?" Christian asked with a puzzled look.

Hans elaborated, "When the DKMA came to me after seeing your lecture and made their offer contingent on you heading the human trials, you could have named your price. I would have paid you ten million dollars, had you asked. That should have tipped me off that you were manipulating me and not the other way around. Anybody else would have demanded the world."

"I'm not a spy, and I wouldn't call it lucky feeling responsible for getting my patient killed and suffering with that guilt for the past two years," Christian replied.

"Christian has very little to hide, and he's clearly not a good liar or manipulator," Britt said, trying to seem impartial, fearing she might reveal her true feelings for him.

"Everyone knows you have an almost flawless ability to tell when someone is lying to you. What does your instinct say about Christian?" She watched as Hans contemplated her question.

"You've got me there," Hans said, conceding to Britt. "Christian never set off any of my alarms."

Britt turned to Hans and Henrik. "I need both of you to trust us right now. Everything Christian knew about your past, he learned from me. I don't trust you enough yet to reveal everything but putting that gun away and helping us will go a long way in building some credit."

Hans put the gun down. "OK, you're holding all the cards since you're the only one who knows the last ingredient. Let's see where this leads, but I'm keeping this!" Hans put the gun in the side pocket of his Patagonia Parka as he leaned back and gazed out the window as they approached Thule Air Base from the southeast.

No sooner had the plane landed and taxied, than a fully armed Black Hawk helicopter swooped down and landed beside the plane as they exited. Two armed soldiers leapt from the chopper and ran towards them. Christian prepared himself to be thrown to the ground and cuffed. This wasn't his first rodeo! Instead, they ran up to Hans.

"Welcome back to Greenland, Dr. Rasmussen. We've been ordered to aid you in any and every way possible, no questions asked. We've been briefed that you need to hunt something, but that's it. Our orders come straight from the VERY top, so this must be a big deal," they said, clearly impressed.

Hans turned to Britt, as did everyone else. "Well, it's your show now," he exclaimed.

Britt walked up to the soldiers. It was clear they were taken aback by her beauty and stature, but they were making an honest effort to remain professional. She read the name tag of the first officer.

"Hello, Captain Jason O'Brien of the US Space Force. Are you boys going to take us to the moon?" She smiled at him.

Jason blushed. "No ma'am, all the spaceships are down in Florida, but a lot of the radar and tracking facilities for outer-space activity are located here in Greenland. The Navy gets sunny San Diego and its beaches, we get Greenland and its glaciers!"

"Well, we're glad you're here!" Britt said with sincerity in her voice. "Do you boys know what a musk ox is?"

"Yes ma'am, it's one of the meanest and toughest sons of bitches to walk this planet, pardon my language, and they're primarily found right here in Greenland!"

"Do you think you could help us find and kill one?" Britt asked matter-of-factly.

Hans, Henrik, and Christian glanced at each other, one step closer to knowing the final ingredient.

"We can help you find it, but killing it's a different story. Every year, Inuits die trying to hunt the musk ox. Most animals will run from an arrow or a gunshot. These bastards will charge and kill you if you get anywhere near them."

"That sounds like a problem," Henrik said, stepping between them and Britt, not liking how comfortable the soldiers were getting with her.

"If you'll allow it," Jason said, "I've got an idea. Follow me."

They all climbed into the Black Hawk and were soaring across the glacier in no time at all. The pilot was using some kind of thermal imaging and within minutes was approaching a herd of musk ox.

Christian spoke into his headset microphone. "Shouldn't we land soon so we can sneak up on them?"

There was some static over the comm, "That would be a negative, sir."

Christian watched in awe and shock as the gunman sighted the head of one of the oxen. They fired one shot from one of the massive cannons mounted on the side of the chopper that reverberated across the glacier. A bright orangish-red bullet streak flew through the air and, a split second later, the musk ox's head exploded, leaving a twenty-meter streak of blood, fur, and brain matter in the snow.

The gunner looked back and, with a pridefully nervous tone peppered with a touch of guilt, said, "Please tell me you didn't need the head?"

Britt quickly responded with a reassuring tone, "You did amazing! We just need a leg bone!" The other twenty musk oxen had surrounded the corpse of their fallen friend, forming a circle with their intimidating horns facing outward, ready to defend from any direction. They eventually broke rank and dispersed as the war machine drew closer. Jason ran out and efficiently removed the lower half of one of the legs and was back to the chopper within minutes.

"That was quick!" Henrik commented, clearly impressed.

"Yes, sir. I grew up on a big ol' ranch in Montana. This is child's play! Where to now, boss?" Jason said, looking at Britt.

As they stood there a few meters from the chopper and a million kilometers from anywhere on top of a three-kilometer-thick glacier, Christian tried to imagine the ancient city of Neith buried so far below them.

Then, he tried to imagine what it must have been like for the holy man to return after so many years, only to discover the desolate ruins of his city from the meteor strike. This visualization triggered a thought that made

Christian seize with fear and wonder.

Hans chimed in, trying to reestablish the chain of command. "If this is all we need, then we should return to Norkap and work on the formulation."

Britt and Henrik concurred, and they all began walking back to the Black Hawk, except for Christian who was just standing there, eye twitching staring into the arctic void. Eventually, everyone began to notice, and a wave of concern washed over the group.

Britt rushed to Christian, grabbing his arm, trying to shake him back to reality. "Are you OK?" She waved her hands and snapped her fingers in front of his face, with no response. Henrik and Hans then took notice and walked over to Christian and Britt.

Very slowly and almost in a whisper, Christian spoke. "What exactly did the medicine man say about the wall surrounding Neith after the meteor hit?"

Hans responded, "I've got a picture of the translation right here on my phone. It reads 'The ghosts of his people were forever trapped in the crumbling wall. A subtle but eternal message from the gods.' I never really understood that part. It was probably part of their belief system that a person's spirit gets trapped if they die a violent death, or something along those lines."

Christian began speaking more clearly and coherently. "What if the medicine man literally observed the shadows of his people burned into the outer wall of the city?"

The others weren't following him as Hans spoke up, "I don't see where you're headed."

"We've seen this phenomenon before in Hiroshima and Nagasaki from the intense light given off from a nuclear detonation. It literally burns the shadows of people into the background. Technically, it bleaches all the other surfaces except the shadow of people or objects in its way. This gives the illusion of a shadow."

Britt was the first to realize what Christian was implying. "That's not possible. It's insane."

"What's insane, Britt?" Henrik asked, looking back and forth between Her and Christian.

"No!" Hans exclaimed, starting to understand. "There's no way a bunch of unevolved cave people could have made a nuclear weapon. I don't care how *enlightened* they were."

"We need to know before any of us leave this glacier," Christian said firmly.

As Hans was about to object, Jason's satellite phone rang, interrupting the conversation. "This is Captain O'Brian," he answered. After a brief pause, he looked at Britt with a puzzled expression and handed her the phone. "It's for you, someone from Interpol—my CO already confirmed it."

Britt answered the phone with a question in her voice. She listened intently before responding. "Alright, we can be there within the hour... sounds good," she said before hanging up. The group looked at her expectantly, eager for an explanation.

"Are you ready to know how I know so much about your past?" Britt asked Hans.

"Absolutely!" was his response with rare enthusiasm.

She then turned to Christian. "Are you serious about the danger that may lie hidden in these memories?"

"More than ever," he exclaimed.

"Then we must go to the outskirts of the Inuit camp to meet the missing piece of this puzzle." Britt said.

She turned to Hans and implored him, "It's imperative you hear this person out and not do anything drastic."

"Of course," Hans replied, "all I want to do is get this behind us, whatever it takes."

Within moments, they were back in the air and on their way to the Inuit camp.

With the camp looming in the distance, Britt asked Jason if he could take them to the outskirts. "Well, I wouldn't be much of a pilot if I couldn't!" he replied as they veered to one side and rocketed towards their destination.

After a safe drop off, Jason returned to the base with instructions to wait for their call to be picked up.

"Why are we so far away from the camp?" Henrik asked, confusion written on his face.

"This is where the Interpol agent wanted to meet us," Britt replied, trying to remain calm and in control.

"Isn't your dad an Interpol agent?" Henrik asked.

"Yes, he is, and that's who's about to meet us," Britt confessed. Several eyebrows raised at this admission as Christian and Britt braced for the impending truth that was soon to follow.

Britt then walked away from the group and motioned for Christian to come to talk in private. "Dmitry is with my dad!" she exclaimed.

"Oh shit." Christian said, immediately recognizing the sparks being added to an already explosive situation. "Dmitry certainly wasn't going to have the warm and fuzzies for Hans, and there's no way Hans will want the Russians knowing what he's been up to."

"How did your dad find us?" Christian asked.

"He apparently never lost us," Britt explained. "Turns out you *can* track a burner phone if you're the owner! It led him straight to Dmitry, and together they figured out where we had gone. They should be arriving on snowmobiles any minute now."

As if on cue, Soren and Dmitry's snowmobiles appeared high on the same ridge Christian had plummeted down just days prior. It was evident that Soren and Dmitry had far better control of their snowmobiles than Christian.

Christian could see Hans and Henrik straining to see who was approaching. He didn't know if Hans would recognize his own brother or Dmitry after all these years, but he wasn't going to chance it.

"Britt and I will go out to meet them," Christian announced. "Please promise us that you'll reserve your judgment and reaction until after we've had a chance to explain everything. As cliché as it sounds, I sincerely believe that the truth will set us all free if this goes half-way decent."

Chapter 53

Soren and Dmitry pulled their snowmobiles to a stop about one hundred meters from the other group. Soren recognized Britt from a distance and sprinted to her.

Britt leapt into his embrace. "I'm so sorry we took off like that, but I couldn't sit by and watch you, Jesper and Papa do something you would forever regret," she said apologetically.

"It's OK. If you tell me things may not be what we thought, I'll trust you and hear what Hans has to say."

Christian added, "Hans has promised to listen to everything everyone has to say and not react."

This clearly rubbed Soren the wrong way, "Well, that's very big of him, isn't it…"

Britt pleaded with her father, "We've heard Hans's side of the story. After you were shot and knocked out at the base camp, the person who shot you went down and killed everyone and tried to kill Hans but ran out of ammo."

"If that's all you have," Soren growled, clenching his lethal fists, "Then I recommend you stay here and let me finish this."

"No, there's more, please listen," Christian begged as he unwisely blocked Soren's path, "It was a bearded man named Henry who claimed to be an

American spy and wore dark sunglasses."

Soren stopped, but was still growling, "You have my attention."

Britt tagged in, "Hans claimed that Henry spoke with an over-the-top ridiculous John Wayne accent. He thought it was a joke at first."

It was clear the last bit of information made an impact on Soren. But before he could respond, Dmitry caught up and they resumed the walk towards the rest of the group.

"I'm so glad you're OK Christian," Dmitry exclaimed, "I assumed the worst when I didn't hear from you, then Soren found me, thank heavens."

Christian turned to Dmitry and expressed his gratitude. "I can't thank you enough for all that you've done. Did you call in another favor to use a state plane?"

Dmitry replied, "Unfortunately, I used up all my favors getting you to Denmark! But one of my old friends runs an executive rental business and was able to charter me a plane."

Christian found this interesting, "Is there a pretty big demand for chartered flights in Denmark?"

Dmitry chuckled. "Not as much as in the US, but this guy deals in all kinds of transportation. He rents out planes, boats, motorcycles, and even classic cars."

Christian's interest grew.

"When we get back to Copenhagen," Dmitry continued, "I bet he can find you a nice vintage MGB to explore the countryside with the top down."

Christian's face lit up. "That would be incredible! I've always loved MGBs."

As the group walked in silence, Dmitry whistled to break the monotony. Christian had a good feeling about the upcoming reunion, but he knew there would still be challenges ahead.

Even if they all agreed on a plan, the problem of The Surgeon remained: giving the secrets of the tablet to the world would be pointless if it only led to the proliferation of weapons of mass destruction.

Christian was entertained by Dmitry's melodic whistling and was surprised that he recognized the tune. "That's The Marriage of Figaro, by Mozart, isn't it?" Alas, his semester of classical music appreciation was finally paying off.

Dmitry was excited that someone shared his passion for Mozart. "Why yes! You have a good ear for music," he complimented with a smile.

Christian's mind raced as they crossed the vast sea of ice and time to reunite a family torn apart by manipulation, miscommunication and murder.

Not bad for my first family therapy encounter since graduating.

As Christian patted himself on the back for a job well done, he was unexpectedly interrupted by a wave of revelation that once again consumed him. He quickly turned around just in time to see Dmitry lighting a cigarette with a golden zippo.

He prayed nobody noticed his face, which had to have been bright red. Christian sped up, reaching Hans and Henrik, ahead of the others.

Once close enough for Hans to see him, Christian slowly and exaggeratedly mouthed the words, *Throw me the gun.* Hans gave a confused look and Christian mouthed the same words again, *Throw me the gun.*

Hans's eyes locked onto Christian's, his face tense with determination. He understood this time, and his uncanny sense for the truth told him Christian could be trusted. With a swift and seamless motion, and not a moment's pause, he propelled the gun forward with all his might, launching it towards Christian. Time seemed to slow as the firearm hurtled through the air, traversing the space that separated them.

To everyone's astonishment, Christian's hand shot up and caught the soaring weapon. In a surprising display of agility, he pivoted towards Dmitry and pressed the barrel of the gun right between his eyes."

Everyone gasped as Britt pleaded, "What are you doing Christian? Please put that gun down."

"I've never told a living soul about my passion for MGBs," Christian declared as he thought out loud, "For Dmitry to know I liked these vintage cars, he had to have been in a chat room with me and seen my user name."

"That's not enough to justify putting a gun to his head." Soren protested.

"No it's not," Christian said in agreement, "But the last time I was in a chat room, was the night I met a woman with the screen name of RelicCollector1, who ended up being the latest victim of The Surgeon."

221

"I still don't understand?" Hans exclaimed as he drew closer.

"There was someone else in that chat named Mozart3000, who tried to stop me from meeting RelicCollector1. I'm pretty sure Mozart3000 is The Surgeon and the only one here who knows I like MGBs."

Confused Britt begged for clarification, "This makes no sense. Just because Dmitry knows you like MGB's and whistles Mozart music doesn't make him The Surgeon."

"You're right," Christian said, "but putting those pieces together triggered another memory, from the flight where Dmitry and I met, en route to Denmark."

"And?" Henrik exclaimed, trying to coax Christian along.

"And," Christian exclaimed with growing confidence, "I remembered the face of the man who tried to steal Dmitry's pen, and in the process, facilitated our introduction. It was none other than the face of Johnny, the man who tried to kill me last week in that cave right over there." Christian said, pointing to the Inuit camp in the distance as he caught his breath.

Christian turned to Soren, "If you don't believe me, maybe you should ask your old Romanian friend Lucas?"

Soren slowly walked up to Dmitry and began inspecting his face.

Christian tried to hold the gun steady as he also took a closer look. "Now, I understand that ridiculous beard and dark sunglasses, Dr. Nilsson, or should we call you Henry?" He said, inviting Hans to have a look.

Hans never made it to Dmitry, as he stared in disbelief at his brother Lars, who he thought died thirty years ago in a cave in.

"Lars? It can't be!" He blew past Dmitry, hugging his brother and sobbing uncontrollably.

Henrik had walked up at this point and just stood there with his arms at his side. "Dad?" he said, looking at Soren in bewilderment.

Hans released his grip, watching as Soren emotionally embraced the son he had only held once as a newborn. "Please forgive me, son," he said, tears streaming down his cheeks.

Soren then motioned a tearful Britt to join them, "this is my daughter, Britt." Hans embraced his niece for the first time as Henrik lowered his head in embarrassment over all of the now incestuous thoughts he had had about his sister.

Britt just smiled at Henrik and quickly yanked him into the hug.

Christian kept the pistol trained on Dmitry as each person recovered from the shock and awe of the unexpected and emotional reunion.

Dmitry began a slow clap so as not to spook Christian. "Bravo! Bravo! There's no use denying what I've done or who I am."

Hans was the first to chime in. "Lars, it was Dmitry who killed both Ingrid and Anya, along with everyone else on the dig!"

Soren walked over to Christian. "I'll take over from here." Christian gladly handed him the gun.

Soren lowered the gun and turned to Dmitry. "Are you The Surgeon, and are you Lucas?"

Hans followed, "And are you Henry?"

Christian finished, "And are you Dr. Nilsson?"

"Yes," Dmitry said bluntly, addressing everyone. "The part of the Lithuanian translation that I withheld from Hans made it clear that all of humanity's memories lead back to a shockingly simple method of converting an ordinary golden cube into an extremely powerful weapon.

"The USSR was giving me unlimited funding and leeway to find that tablet, but it all ended in 1989 with the fall of the Berlin Wall. The Politburo mothballed the program and forbade me to pursue it any further. Since then, I've been working with a handful of true believers from throughout the former Soviet empire to finish the mission. Our governments have no clue what we are doing, but they will have no choice but to bend to our will once we unlock this weapon."

Soren raised the gun back to Dmitry's head. "Well, I hate to disappoint you and your friends, but this all ends right here. Tell me who your co-conspirators are."

As Soren was cocking the gun, Christian jumped between the weapon's muzzle and Dmitry. "No! Look at Britt!"

Everyone looked at the two green dots converging on Britt. One on her forehead and one on her heart. Soren immediately dropped the gun and raised his hands. "No."

Dmitry picked up his gun. "You were right about one thing—it will all end here today if you don't give me the final ingredient. But if you give me what I want, I will leave you alone to enjoy the short amount of time you will have together before the world bows to me and the reborn Soviet Empire!"

"It didn't have to end this way," Dmitry said to Soren. "If you had simply done what you said you would do, Anya and all my experimental subjects, would be alive today."

Hans looked at Soren. "You agreed to kill us?"

Before Soren could refute this, Dmitry answered for him. "Lars agreed to carry out my request after a little persuasion. Unfortunately, I had a feeling he wouldn't follow through, and I was right. He and Anya were going to collapse the dig site and fake their deaths. That's why I took matters into my own hands."

Soren was shocked and exclaimed, "All these years, I was so certain it was Hans!"

Dmitry replied, "I guess it must've looked like that. I watched from a distance all those years ago when you attacked Hans as he tried to remove the explosives from the cave wall that I had planted. When you dove into the cave, I assumed you and the bottom half of the tablet were lost forever. You must have made it to the temple and found the bodies before escaping. You obviously didn't see me knock Hans out and take his half of the tablet after the cave-in. I decided to let him live, in hopes that he would one day go back and unearth the bottom part of the tablet.

"You can only imagine the shock when I saw you on Johnny's bodycam after you so easily snapped his neck the other day. Very impressive. It was more than I could have dreamed of. I hope you don't mind, but I've had a few of my new associates tag along, seeing that you disposed of Johnny and Brian."

Dmitry motioned to the green dots on Britt as two men with scopes on her slowly approached from their hiding place among the boulders.

"I knew you wouldn't risk your precious daughter's life, even if it meant revenging your lover's murder," Dmitry continued. "If it makes you feel any better, Anya's death wasn't instant. She refused to die. I had to put another bullet in her head before she'd stop fighting."

Soren was trembling with rage as Dmitry continued, "I have hated myself ever since then, because had I not wasted that last round on Anya, I would have had one bullet left for Hans, and the complete tablet would have been mine."

Dmitry raised the gun, as Soren's life hung in the balance. Christian could only watch as Britt begged for her father's life. Dmitry's gunmen were closing in, and there seemed to be no way out.

"Tell me what the last ingredient is!" Dmitry demanded.

Britt shouted, "It's the bone marrow of a musk ox! Please, don't kill my father!"

"Thanks for not making this harder than it had to be," Dmitry said. "I have to keep some of you alive, at least until I confirm this concoction works."

Turning to Hans, he said, "I don't know how you did it, but I assume you somehow made a copy of the top half of the tablet before I knocked you out?"

Hans replied, "Your assumption is right. But you won't get away with this."

"I think we'll start thinning the herd with you," Dmitry said as he pointed the gun at Hans.

Unsure where the courage was coming from, Henrik dove between Hans and Dmitry ready to take the bullet meant for his uncle. Soren effortlessly stopped him dead in his tracks a split second before a series of three clicks echoed in the distance. Another split second later, a swooshing sound passed by the spot where Hernik's head would have been, striking Dmitry in the neck.

Dmitry's made no effort to stop the blood spurting from his neck as he watched his two shooters crumble to the ground in the distance. He just smiled and gurgled as he raised the gun to Britt's head, "I still win."

Everyone but Hans screamed and lunged to stop Dmitry from pulling the trigger, all of them knowing it was too late.

The last thing Britt saw was the hammer of the gun moving back as Dmitry squeezed the trigger.

The smile slowly faded from Dmitry's face as the impotent click of the gun yielded no bullet.

Everyone then watched in disbelief as Dmitry slowly fell backwards into the bloody snow with a muffled thud. All the while squeezing the trigger over and over with the same unsatisfying result.

The group's attention then slowly panned to Hans, who simply shrugged his shoulders, "What? It's a statistical fact that you or one of your loved ones, is fifty times more likely to die from a loaded gun than a potential assailant who the bullets were originally meant for. The first thing I did after stealing the gun from Christian back on the jet, was to take the bullets out!"

Hans's explanation was interrupted by the emergence of two men in the distance; fully loaded rifles slung over their shoulders, and clad head to toe in arctic-white gear. At first, it appeared to be a man and a child. But as they drew closer, everyone breathed a sigh of relief at the sight of Jesper and Andre.

Andre arrived, looked down upon Dmitry, and spat on his twitching body, "That is for my daughter Anya."

Jesper walked up and just looked down. "I hope you burn in Hell for what you did to my father and everyone else."

Soren didn't give a second glance as he resumed his embrace of his long-lost family.

Dmitry stared up at them as his last heartbeat produced one final spurt of blood that was gladly absorbed by the white snow of the ancient glacier.

Chapter 54

Gazing at the eclectic group of people in front of him, Christian experienced a rush of both elation and pain. Justice and restitution were long overdue, but he knew this was just the beginning of their journey. He didn't know how much to reveal, aware that there were no safe options. "I fear this secret may have to be taken to the grave."

"What do you mean, Christian?" asked Hans, his frustration evident. "This is a second chance to clear Lars's name, expose The Surgeon, and unlock the secrets concealed in those memories."

"I believe there's a powerful but dreadful secret hidden in our memories," Christian said. "As Dmitry admitted, according to the Lithuanian scroll, there may be a painfully simple formula to create a weapon of mass destruction from a simple golden cube buried deep in our collective memories."

Britt chimed in this time with furious denial in her voice, "No, no, no. My father must be vindicated, and his name cleared!"

"We all want that," Christian said soothingly. "But what do we tell the police? We just killed a Russian ambassador who was a serial killer and the head of a secret society bent on reviving the USSR to its past glory. And what about the rest of his secret society? They are still out there and will stop at nothing to win this prize. I vote we dump these three bodies in the same bottomless glacial pit with Johnny and Brian."

Hans was shaking his head and it was clear Britt was not happy with Christian's suggestion. As she was about to speak out, Soren interrupted, "I appreciate the desire to clear my name, but Christian is right. Nobody can ever know what transpired today."

Hans reluctantly agreed that Christian's plan was a good one. "How does this sound: Jesper and Soren can use the snowmobiles to get rid of the evidence, and I'll take Andre, Britt, Henrik, and Christian to the Inuit village. I've been working with this village for over thirty years. They will gladly set us up for the night, especially once we let them know about the freshly killed musk ox. The entire village will journey to the site to camp, celebrate, and butcher the ox. It can feed them for weeks and provide clothing and a host of other useful resources."

"I still don't like it," Britt said reluctantly, "but I understand."

"Sounds like we have a plan," Christian said as he picked up the musk ox leg and began inspecting it. "Hopefully, they'll have some supplies we can use to mix things up!"

Christian was impressed with Hans's predictions; he was right on all points. The Inuit Chief Aknar was elated about the news of the ox, and the entire village set off that evening to find the ox before polar bears and wolves could get to it.

As a gesture of appreciation for the ox, Chief Aknar had the cave set up with everything they required; sleeping furs, firewood, food, drinks, and useful utensils. The cave, located on the cliffside where Christian was previously attacked, served as the Inuit village's gathering place for special events and ceremonies. The last time he was there, the villagers had been out on a similar hunting-gathering trip, so there had been no witnesses to his attack or escape with Soren.

They settled into the cave, and Hans took out a small case like the one he had given Christian. Britt had extracted a small scoop of bone marrow from the ox leg, which they mixed with a sample of ReminEssence and heated over the fire. Hans turned to the others as he poured a small portion of the liquid mixture into a metal coffee cup and asked, "Any volunteers? I assume we're skipping all the R&D and animal trials and going straight to human trials!"

"Should we wait for Dad and Jesper?" Britt asked, as Christian reached for the cup.

"Let's get this over with!" Christian replied, and Britt made no objections. Hans passed the cup to Christian. "Skål!" Christian guzzled the foul-smelling concoction and moments later began crumpling over. Henrik and Britt caught him as his body fell lifeless onto the sleeping furs.

Chapter 55

C hristian was aware, yet of what exactly, he couldn't discern. The elixir had disabled his senses, leaving him in utter darkness. Paralyzed and numb, he tried to move, but there was only emptiness, devoid even of the faint ringing that emerges in profound silence. The vile taste and smell of the elixir had vanished, as if his mind had entirely detached from his body.

A chilling thought surfaced: was he dead? But no sooner had it arisen than he became acutely conscious of every single cell in his being. He could sense every hair follicle on his little toe, right down to each individual hair, and he instinctively knew everything within that toe was working as it should.

Intrigued, Christian speculated whether the elixir was designed to induce a kind of anatomical diagnostic mode. Seeking to validate his theory, he concentrated on a muscle in his shoulder he'd injured during the snowmobile chase the previous week. He perceived every detail within that region, right down to the specific muscle fibers that had torn. His body was actively mending the damage, which explained the lingering pain.

While engrossed in the details of his shoulder, he detected an anomaly in his head. Redirecting his focus, he suddenly became conscious of the stitches on his scalp. His body was healing the wound, and he even sensed the exact duration of recovery.

Feeling like the commander of an exceptionally advanced vessel, Christian yearned to delve deeper. He had been merely observing thus far; now he wished to exert control. Almost effortlessly, he honed in on his ears and overheard Britt assuring the others that his vital signs were stable.

Suddenly, the puzzle pieces clicked into place. It was as if he was a remote operator of his own body. He directed his attention to his eyes, opting to keep them shut, wary of unnerving the others. Yet even behind closed lids, he perceived the cave's ceiling and the erratic dance of shadows from the fire. It felt as if he were an observer, removed from the scene. Simultaneously, he grasped the intricate computations enabling his eyes to capture and translate visual stimuli. The conscious entity with which he was thinking seemed distinct from his physiological operations. An epiphany struck: could this be his subconscious?

But as Christian endeavored to assimilate everything, an alarm signaled an issue with his right eye. When he tried honing in on the problem area, there was no response. He kept focused and waited, and suddenly it happened again, only to disappear as quickly as it appeared. This time, Christian was able to determine that there was no physical problem with the eye. The alarm had come from a nerve that went into his eye. He then recalled the nervous twitch that had plagued him since childhood and was becoming worse by the day.

Having pinpointed the issue and its origin, he traced the nerve to the brain section overseeing ocular movements. As he journeyed deeper into the cerebral networks governing vision, he marveled at the countless chemical interplays facilitating the conversion of visual inputs into cognitive understanding. The nerve trail led him through the optic nerve processing zone, and before he realized, he had ventured beyond. Abruptly, his path was blocked.

Although the path seemed to extend further, an insurmountable barrier lay ahead. There was a never ending flow of signals crossing this invisible and impenetrable barrier, yet he could not pass. A primal warning pulsated, discouraging him from trespassing. This only amplified his resolve.

He began exploring other signals leading into this area. There were signals from his ears and nose transmitting the sounds and smells from the cave. Then he identified signals from his mouth transmitting the awful taste of the elixir. Another signal from his back transmitted the pressures felt from lying on the cave floor. Everything suddenly made sense as he observed the signal from his eyes transmitting the fuzzy images of the flickering flames on the cave ceiling from his loosely closed eyes.

Christian was standing at the border of the mythical demarcation between his finite body, and his immortal DNA. He was at the precipice of the thing that had eluded him for so long. All of his memories were flowing through the barrier into his DNA like a rushing river after a rain storm.

Now that he understood what he was observing, Christian somehow knew he could cross the barrier just as easily as his memories. But something prevented him from taking the plunge.

Like a stray tributary diverging from the river, Christian couldn't ignore the malfunctioning signal that was somehow connected to his twitching eye. Going against his better judgment, Christian dove into this dysfunctional branch.

Chapter 56

He had transitioned into a realm beyond description. Immersed in absolute darkness, it felt as though he was being blasted naked through an endless gun barrel, its interior lined with razors and salt. Every fraction of his being was instantaneously torn apart, the resulting wounds searing with unimaginable pain. What felt like an eternity of horrific suffering had been concentrated into a mere fraction of a second. Then, like a bullet puncturing a water balloon, he was propelled from the abyss of pain and darkness straight into a vivid childhood memory.

This memory surged with clarity, more vibrant than anything he could recall—surpassing even the most advanced virtual reality experiences imaginable.

Remarkably, the adult Christian remained acutely aware of his own emotions and senses, while simultaneously reliving the feelings and perceptions of his younger self within the memory.

He found himself revisiting a serene moment at nine years old, trekking through the North Carolina mountains alongside his father. "See this tree, son? It's called mountain laurel. Notice how its leaves are narrower than those of a rhododendron."

Gazing upon his father, who had passed away over two decades ago, was a deeply emotional experience. A nascent sense of unease began to surface. Though he and his father had embarked on numerous hikes in the mountains beyond their horse farm's slopes, Christian couldn't place this particular memory.

As they hiked further into the mountains, the initial discomfort slowly intensified into a foreboding panic. Adult Christian felt an overwhelming urge to retreat, but he couldn't pinpoint the reason. His father's voice was a beacon of safety, guiding him through the forest: "Let's explore this trail, buddy; we've never ventured this way before." Despite the unfamiliarity of the memory, the mounting panic evolved into a pervasive and suffocating dread.

The trail meandered over a hill and descended into a narrow valley, opening up to reveal an expansive field dotted with cannabis plants. Beyond lay a weathered double-wide trailer, its multiple chimneys spewing plumes of white smoke. Christian sensed his father's grip on his hand tighten, a mask of worry overtaking his features. "We need to turn back immediately, son. Stay silent and stick close to me."

No sooner had they turned back than they saw their path blocked by four unkempt men dressed in ragged clothing. They were heavily armed, weapons at the ready.

"Where y'all think yer goin'?"

Christian's dad was calm but authoritative, "We didn't see anything. We just made a wrong turn. So sorry for any trouble. We'll get out of your hair." Christian had never heard his dad use that tone before.

"The hell you will," one of the men said as the others laughed.

"We don't want any trouble. I was just hiking with my son."

One of the men looked at Christian. "You got a real perty boy. We're all gonna have some fun with him, then I reckon the rest'll sort itself out."

The other three men roared with laughter, exposing jagged rows of rotting black teeth, encrusted with years of decay and neglect. Young Christian jumped as one of them violently cocked a shotgun and another began unbuckling his belt.

Christian's dad squeezed his hand and looked down at him. "When I say run, you run, and DO NOT look back till you're far from here and safe. I love you so much, son."

Like a ghost, his dad vanished, and a split-second later Christian saw the blur of him flying towards the closest man. With one fluid motion, he broke the man's arm, took his gun, then snapped his neck as if it were kindling for a fire. He used the lifeless man's corpse as a human shield to block the gunfire erupting from the others.

In another split second, his dad pivoted and shot the man unbuckling his pants, once in the crotch, and once in the forehead. He then turned away from the other two men as he pleaded with Christian, "Run, buddy, please, get out of here!" But Christian didn't run; he was paralyzed with fear.

As his dad turned back to the remaining two men, a rifle shot echoed through the valley, and Christian watched in horror as the bullet blew through his dad's chest, spraying blood behind him.

If I had listened and ran, my dad would be alive today. It was my fault he died.

Unfazed by the bullet, his dad aimed and squeezed the trigger, but nothing happened—the gun was out of ammo.

"Run, Christian!"

But he was still frozen.

Unable to look away, he watched his dad throw the pistol at the man reloading his rifle. Distracted by the flying gun, the man never saw Christian's dad draw the seven-inch razor-sharp KA-BAR knife that had served him well since his early days in the Navy.

As the pistol hit the man, his dad closed the gap and buried the knife deep in the side of the man's neck. He then turned the handle and pulled it towards him. There was an eruption of blood, as the man's partially decapitated head fell to his back like a PEZ dispenser.

A loud bang erupted from the last man's shotgun as Christian's dad was turning towards him. His dad used the force of the impact to propel him around faster and projectile the knife seven inches deep into the man's eye socket.

Falling to one knee, Christian's dad reached out to him. He ran into his father's blood-soaked arms, the bodies of the four men scattered around them, either dead or dying, "Listen carefully to me, son," he said, gasping and coughing as he drowned in his blood-filled lungs. "None of this is your fault. I'm the luckiest man in the world because I got to be your dad."

"No!" Christian pleaded, "Don't leave me. I love you."

"Look at me," his dad said, his breaths slowing and turning into reflexive gasps, "You are so special and can accomplish anything you want. Remember everything I taught you. You're ready for this world. Never let anyone tell you otherwise. I love you, son."

With those last words, Christian could no longer support the weight of his dad's lifeless body. He had to let go and watch his father collapse dead on the ground.

In shock, Christian didn't say a word. He simply laid down beside his dad and pulled his arm over him as he had done a thousand times before. He then lost consciousness, and the next memory was of waking in a hospital bed.

In shock, Christian tried to reconcile what he had just seen and felt. The trained therapist in him now understood the true scope of damage young Christian had suffered. The damning insult wasn't from the violence witnessed, or the shame of thinking his dad was a drug addict and dealer.

It was the guilt of believing he was responsible for his dad's death. Young Christian must have believed that if he had just listened and run away, his dad would have easily finished off those men and still be alive to this day. He had seen this a thousand times with kids of abuse or divorce, always believing it was their fault.

Christian could see the value of this elixir extended far beyond monetary wealth. He wondered if Norkap's ReminEssence was this effective without the musk ox bone marrow. He also tried to imagine the benefits of this medication for war veterans, like his father, who suffered from PTSD.

All Christian wanted to do now, was go back and relive the countless wonderful times with his father and never let go again. Alas, he knew this wasn't possible.

As dark and terrifying as his repressed memories were, he suspected something even darker and more terrifying was lying in wait. He hoped with all his might that he was wrong, but knew it was up to him to find out.

Christian could feel the divergent tributary created by this traumatic event merging back into his mainstream memory. Just as quickly, he was back at the invisible barrier watching the river of memories flow through.

Something had changed in him, but he wasn't sure what, and didn't have time to analyze it. He worried the elixir could wear off at any moment.

Without hesitation this time, he followed the river of memories through the invisible barrier with no resistance. This time, there was no pain or suffering. It felt as if a wormhole had opened, and he was suddenly traveling at light speed through the universe.

He didn't understand it, but he was somehow viewing every moment of his life all at once. There was no question where he wanted to go first.

In an instant, he was viewing memories of his first weeks of life. It was there that he saw his mother for the first time that he could remember. Up to that point, he had only seen pictures, since she had died from an undiagnosed complication just a month after his birth.

She was holding him in her arms as he looked up at her lovingly. She was beautiful and could not take her eyes off him. Beside the bed was his father, beaming with pride and love.

Emotions welled up inside him; his heart yearned to stay there and just watch, but reason prevailed. With a painful goodbye to his mother and father, Christian continued the journey.

By the time he had reached his memories of the delivery room and the birthing process itself, everything was dark. This made sense since he was essentially watching a recording, and his infant eyes needed time to adjust before they could clearly record visuals. Fortunately, he was very much aware of the other developing senses like touch, taste, smell and hearing.

Christian felt the crushing sensation as he was passing in reverse through the birth canal, and he even remembered feelings from inside the womb.

Then, without warning, the memories stopped.

Logically, he knew this would happen, but a part of him—the part engrossed in two years of searching for genetic memories—craved more.

He had never imagined he would discover everything he had so far, but he knew this wasn't the end. If there were ever a chance to access ancestral memories, it would be here.

Christian sat there, paused on the first memory his developing mind had recorded, knowing there was more with no idea how to proceed. Trying to go further back yielded no results. How could it? His mind had not recorded any memories prior to his first.

Nothing was working, and a sense of panicked claustrophobia began creeping in. Trying desperately to clear his thoughts, Christian suddenly remembered the AncestryDNA diagrams that helped him match so many of Collin's memories with his past ancestors.

For every generation, one had to choose a branch to continue tracing the lineage. You could either follow the mother's or father's line each time you wanted to look back a generation.

Of course—why hadn't I thought of this sooner?

Christian quickly decided to follow his father's line of memories. The instant the thought occurred, he was back in the wormhole traveling at light speed through the universe.

A split second later, Christian arrived to something that would surely scar him for life.

Chapter 57

He arrived to the vision of his naked mother underneath him climaxing with orgasmic pleasure. There was nothing he could do, and nowhere he could run. Clueless as to how to shut the memory down, all he could do was wait and watch in crushing disbelief.

His only saving grace was the fact that he had just met his mother a few moments earlier before jumping into his father's memories.

This provided little comfort and would certainly give the Freudians plenty to debate for years to come. Eventually, the memory simply stopped as he experienced, in shocking detail, every feeling and sensation of his father climaxing.

And then there was nothing.

He just sat there in the empty void, metaphorically kicking himself for not having thought of this sooner. It made perfect sense. His father had been recording memories into his DNA right up until the moment when he released the life-giving seed that would eventually become Christian.

If he had chosen the maternal pathway, he would have been looking up at his father, which would have carried its own set of complications. Either way, there would be some serious therapy in his future. He made a mental note to warn the others of this little surprise before they took the plunge.

To make the situation worse, he had no idea how to navigate these memories. They were different from his own. He couldn't see his father's entire life all at once, the way he had seen his own life.

As Christian wrestled with the intricate aspects of his situation, a realization struck him. He had just discovered the genetic memories that had been his life's quest up to this point.

At the end of the day, it wasn't the rigorous scientific procedures that brought him here. Instead, it was his unyielding pursuit of the truth. This quest for enlightenment exposed him to a series of unpredictable challenges. The reward for persevering and surmounting each of these hurdles was access to the elusive genetic memories.

As the exhilarating rush of achievement waned, Christian's determination surged. He knew that somewhere within his familial past lay the remaining answers he sought.

Without a personal framework to serve as a guide, Christian simply tried to focus on moving backward in time. It worked. This technique allowed him to navigate through his father's life. With a little practice, he was able to instantaneously and effortlessly move backward and forward through his father's memories.

Reaching the beginning of his fathers memories, Christian decided to visit his saintlike grandmother next as he hadn't seen her since she passed a year after he moved to Rhode Island. This time he was able to skip the traumatic parts with his finely honed navigational skills.

Christian recognized that he could easily spend a lifetime poring over the memories and history of this incredible discovery. However, he was consumed with an overpowering drive to continue moving back in time.

Moreover, a nagging thought was ever present in his mind. This was the very real possibility that everything he was experiencing was all just a figment of his imagination. All factors considered, everything Christian had seen would be much more logically explained as a hallucination rather than a real experience.

It would make much more sense that this was an illusory construct of Christian's imagination. After all, he had just taken the most powerful hallucinogen known to mankind and just happened to see the exact innermost desires of his heart.

As a scientist, Christian knew he needed to have his findings verified by others with as little bias as possible.

Chapter 58

With renewed urgency, Christian focused on moving further back in time. A single thought propelled him back ten thousand years and two hundred generations. Christian knew he should keep going, as his destination was at least one hundred and fifty thousand years in the past.

But something unfathomable caught his eye...

It took a moment for Christian to accept what he was seeing through the eyes of his ancient ancestor. In front of him was a breathtaking hilltop vista overlooking the Pyramids of Giza. Christian wasn't much of a historian, ironically, but he had always been under the impression that the pyramids were built closer to five thousand years ago, yet here they were, much older than anyone had imagined.

There was just a sliver of the setting sun remaining above the horizon. This remnant of sun was just enough to illuminate the highly reflective tops of two of the three massive pyramids sitting on the Giza Plateau, roughly a kilometer away from him.

As Christian watched this Egyptian sunset in the cool desert breeze, he noticed that the surfaces of all three of the pyramids were covered in a highly reflective, smooth, flat surface; gone were all the steps, tomb entrances and giant stones one typically imagines when thinking of the pyramids. They looked like massive triangular mirrors.

Over the years, of scouring the internet in an attempt to better understand Collin's affliction, Christian had unintentionally acquired a vast and eclectic knowledge base of interesting facts. For example, he had read that the Giza Pyramids were covered in a flat layer of highly polished white limestone. But how did they polish it to the point of resembling a mirror? Then he recalled a documentary detailing reservoirs of mercury being discovered in secret chambers underneath pyramids around the world. Could the pyramids have once been coated with mercury to obtain this reflective surface?

He had also read that the four sides of each pyramid had slight concavities down the middle that created eight sides, which were only discernible from the air at certain times of the year. With the mirror-like surfaces, he was able to easily see how each side was, in fact, two smaller triangles in the setting sun.

With the last light of day fading, Christian's ancestor began walking along the ridge of the hill towards a massive square black marble building with a domed roof. Several soldiers were escorting him. One of the soldiers called him Djau.

As Djau drew closer, Christian realized the structure must have been at least five stories tall and equally as wide on each side. It was positioned in a way that one of its corners was directly facing the three pyramids in the distance. Built into the corner of this massive black structure was a giant window that faced the pyramids. There were also smaller windows directly in the middle of each of the flat sides of this perfectly square structure.

Without warning, Djau became overwhelmed with emotion. Christian was unable to discern the exact emotion, but he suspected it was a combination of anger and fear based on the elevated heart rate, respiration, body temperature, and, of course, the dry mouth that Christian knew all too well.

Djau began screaming and pointing to a fire that someone had just lit far below, roughly half a kilometer between him and the pyramids. Christian watched in shock as a group of twenty soldiers sprinted the half kilometer at full speed and violently butchered the man who had ignited the simple campfire.

"What kind of monster have I descended from?" Christian wondered as he watched in shock.

The soldiers quickly doused the campfire with water, sending a large plume of smoke billowing towards the heavens. Daylight was almost completely faded now, and the brightest stars were slowly beginning to appear at various points in the sky. There was no moon that night, but the night sky was crystal clear. As the smoke plume rose to the altitude of the large structure where Djau was headed, Christian witnessed something that would certainly be added to the growing list of mind-numbing experiences he would not soon forget.

The smoke revealed three barely visible beams of light originating from the sides of the three pyramids facing him from a kilometer away. The entire triangular side of each pyramid reflected a huge beam of faint starlight. Each of these three beams slowly tapered from the size of the pyramids to small rays, all converging directly into the large corner window of the building that Djau was approaching. Christian wondered if the unique eight-sided design of the Giza Pyramids allowed them to form these convergent beams of starlight.

As the smoke cleared, the beams of light became less obvious, but Christian could still see them. It was at this point that the very last vestiges of dusk vanished. With the daylight gone, the remaining millions of stars in the heavens became acutely visible, and the three beams of light exploded with an intensity rivaling the brightest laser beams Christian had ever seen.

At that moment, Christian witnessed something even more spectacular, if that was possible.

Kilometers away, to the right, to the left, and directly behind the three massive pyramids, were the same three beams of light emanating from the remaining sides of each pyramid. There were three other mega-structures just like the one Djau was approaching on each side of the pyramids where these beams of light converged. The flat sides of each of these massive square structures faced each other perfectly, with their corners all facing the pyramids.

This perfect symmetry would not have been possible if the three pyramids had been constructed side by side, but they weren't. The pyramids were constructed diagonally, corner to corner, in a way that allowed all four sides to send their reflective beams of starlight in all four cardinal directions: north, south, east, and west—directly into the four black megastructures without any interference with each other.

Across the plateau, a faint mechanical sound rang out from the structure on the opposite side of the pyramids from Djau's building. A split second later, beams of light shot out of the smaller windows on each of the flat sides of that structure. Those two beams on either side of that structure shot across the Giza Plateau and fed into the other two megastructures to the left and right of Djau's building. Instantaneously, beams of light shot out of those two structures and into the two small side windows on each side of Djau's building. This completed a perfect square of light around the three giant Giza Pyramids, creating a square-wheel-and-spoke laser show.

Christian had once attended a Pink Floyd laser light concert. As impressive as that show was, it couldn't hold a candle to this.

Christian desperately wanted to see inside this structure that Djau was rapidly approaching, but he was also worried about his greater mission and began to fear that the elixir would wear off before he could complete his task. Fighting the urge to continue jumping back through the generations and time, Christian forced himself to enjoy a few more minutes of this enchanting Arabian night.

Djau finally reached the huge black structure. He entered through a small door several stories below one of the side windows with a blinding beam of light flowing through it.

Inside the structure high above, there was an intricate framework of giant glass lenses and mirrors that were capturing the light beams from the pyramids and the two perimeter structures. To the side was a giant mirror that was not in use. Christian wondered if its purpose was to utilize or possibly weaponize the powerful beams of sun that would surely enter during the daytime. These lenses somehow fused the beams of starlight together to produce a three-dimensional image of the celestial sky that defied any description.

This one-hundred-and-eighty-degree view of the night sky, filling the twenty-meter-wide dome above him, was crisper and clearer than any image Christian had ever seen.

Djau reclined in a large chair surrounded by levers with wires and pulleys connecting them to all the lenses and mirrors. Christian watched in amazement as Djau gripped two of the many levers, one in each hand. While staring into the dome above, he made an almost imperceptible motion with each lever, and the image rapidly magnified a thousand times toward a small section of the night sky. Another slight shift of two other levers zoomed in even further on the night sky.

Now filling the massive dome was a crystal-clear live view of Jupiter with it's many moons orbiting, and its raging storm spinning, all in real time.

Djau said something in Egyptian, and then he looked to the side. It was then that Christian saw fifteen scholars sitting at desks feverishly writing and drawing on papyri, following Djau's every word.

Christian was no astronomer, but he knew enough to realize that the pyramids and the four megastructures formed some kind of light telescope complex. The sides of the pyramids collected massive amounts of light from all corners of the night sky and focused them into the four megastructures. Each structure captured a section of the night sky and shared the images with each other, stitching them together to create a complete one-hundred-and-eighty-degree view of the night sky with magnification abilities that would rival the most sophisticated modern-day telescopes.

Christian feared he was traveling on borrowed time. As much as he wanted to stay and discover the many secrets of who built the pyramids and how they did it, he knew this wasn't on the agenda.

Reluctantly, he bid an ambivalent farewell to Djau and the pyramids. With one simple thought, he was back into the time warp.

Chapter 59

Christian journeyed back through time and generations, spanning hundreds of thousands of years, watching his ancestors slowly devolve into cave people right before his eyes. Christian fully expected his ancestors to continue devolving into primate-like creatures as he traced further and further back.

But then, something very unexpected happened.

Within a span of a thousand years, the primitive cave people began to walk more upright, becoming increasingly more Homo-sapien-like the further back he went. After a few more generations, Christian was observing the memories of ancestors who were taller and far more sophisticated than any modern-day humans, communicating in an unintelligible yet intricate language. This only lasted for a few generations before everything suddenly and unexpectedly went dark with one leap.

There was always a clear and unmistakable demarcation each time he passed from one generation to the next, but this time it was different. Despite a sense of time passing, there was no transition from one ancestor to the next. He moved back tens of thousands of years, but it remained the same simple darkness of one person's memory.

Christian became increasingly worried and began jumping back in increments of a hundred thousand years, then in millions, and finally billions of years. The unending darkness was overwhelming, spanning over four billion years.

This has to be a mistake...

Suddenly, the memories of this four-billion-year-old individual resumed without warning. Christian could sense he had traveled roughly a day before the darkness. He stopped and decided to observe from this point to find out what could have led this person into a four-billion-year blackout.

As morning broke, the individual Christian was observing awoke in a dilapidated apartment with broken windows, cracked walls, and old, flaking paint. Then, someone opened the front door and walked in.

Christian observed as the stranger approached and exchanged a greeting with his ancient ancestor. The stranger called him "Luf."

Luf followed the other man outside, and they quickly ducked behind a burned-out vehicle, gazing up as a metallic black triangular aerial vehicle silently darted across the sky at unimaginable speeds, making ninety-degree instantaneous turns that defied all physics. They continued this routine for at least a kilometer, running from one hiding spot to the next, never taking their eyes off the sky. They were in a war-torn city with massive, toppled skyscrapers and plumes of smoke randomly dotting the horizon.

Eventually, they reached the city's edge, which gave way to a vast ocean with hundred-foot-high crashing waves. The beach between the ocean and city stretched for at least a kilometer and was littered with giant boulders, destroyed ships, and decomposing bodies.

After a brief break to catch their breath, they made one final sprint to a lone boulder on the beach. Luf brushed the sand away to reveal a metal trapdoor at the base of this boulder. After entering a six-digit code, the door clicked open, revealing a ladder leading into an underground bunker. They both looked around before slipping inside, sealing the hatch behind them.

Inside the bunker, Christian saw two women in front of computer terminals. The room was well lit, with stainless steel panels covering the walls and ceilings. Christian watched as they activated the computers with a wave of the hand.

They spent the first few hours using a three-dimensional cube design program. Eventually, they stopped working and moved to the front of the bunker, where a narrow window, ground-level with the beach and ceiling level with the bunker faced the ocean. Below the window was a monitor with complicated joysticks and buttons.

Christian deduced that they were scientists working on a mysterious project. He watched as the four of them gathered around the monitor, and an image appeared. It was a square block of gold with a solid white background, hovering above a round white platform. It was impossible to determine the scale of the cube. It could have been the size of a house or the size of a grain of sand.

They used the control panel to guide a robot arm towards the cube, making dimples in various numbers and patterns across its six surfaces. These dimples resembled those of a golf ball or game die. Once finished, the robotic arm moved out of the picture, and one of the scientists pressed a button, creating a buzzing sound.

All the scientists looked over at yet another screen, which showed the cube through some sort of filter.

The background was now pitch black, and the golden cube appeared fluorescent green. The camera zoomed in on the two divots at the top of the cube, and the screen flickered. Suddenly, the image went dark, but then the top surface of the cube slowly emerged into focus.

This time, streams of light emerged from one divot and arched over into the other, producing thousands of multicolored neon light rays. Most of these microscopic beams formed a perfect arch from one divot to the other. To their clear dismay, there were a few beams of light that did not follow the arch and shot straight out. Panic and disappointment were evident on all their faces as they looked at one another with hopeless abandonment.

A nearby explosion interrupted this moment, shaking the bunker. The scientists turned to another monitor that displayed thousands of the black triangular ships swarming over the beach and city several kilometers away. These ships repeatedly fired energy beams at random intervals without any apparent targets. The ships were heading towards the bunker, destroying everything in their path.

The scientists rushed to their terminals and worked feverishly on a new simulation, finishing within minutes. They then rushed to the large monitor for another test, as a new golden cube emerged on the platform.

The robotic arm began placing the divots, and it was clear that the location, size, and pattern of the divots were not important. The only thing that mattered was the number of divots on each of the six sides. The number was the same on the first five sides; however, the last top surface had a different number of divots.

The first surface had five divots, the surface to its right had seventeen, the next had eleven, and the fourth had thirteen. The bottom surface had seven. When the robot arm arrived at the top surface of the cube, it placed three divots instead of two.

The scientists quickly switched to the filtered view as the explosions outside drew closer. It took some time, but the magnified image of the three top divots finally appeared, and there were thousands of perfectly smooth arches leaping from one divot to the next with no outliers. The camera zoomed out to reveal that all the divots on all the sides had these perfect arches of light.

Christian noticed Luf trembling with fear and excitement as he observed the perfect arcs of light flowing like a river between all the divots. It was a living rainbow of lights, one of the most beautiful things Christian had ever seen. The other male scientist rushed to the back wall and picked up what Christian assumed was a phone, but the female scientist quickly took the phone and placed it back on the wall.

Amidst their quarreling, a massive explosion violently shook the bunker, causing the scientists to stumble and fight to maintain balance. They all gathered around the main screen as it flickered from the explosion. Luf navigated the robotic arm over the golden cube. He pressed a button, and a nozzle emerged from the robot arm, pointing directly at the cube.

There was a moment of silence as each person in the room placed a finger on a second large red flashing button. Then, after a brief countdown, they all pushed it simultaneously. Christian watched as a tiny flame shot out of the nozzle towards the golden cube. As the flame made contact, the screen went blank.

Luf stood motionless, staring at the screen, while the other three scientists frantically rushed to the back of the bunker. Suddenly, the horizon flashed with a blinding light, and a few moments later, the planet began to shake. The sky above became an all-consuming dome of orange, red, and blue flames, eviscerating the triangular destroyers instantaneously. As Luf watched in horror, a kilometer-high wave approached them while the ground continued to violently quake.

The sight jolted Luf back to reality, and he sprinted towards the others at the back of the bunker. With haste, he punched in a code on the bunker's wall, and a door leading even further underground flew open.

They fled into the tunnel as the rumbling from the tidal wave grew louder. Once inside, they boarded a capsule-like vehicle that was hovering above what appeared to be a magnetic rail. It took off like a bullet, and within moments, they arrived at an incredibly vast underground circular chamber. Thousands of similar tunnels exited into this chamber from all directions, but nobody else seemed to be arriving. They sprinted hundreds of meters across the shaking chamber floor to reach a massive elevator.

Tens of thousands of people could have fit into the Madison Square Garden-sized elevator; however, it was still just the four of them. They began to argue once again but were cut short this time by the collapsing ceiling as the massive chamber began to crumble.

An alarm sounded, and the elevator doors slammed shut. The elevator began to descend at free-fall speeds, and the team scrambled to find balance while holding onto the walls for support. The descent was so rapid that gravity vanished, and they started to float several inches above the floor. It was impossible to determine how far they had traveled, but it must have been kilometers beneath the planet's surface. Gradually, the elevator decelerated, and gravity returned.

The doors finally opened, revealing an incomprehensibly vast chamber that was so enormous they could not see the other sides or the ceiling for that matter. The chamber was filled with small white pods that stretched as far as the eye could see, enough for billions upon billions of people.

With a final panicked glance at each other, the team climbed into separate capsules that sealed shut moments later. The capsules began to fill with fluid, and Christian could feel Luf resisting the fluid. After roughly a minute, he took a deep breath, and the liquid flooded his lungs. Slowly, everything faded to black, and then there was nothing.

Christian now understood why Dmitry went to such lengths, and he also knew that if this knowledge were to get out into the world, everything would end. He sat there in the darkness, trying not to believe what he had just experienced. Part of him wanted to stay there forever, while the other part knew that he had to warn the others.

He figured the elixir would eventually wear off, and he would wake up— hopefully. With that in mind, Christian decided to see just how far back he could go in his memories.

No sooner had the thought crossed his mind than everything began to swirl and fade as he was pulled through the wormhole.

Moments later, he was back in the Inuit cave.

Chapter 60

Struggling to open his eyes, the images of Britt, Henrik, Hans, and Andre slowly came into focus as they looked down upon him, expressions of puzzled concern etched on their faces. "How long was I out?" he asked, a sense of urgent disorientation in his voice.

"Real funny," Henrik chuckled. "Get up and help us figure out why it didn't work."

"Didn't work?" Christian's confusion deepened. "I must have been out for weeks, or even months. I journeyed through billions of years of memories."

Britt regarded him with compassion, "Poor thing. I thought the fur cushioned your fall, but you must have hit your head again. We're not joking; you were out for just a few minutes."

Either I've finally lost it, Christian thought to himself, *or I could really use the expertise of that quantum physics student right about now.*

Andre watched Christian intently. "You're serious, aren't you?"

"I am," Christian replied gravely.

"What did you see?" Britt asked, uncertain if she really wanted to know.

Christian stood up, rubbing his head, as he addressed everyone. "I can't tell you. I need each of you to go into this with as little background as possible..."

Christian's voice faded mid-sentence as he caught Henrik's puzzling, inquisitive stare. After a few uncomfortable moments, Christian finally asked, "What is it, Henrik? Is there something on my face?"

"No," Henrik replied, tilting his head to focus more on Christian's face.

Then Britt and Andre began to take notice as Christian slowly backed away, feeling more unnerved. "You guys are really starting to freak me out," he said.

"Why are you speaking with that Southern accent?" Hans asked as they slowly closed in on him.

"And why do you seem even taller than before?" Britt added, taking another step closer.

Christian was about to answer, but before he could, Henrik continued, "And where did that twitch in your right eye go?"

Christian raised his right hand to his eye, realizing that the tic was indeed gone. He also felt himself standing taller with his head held high and shoulders back. His true Southern accent flowed freely and fluently, with no filter.

The elixir had not only solved the greatest mystery of his life, it had also reformatted his body and history, erasing all his shame, guilt, and pain without a trace. His father was now a hero of the highest order. Christian felt an immense sense of pride, warmth, and belonging that had eluded him since his father's death.

He now had a newfound appreciation for one of his father's favorite sayings: "It's a sad dog that won't wag its own tail."

Christian was no longer that sad, tormented dog.

"The therapeutic potential of this elixir is beyond anything anyone could have ever imagined," Christian said with awe in his voice. "But right now, we have bigger fish to fry. I need each one of you to confirm what lies hidden deep within these memories."

To Christian's great relief, they reluctantly accepted his explanation and slowly backed away.

"This won't make much sense right now, but it'll be worth its weight in gold once you take the elixir," Christian added. "First, you will need to trace one of your five senses through your mind until you hit an invisible barrier. The moment you recognize that barrier as the crossover point between your body and your DNA, you will be able to cross over. There's a big difference between your memories and those of your ancestors. I suspect this is because your memories follow a natural timeline that is familiar to you, unlike those of past generations. Once you get to past family memories, you must focus on either going forwards or backwards in time."

Everyone stared at Christian in disbelief. "Please trust me; you'll understand soon enough, I hope," Christian continued. "Now, once you reach the beginning of your memories, you will be in your mother's womb. To transition from your memories to those of your parents, you'll need to concentrate on the lineage of either your mother or father. Remember, you have access to both their memories and the memories of all their ancestors. After that, you can quickly navigate through the maternal or paternal line and switch over at any time."

At this point, Christian noticed more strange looks and tilted heads, making him worry that he was pushing the boundaries of their willing suspension of disbelief.

Despite their reactions, Christian pressed on, issuing a stern warning. "Pay extremely close attention to what I'm about to say. The last memory your parents stored - the moment of your conception - will be the first memory you encounter."

Christian paused and took a deep breath, giving them time to process the gravity of his warning. He watched patiently as each of them, one by one, experienced a physical jolt and gasped upon grasping the full implications of his words.

Henrik was the first to break the silence, his voice heavy with sarcasm and disbelief. "You're telling us the price of admission to this little trip down memory lane involves witnessing intercourse with one of our parents?"

"Not just witnessing," Christian cautioned tersely, "Remember, all five senses will be present as you navigate these past memories - vision, hearing, touch, taste, and smell. Once you make that initial leap from your own memories to those of one of your parents, there's no place to escape. You should prepare yourself emotionally for the experience and ponder carefully which parent's memories you'd prefer to explore. If you become adept quickly, you can leap back further in their memories, thus minimizing the trauma."

Henrik paced around the cave, biting his lower lip and shaking his clenched fists in the air as he wrestled with this impossible concept. "Do you have any idea how utterly insane you sound right now?" he asked.

"I do," replied Christian with great empathy. He walked over and placed a comforting hand on Henrik's shoulder. "Part of me hopes you're right. I would be ecstatic if this were just one really, really, really crazy trip."

"Me too!" Britt broke in, realizing that Christian was genuinely convinced of what he was telling them.

"Either way," Christian declared, "there's only one way to find out for certain. I need each of you to travel back until you hit a prolonged period of darkness. Then observe the last day before that darkness begins, and tell me what you see."

"On it, Captain!" Henrik responded with an exaggerated salute to Christian, making a light-hearted attempt to ease the tension for both himself and the others.

"One last thing—when you're ready to wake, and if the elixir doesn't wear off, try focusing on going to the very beginning of all memories. I think that's what woke me up."

Hans stepped forward. "I want to go next." There were no protests, and Hans followed Christian's instructions, lying down on a piece of rolled fur.

Everyone watched as he swallowed the foul-smelling elixir, quickly losing consciousness. Several minutes later, they all recoiled as Hans jolted upright, exclaiming, "No, it's impossible, the world will burn..."

Christian shushed Hans before he could divulge more. "Don't relay what you saw to anyone else but me right now. Each person must witness it individually to prevent bias in the truth. Whisper it to me."

Still trembling, Hans walked over to Christian and murmured, "Four scientists, a beach bunker, a planet devastated by a golden cube, and about four billion years of cryogenic sleep, I'd guess. After that, I'm left with far more questions than answers. Did those four scientists populate the earth? That gene pool would be a ticking time-bomb, but it would explain why they started to devolve after merely a few generations. It might even account for the elusive missing link between primates and humans."

Christian was both elated and devastated. His quest for the truth was complete, and every question had been answered beyond his wildest dreams. His jubilation was swiftly followed by a bone-chilling exhalation of fear. Could our entire species have originated from those four scientists? Might it be as simple as a golden cube with divots on each side to obliterate the planet?

Soren and Jesper walked in just as Hans finished sharing his revelation with Christian.

"Did we miss anything?" Jesper asked, his words heavy with the palpable tension that hung in the air.

One by one, the others consumed the elixir, each affirming the daunting truth Hans and Christian had unearthed.

Soren was the first to regain his composure and address the group as they looked at each other, grappling with the splendor and dread of their discovery, "My dear friends and family, unless a better explanation surfaces, we must presume the harbinger of humanity's demise is embedded in the memory of every human being who has ever, or will ever, tread this planet." An undeniable wave of agreement resounded from everyone present.

Hans interjected, "You all know me, and you know there is no obstacle on this planet that can stand between me and my profits. But this is something different. All the money and power in the world amount to nothing if there is no world."

Christian stepped up to the fire as everyone contemplated the gravity of their situation. His demeanor was calm and steadfast, with no traces of the pain and suffering that once consumed him. Everyone watched as the flames played a symphony of light and shadows across his resolute profile. "We must each swear an oath, right here in this cave tonight," his voice faltered for a moment as the enormity of what lay ahead settled in, "a vow to protect humanity from this secret and to discover the extent of Dmitry's organization, no matter the costs."

With renewed purpose and growing hope, each one of them solemnly accepted this charge with a silent nod to each other and to Christian, understanding all too well the price of failure, having already witnessed it.

A new peace settled upon the glacier as an Arctic wind danced with the roaring fire, whispering the gratitude of countless generations.

~*~The End~*~

Thank you for taking the time to read my debut novel. Your feedback and reviews are greatly appreciated as I prepare for the next installment!

Sincerely,

Hugh